C.
IN ~~THE~~
BOUTIQUE

A fiercely addictive mystery

CATHERINE MOLONEY

Detective Markham Mystery Book 18

JOFFE
BOOKS

Joffe Books, London
www.joffebooks.com

First published in Great Britain in 2022

© Catherine Moloney 2022

This book is a work of fiction. Names, characters,
businesses, organizations, places and events are either
the product of the author's imagination or are used
fictitiously. Any resemblance to actual persons, living
or dead, events or locales is entirely coincidental.
The spelling used is British English except where fidelity
to the author's rendering of accent or dialect supersedes
this. The right of Catherine Moloney to be identified as
author of this work has been asserted in accordance with
the Copyright, Designs and Patents Act 1988.

Cover art by Dee Dee Book Covers

ISBN: 978-1-80405-712-4

PROLOGUE

Stella Walker felt somewhat self-conscious as she pressed her palm against the glossy surface of the Confetti Club's black marble floor, but she loved the sensation of chill silkiness beneath her fingertips. Marble signalled wealth and exclusivity. . . enjoyed by people who didn't have to count the pennies like she did.

Unusually for a Sunday morning, Stella was cleaning the third-floor boutique by herself due to Moira Clegg having come down with tonsilitis the previous day. Antonia Rambert wasn't happy about it — the senior sales consultant being notoriously mistrustful of her underlings — but Stella had convinced the woman she was up to the job.

Actually, Moira was such a motor-mouth that it was a treat to have the place to herself without having to listen to salacious details of her colleague's colourful love life.

Stella had never had a boyfriend and, after months of Moira's confidences, was in no hurry to acquire one. Which wasn't to say she was immune to the romance of all those ethereal gowns, foaming with frills and lace, displayed beautifully around the room.

Stella knew Moira wasn't as smitten with their surroundings, saying that she supposed it was okay when customers were around and the place was bustling and lively. But after everyone had gone home, there was something downright spooky about the headless mannequins trailing their ball dresses. As though the women inside the costumes were long dead.

> With her head tucked underneath her arm
> She walks the bloody tower
> With her head tucked underneath her arm
> At the midnight hour.

It totally creeped Stella out when Moira warbled that horrible song, but the other just grinned at her protests.

'Heard it from my nan,' she would say unapologetically. 'All about Anne Boleyn haunting the Tower of London. I can only remember the chorus.' Which suited Stella just fine. Ghosts and headless women were the last things she needed to imagine.

At a level, though, she admitted to herself that she knew what Moira meant. Out of hours, it *was* a bit like being in a waxworks museum.

She'd never told Moira, but she tried to avoid the store-room filled with rack upon rack of plastic wardrobes which made her think of graveclothes and shrouds and morbid stuff — like in pictures of Jesus and Lazarus and people in the Bible rising from the dead.

Winding sheets. That's what awful Mrs McGillivray had said when they did RE in junior school. Something about tombs bursting open when Jesus died and the bodies of prophets coming out of them and walking all over the place. . .

Yeah, thanks to that old witch she could never look at those garment bags without thinking of 'bandages' and 'burial strips', and gruesome things like that. In the circumstances, she was always pleased to leave the backroom area to Moira who enjoyed pawing through the merchandise as she cleaned.

With prickles of sweat breaking out on her forehead, Stella realised that today there could be no shirking of tasks she found distasteful.

Uneasily, her gaze wandered across to the curtained cubicles that lined the right-hand wall, gold brocade drapes drawn chastely across to screen their interior.

Stella preferred it when the swags were looped back. She had never forgotten Moira jumping out at her one time and almost giving her a heart attack.

'If you stand on the pouffe thingy,' the other girl crowed gesturing to the grey velvet tufted banquette at the rear of the cubicle, 'nobody can see your feet. . . so they don't know you're there!'

The stealthy ambush had given Stella a most disagreeable sensation.

Now, heart beating fast, she peeped inside each of the half dozen booths, feeling faintly ridiculous, like a child checking under the bed for bogeymen. There were more cubicles at the rear of the shop on the other side of the store-room . . . but they could wait until her heart had stopped racing.

What the hell was wrong with her? she wondered irritably. It was mild and sunny outside, with Easter just a fortnight away. And this was her big chance to show them how trust-worthy and reliable she was. If she put her back into it, they might even put in a good word for her with the cleaning agency. She was still on probation with Executive Marigolds, but a recommendation from the bridal boutique would definitely count for something, particularly given its upmarket clientele. It was far and away the smartest store in Bromgrove Shopping Centre, a real step up from Primark and the naffer outlets on the two floors below — to say nothing of the unisex toilets on the ground floor that reeked so strongly of ammonia they made her eyes sting. The Confetti Club's 'ladies' powder room', redolent of citrus and lavender, with its tub chairs upholstered in purple velvet, felt like heaven after *that*. It was the same with the men's restroom just off the boutique's entrance vestibule, the décor more restrained but equally expressive of a luxury brand. As Moira said (though not when Antonia Rambert could overhear her), posh folk liked to think their pee smelled of violets and always talked about washing their hands when they meant go to the bog.

Recalling her colleague's cheerful irreverence momentarily raised Stella's spirits and she took a deep breath.

The slightly built cleaner swiftly braided her sandy hair into a neat plait. It was all a question of having a *system*, she told herself. And making sure that by the time she had finished, the shop was so immaculate you could eat your dinner off the floor.

The backroom areas could wait till last, she decided. She would start by polishing the floor-to-ceiling mirrors that lined the left-hand wall before hoovering the overstuffed chintz armchairs and dusting the Shaker ivory coffee tables. After that, she would sort out the tiny staff kitchen and loos (no expensive floral scents wasted on employees there) before cleaning the floors and changing areas. Then, after a quick coffee, it would be time for Mr Everard's office.

Mr Everard. Proprietor of the Confetti Club.

A misty expression stole over Stella's pinched features at the thought of Gino Everard.

'That fella's no more Italian than Mister Whippy,' was Moira's grudging refrain, but Stella didn't care. And besides, Mr Everard didn't make a big thing about being continental or anything like that. The family came from Somerset, though to be sure there was Italian ancestry on his mother's side, while his artfully layered silver bob, come-to-bed eyes and languorous, caressing accents — home counties overlaid with a hint of something more exotic — suggested gilded origins far from the common run of provincial dress designers.

Moira wasn't having it. 'He's a big fat phoney,' she scoffed in response to Stella's raptures. 'An' as for that barnet, well, makes it look like he's in drag. . . Y'know, pantomime. . . impersonating Miss Marple or that housekeeper woman in *Father Brown*.'

Stella took no notice. There was something magical about the way Mr Everard made every girl feel like a princess. When they went to the Wedding Show at Carton Hall last year, even her mum had to admit he had star quality. You felt that he actually *liked* women. . . that the old-world gallantry — calling everyone 'darling' and the courtly hand-kissing — wasn't just some big act. The *Gazette*'s 'Celebrity Corner' hinted that he'd dated men (in addition to there being an ex-wife), but it made no difference to Stella. He had *glamour* that made her knees turn to jelly. Wistfully, she acknowledged that he probably wasn't aware she even existed, but just taking care of his office was something special. . . something to be saved till after the boring chores were out of the way.

Her dreams of Gino were interrupted when suddenly a door slammed somewhere in the shopping complex, causing her to jump.

* * *

The noise should have made her feel safe, reminding her that other janitorial workers were busy in the vicinity, trundling round the retail units with their mobile trolleys of all shapes and sizes.

But, unbidden, another of Moira's ghoulish *bons mots* came into her mind.

'You could hide a body in one of those housekeeping carts,' her colleague had observed casually one day as they watched a weedy little bloke wheeling a three-shelved stainless-steel number around the third floor. 'Clobber someone and then wheel them out of here under everyone's noses. Easy peasy.'

'It'd have to be someone fairly small,' she'd objected, only for the Incorrigible One to reply, 'I reckon *you'd* fit.'

At the time, Stella hadn't been able to help laughing, but now the thought of those rubber-wheeled gurney-like contraptions made her shiver.

It was all right joking about psychos on the loose when there were two of you, but it was not helpful now that she was here on her own in the silent boutique with its mirrors and curtains and spotlights. . .

Time to get a bloody grip, she told herself savagely.

She didn't intend to stay a cleaner for ever. One day she meant to swap her squeegees for stilettos and a business suit. Already she was picking up the consultant's jargon: 'a customer's *entourage*. . . her preferred *silhouette*. . . *mermaid or princess*. . . *sweetheart neckline*. . . *illusion bodice*. . . *bling*. . . *embellishments*. . .' At first it was like Esperanto, but now the words felt like old friends.

When she'd shyly told Franco Santini — the boutique's director of operations and rumoured 'power behind the throne' (as well as an Italian 'real deal') — about her ambitions, he hadn't made fun or been dismissive. Instead, he had flashed his engaging lopsided smile and quoted poetry at her.

'The inferior priestess, at her altar's side, Trembling, begins the sacred rites of pride. This casket India's glowing gems unlocks, And all Arabia breathes from yonder box.'

Apparently, it was sending up the beauty industry or something like that. At any rate, she liked it a hell of a lot better than Moira's rhyme about Anne Boleyn. . .

An hour and a half later, glowing and sweatily virtuous after the application of some serious elbow grease, Stella headed towards the storeroom.

Ruthlessly suppressing all thoughts of Lazarus and bandages, she began mechanically to work her way through the rows of clothes racks, carefully wiping down the steel rails and garment bags as she hummed the latest Ed Sheeran ditty.

Finally, Stella came to the fitted wardrobes which covered the whole of the back wall and held the most expensive samples. Her pace quickening with relief, the end was in sight. She moved from right to left, methodically parting plastic covers and cellophane until she reached the far end of the cupboard—

And screamed as a face swam towards her that belonged to the phantasmal sheeted dead, like one of the prophets in those RE lessons, luxuriant silver hair waving about the livid features like a halo. . . a saint or holy man rising up from the depths.

As she staggered backwards, Stella realised this was no celestial apparition but something infinitely more diabolic.

Gino Everard, proprietor of the Confetti Club . . . was unmistakeably dead.

1. OPENING MANOEUVRES

Early morning on Monday 4 April found DI Gilbert ('Gil') Markham lost in thought on his favourite bench in the graveyard of St Chad's Parish Church overlooking the police station, this being his invariable habit at the start of a new investigation.

The air was mild in the bosky little terraced cemetery, with wood pigeons warbling throatily to each other in the yews and the odd squirrel whisking between lichened headstones and baroque monuments. Clumps of daffodils, bluebells and primulas offered little bursts of colour amid the granite and marble, so the scene was altogether a pleasing prospect.

Markham's enjoyment was heightened by the knowledge that at this hour he was safe from the evangelical predations of St Chad's new incumbent, a former bank manager, who had shown every sign of being determined to corral the aloof inspector into his fold. Formerly, Markham's wingman George Noakes had offered some protection from the clergyman, who hadn't exactly been convulsed at quips about Anglican clerics having a better half while RC priests had better quarters. Noakes's favourite headstone joke about *Lucy. Whose price was above Ruby's* elicited an even frostier response,

8

the pastor thereafter giving the two men a wide berth whenever they took a stroll round the graveyard.

The DI's austere features softened at thoughts of his ex-sergeant whose proudly un-PC credentials made him something of a legend among his peers (though distinctly unpopular with the 'gold braid mob'). Never had anything seemed more improbable than that he and Noakes should find each other infinitely simpatico, but so it was, the stocky veteran's lack of filter very much to his taste amid the politicking and sycophancy of CID. Notoriously uncouth and sartorially a walking disaster with prize-fighter's features and an addiction to junk food, Noakes had a surprisingly sensitive, poetic side — albeit one that he generally kept well hidden. Combative and outspoken in puncturing pomposity or wokeness, he never dropped a clanger in his dealings with underdogs or the vulnerable. And he was fiercely, unflinchingly loyal to Markham whose childhood trauma as the victim of an abusive stepfather he instinctively fathomed though few words on the subject had ever passed between them.

Noakes had shown the same dogged fidelity to Markham's ex — the willowy English teacher Olivia Mullen, seduced alike by her Pre-Raphaelite looks and mischievous sense of humour. When Markham and Olivia had split up, the burly sergeant was almost the most distressed of the three. Markham knew he continued to harbour wistful hopes of an eventual reconciliation.

Noakes's bossy social-climbing spouse Muriel, however, was by no means displeased with this turn of events, being decidedly partial to Markham while deploring that he had ever been caught in the toils of an 'uppity, sardonic, too-clever-by-half schoolmarm'. As far as she was concerned, it was high time the scales fell from the handsome inspector's eyes and his attention turned to someone more suitable (that is, someone in the mould of Muriel herself).

Naturally, Markham was well aware of all this, just as he knew that Noakes's susceptibility to Olivia's charms thoroughly irritated his wife. The nature of the Noakeses' union was in many respects baffling to him, but he had no doubt of their mutual devotion. Having met (of all things) on the ballroom-dancing circuit, theirs was a solid marriage that had weathered a brief crisis when Noakes discovered that he was not perma-tanned beautician daughter Natalie's biological father (that Natalie was the apple of his eye made things worse at the time). Temporarily going off the rails, his relationship with Markham and his professional reputation nearly became casualties of the discovery, but somehow he pulled through with both intact.

It had been a blow to Markham when Noakes finally retired. Of course, DCI Sidney ('Slimy Sid' to the troops) had been trying for years to have Noakes put out to grass, seeing him as the absolute antithesis of modern policing and a 'deplorable anachronism', but in the event, it was his old nemesis himself who chose the time and manner of his departure. The retirement party and Noakes's farewell gaffes, like the man himself, had passed into legend. Markham still savoured the remembrance of Sidney's apoplectic expression when Superintendent Bretherton made some typically trite remark about 'never resting on his laurels' only for a well-refreshed Noakes to retort that he must be wearing them in the wrong place.

Even then, poor old Sidney hadn't seen the last of Noakes who promptly took up a post as security manager at an upmarket retirement home only to find himself slap bang in the middle of a murder, investigated by Markham. The DCI had been almost resigned when Markham brought Noakes in as a 'civilian consultant', wearing the look of one who knew his reprieve was too good to be true.

Noakes's replacement, DS Roger Carruthers (or 'Roger the Dodger' as Noakes immediately christened him), had initially seemed like a poor exchange, being a pallid protégé of Sidney's and almost certainly his spy on the side. But from unpromising beginnings, the newcomer had somehow bonded with DI Kate Burton and DS Doyle, the other members of the team. And as Doyle — even more fanatical than

Noakes about football — was wont to say, no one who liked the Beautiful Game could be all bad.

Markham's growing regard for DI Kate Burton had been one of the reasons behind his breakup with Olivia. Earnest, politically correct and serious-minded — in many ways Noakes's polar opposite — the psychology graduate faced stiff parental opposition in her choice of career ('no job for a woman', said her father) and was never entirely at ease with the more raucous aspects of CID canteen culture. She and Noakes had enjoyed a love-hate relationship which gradually evolved into genuine affection, not least given their shared enthusiasm for true-crime documentaries, commitment to the job and unshakeable devotion to Markham. It was true that Noakes had never been entirely converted to the cause of criminal profiling nor developed an appreciation for Burton's beloved Diagnostic and Statistical Manual of Mental Disorders, but Markham knew the two sparring partners secretly missed each other, notwithstanding Noakes's habit of referring to Burton's fiancé as 'Shippers' on account of his startling resemblance to the serial killer Dr Harold Shipman.

Burton seemed to have blossomed since becoming engaged to Professor Nathan Finlayson, clinical psychologist and head of the criminal profiling unit at Bromgrove University. Over time, she became more confidential with Markham, opening up about her background and displaying an unexpected vulnerability that surprised and touched him. A wryly mischievous sense of humour had also gradually emerged that reminded him of his ex-partner. . .

Perhaps therein lay the rub.

Was it possible to love two women at the same time?

The startled expression of a squirrel gambolling yards away made him realise he had spoken the words out loud.

Smiling ruefully at himself, he meditated on the conundrum.

It was disconcerting to discover that he had felt jealous when Kate Burton took up with Nathan Finlayson. He was aware — not least through Noakes's blunt remarks and Olivia's increasingly jaundiced observations — that his colleague had nursed a crush on him ever since her arrival in CID as an ambitious DS. He could admit to himself that Burton's hero-worship had flattered his ego, but in any event, he had rapidly come to feel both respect and a liking for the preternaturally solemn and punctilious detective whose po-faced appearance belied a deeply sensitive nature. Initially dowdy with a penchant for 'Chairman Mao' trouser suits in endless shades of beige, Burton had finally come out of her chrysalis and these days looked positively glamorous, her geometric chestnut bob and blonde highlights set off by cashmere midi dresses in a range of eye-catching colours. She still never hesitated to whip out the spectacles that magnified her eyes to enormous brown lollipops, but these days the fashion statement frames were what got people talking. Physically very different from Olivia, being petite and curvy, Burton had acquired a sophistication — possibly an armour — that served her well.

The bottom line was, he found her appealing and somehow soothing (where Olivia was sparky, sharp-tongued and highly strung). It wasn't the same electric connection — the sexual fireworks — as he had with Olivia, but there was still something. . .

Perhaps, he thought wryly, it was connected with Burton's flattering subservience towards him — not an agreeable reflection, but he knew himself to be as capable of chauvinism as the next man. On the other hand, the newly minted DI was no simpering pushover, and there had been many occasions when she spoke her mind. After all, she would never have lasted the course with Noakes and the others without a certain steely inner resilience.

Whatever the nature of the attraction, Olivia had sensed his increasing warmth towards Burton (perhaps he himself had realised it) and been threatened by it, so in the end his colleague had inadvertently come between them.

He cringed at the thought of Burton discovering that Olivia regarded her as one side of an Eternal Triangle, but believed that, to date, his domestic secret was safe. As far as his colleagues were concerned, the breakup had occurred due to the pressures of his job.

And there was undeniably some truth in this version of events, since he could not deny his tendency to live the job in a way that had undoubtedly provoked resentment. However, Olivia's troubled past — which included a botched abortion that precluded them having children of their own — was also part of the mix. His suggestion that they should marry had been turned down so decisively that he was discouraged from proposing again.

And now Olivia was being squired everywhere by Mat Sullivan, their mutual friend and the deputy head at Hope Academy where she worked. Sullivan — beanpole thin, lanky with an ironic turn of phrase — had come out as gay during the Ashley Dean investigation (during which he was briefly a murder suspect), but since he was showing every sign of being infatuated with Olivia there was precious little comfort in that.

Markham supposed it was possible that Olivia, now renting a flat in town, had reached out to her colleague and he was now doing his best to jolly her out of the doldrums; after all, the two had always shared a conspiratorial bond, particularly their passionate abhorrence of wokeism in schools. But something in Sullivan's demeanour suggested a more unsettling dynamic. Noakes — who had formed an unlikely bond with Sullivan during the Ashley Dean case, appreciating the teacher's subversive streak — was all for 'having it out with him'. But 'Fools Rush In, Noakesy,' Markham had responded before dissuading his old ally from interfering.

And anyway, at the moment Noakes had quite enough on his plate what with daughter Natalie's unexpected connection to this latest investigation. . .

During the Rosemount Retirement Home murder investigation, Markham had been startled to learn that Natalie's engagement to Rick Jordan — the highly eligible heir to a fitness empire — had foundered, leading her to embark on a somewhat dubious voyage of personal discovery that included plans for a 'self-marriage ceremony'. She had apparently fallen in thrall to one Gino Everard. . . proprietor of the Confetti Club and now murder victim.

It was an extraordinary and disconcerting coincidence, not least as Noakes had even solicited Olivia to visit the bridal store so that she could reassure him and 'the missus' that 'Gino Ginelli' (Noakes could never resist a nickname) wasn't up to anything nefarious.

Olivia and Natalie were not exactly soulmates. Indeed, Markham suspected that Noakes's brassy, buxom offspring disliked Olivia at least as much as her mother (while exhibiting a marked penchant for Markham). But Olivia hated seeing Noakes worrying himself sick over the prodigal daughter and readily undertook the mission. Apparently, she reported back to Noakes, there was no great harm in Gino Everard, and it was simply a case of Natalie enjoying the glamour of doing 'wellbeing' consultations there and being a sucker for the man's theatrical mannerisms. As for Natalie's self-marriage scheme — apparently quite common these days for all its wackiness — she was fairly sure it would 'die a death'.

Only now it was Gino Everard who had died. In highly suspicious circumstances.

Markham's thoughts turned to the previous day's call-out with Doug 'Dimples' Davidson the police pathologist, a bluff medic with more the air of a country vet than sawbones. Certainly, he was the spit of Siegfried Farnon in both appearance and manner. . .

'Strangled,' was Dimples' succinct verdict after he had supervised removal of the corpse. 'Then tied to this manne-quin pole thing or whatever it is and wedged inside the plastic wardrobe. . . ready for some poor soul to have a coronary when his face leered out at them.' The medic was sombre. 'I'd say your killer enjoyed rigging him up like a puppet on a string. . . making him look ridiculous.'

'Do you think it was a man or woman?' Markham wanted to know.

'From the marks round the throat, I'd say whoever did it used a sequin sash belt or some kind of blingy garotte.' The pathologist's eyes scanned the shop. 'Some rhinestone accessory or other . . . With the element of surprise, a woman could have done it . . . Your victim was actually quite slight, which meant he was manoeuvrable. The hardest part would have been strapping him to the clothes rod and getting him into the wardrobe. But doing it in stages — first moving him onto a chair perhaps, while he was still supple — would have been perfectly manageable. . . especially if the adrenalin was flowing and they knew they had all the time in the world.'

The adrenalin would have been flowing all right, Markham thought grimly.

'Time of death?'

'Tut-tut, Inspector, always so impatient.'

Markham knew it was a token protest and waited.

Dimples pursed his lips. 'Don't quote me, but I'd say late Saturday night, before midnight.' He looked around the chi-chi interior with its chintz, gilt mirrors and flouncy mannequins, raising a bushy eyebrow. 'Presumably he wasn't here for a business meeting at that time of night.'

Markham wasn't ready to delve into the specifics.

'Do you know this place, Doug?' he asked, deflecting any analysis of Gino Everard's motivation for his rendezvous with death.

'The wife was in and out by the minutes when our eldest got married,' the other replied before adding with a grin. 'The only book she's ever really been interested in is my chequebook.'

The two men exchanged a long look of masculine complicity.

'What did she make of Everard?' Markham enquired.

'Said he was a real smoothie. Lots of "Fabulous, dahling" and all that jazz . . . He did some minor royal's wedding dress back in the day. . . been trading on it ever since by the sound of things.' The portly medic bit his lip with momentary compunction. 'The guy was a real Flash Harry, but there was no great harm in him. He had a nice thing going here and the television people had come calling.'

'Indeed?'

'Yes, Bromgrove TV were sniffing around, think they even did a pilot. Apparently, Everard was poised to cash in on the trend for reality TV programmes that follow brides in the run-up to the big day. It's all the rage these days. My lot are hooked on the stuff.'

Markham was amused to note that Dimples couldn't have looked more embarrassed than if he had admitted to snorting cocaine. Clearly this dabbling in popular culture was something to be indulged in by stealth.

He continued to pump this most unlikely of informants.

'Anyone with grudges against Everard?'

'Some hairy legged feminist at the *Gazette* wrote a few snidey pieces about him.' Dimples grinned. 'Presumably he hadn't wasted too much hand-kissing on *her*.'

Markham sighed inwardly. He knew there was no point remonstrating with the other about his antediluvian attitudes. He was worse than Noakes when it came to that.

And yet, like Noakes, the pathologist possessed a compassionate humanity that Markham knew cared nothing for creed, colour or class. The two men were products of their generation but infinitely preferable in the DI's book to virtue-signalling, upwardly mobile careerists.

All the same, he was grateful that Kate Burton wasn't around to hear the pathologist's dithyrambs against the *Gazette*'s hapless columnist.

'Anyone else while we're at it, Doug?'

'I seem to remember the wife saying there were various people he'd pissed off. . . pardon my French.' Davidson had to be just about the only person who ever used the phrase these days. 'Some designer he'd badmouthed. . . and a pretty boy he thought stole his thunder in the pilot thing.' The medic suddenly looked wary. 'But don't quote me on that.'

Markham dismissed his worries with a wave of his hand. 'Perish the thought.'

16

Now, thinking back to the aftermath of the murder as he sat in the tranquil little cemetery, Markham concluded that with this one he had his work cut out.

Designers, fashionistas, demanding clients, distraught brides. . . Quite a cocktail.

He took one last look around the graveyard, his gaze coming to rest on a nearby tombstone which stoutly proclaimed: 'Every tear shall be wiped away'.

Well, whatever the celestial outcomes, it was up to him to snare a murderer and ensure justice for Gino Everard here on earth.

Another grey squirrel peeped out from behind a headstone as though to say, 'Good luck with that, mate.'

* * *

Despite the early hour, his team was already waiting in Markham's poky office with its unrivalled view of the station car park, all bright eyed and bushy tailed.

Carruthers had sorted the refreshments.

'Black coffee for you, sir. Vanilla soy latte, ma'am, and flat whites for me and Doyle. . . with triple chocolate chip muffins on the side and, er . . . a granola bar.'

He didn't say, 'Yours is the birdseed crap, ma'am,' but Noakes's immortal description hung in the air.

Talk about Banquo's Ghost, the DI thought with an inner smile. Noakes was temporarily somehow more vividly present than if he had been there slouched across the table, setting the swinging balls of Markham's cradle desktop toy in motion with childlike glee and the perennial pronouncement that he 'didn't know why the boss bothered with all that Zen shit'.

Carruthers, for all his blond albino pallor and horn-rimmed spectacles, appeared far more congenial these days, Markham had observed. Like Doyle, attired in skinny chinos and crew neck, the former attenuated intensity had mutated into something altogether more acceptable. Less Kim Philby crossed with Herr Flick and more Liam Gallagher or some other scrawny contemporary icon.

At any rate, there was an easy camaraderie with Burton and Doyle that augured well. And all three radiated an unmistakeable eagerness to crack on with this latest homicide investigation.

Seeing that Burton had already whipped out her designer specs and notebook, Markham invited her to brief them on the victim and suspects.

'Gino Everard, sir,' she said, twitching the crib that Markham was reasonably sure she had memorised by heart. 'Proprietor of the Confetti Club for the last twenty years and fodder for the gossip columnists. Did some royal cousin or other's wedding dress and made a living out of it. Divorced his wife Claudia Everard yonks ago amid a big falling-out over who should have had the credit for the costumes at some aristo's nuptials.'

'Have we been in touch with Mrs Everard, Kate?'

Markham was famously reluctant to make his subordinates undertake the dreaded bereavement visits.

'She's abroad right now, sir, but I've got people on it. They didn't have kids. . . Family liaison's checking out relatives.'

'Thanks, Kate. How about the rest of the *Dramatis Personae*?'

'Right, sir.' Her tone was crisp as she resumed. 'In terms of the boutique's management structure, we've got Franco Santini, Mr Everard's number two and oldest friend. . . Then there's Lucille Chilton his PA and Antonia Rambert the senior consultant—'

'Bet the names are all made up,' Doyle interjected. 'Sounds too French Riviera for words.'

'Most likely,' Burton agreed equably. 'But it's like that in their line of work.' She grimaced. 'Plain Jane Doe's never going to cut it.'

'Who else, Kate?' Markham persisted.

'Antonia's assistants are Maria Hagan and Christina Skelthorne,' Burton replied. 'Those three handle front of house, while a bloke name of Randall Fenton takes care of the seamstresses and,' Burton air quoted with a quizzical expression, 'the "creative team".'

'What about disgruntled employees?' Markham asked, remembering his conversation with Dimples Davidson.

'There is a designer, Joanna Osborne. . . She quit after Everard apparently bitched about her during some TV pilot,' Burton replied. 'Plus, a young guy, Jamie O'Neill. He got fired shortly after they made the pilot. Word on the street is, Everard thought O'Neill was upstaging him. . . apparently, he was too good looking and charismatic by half.'

As anticipated, the cast list was proving complex.

And somehow Markham knew they weren't finished yet.

'Danielle Rigsby at the *Gazette* seemed to have it in for Everard,' she said frowning. 'Did a couple of hatchet jobs on him. . . He'd threatened to sue over a feature she did about the TV pilot.'

Ah, presumably this was Dimples' 'hairy legged feminist'.

Wonderful, the DI mused with an inner eye roll. The ladies and gentlemen of the press getting their oar in was bound to complicate matters, as well as being absolutely guaranteed to bring DCI Sidney and the top brass out in hives.

Burton still wasn't done.

'And there's this local businessman who had some kind of vendetta against Everard on account of his daughter.' Burton squinted at her notes, clearly finding the entire topic distasteful. 'He felt the TV pilot made her out to be a . . . "half-witted slag".'

'*Name?*' Markham already felt a headache building behind his temples.

'Mark Harvison, sir.' Burton looked apologetic. 'You may remember him from the Citizens-Police Liaison Committee.'

Oh God, only too well. Florid Colonel Blimp type. Champing at the bit to portray Bromgrove CID as a complete waste of space. Markham shook his head.

Burton cleared her throat nervously, which could only portend more bad news.

'Er, finally sir, there's Shay Conteh,' she said.

'Wait, he got to the Commonwealth Games boxing finals,' Carruthers interposed eagerly. 'Doing an MA in sports science at Bromgrove Uni, sir. Big on equality and all that. . . the *Gazette* interviewed him about sexism and women being commoditised.'

Damn and triple damn, Markham thought. *That's all he needed. A bunch of liberal do-gooders gagging to portray Bromgrove as some kind of ghastly neanderthal backwater where discrimination and social oppression were rife. The hits just kept on coming. . .*

'Presumably Mr Conteh wasn't happy about Gino Everard's endorsement of bridal patriarchy,' he said flatly.

'That's about the size of it, sir,' Burton agreed. 'But it doesn't look like the Confetti Club ever became a flash point . . . at least not in *that* way.'

'Thanks, Kate.' He did his best to sound brisk and authoritative. 'Is that it?'

'For now, sir,' came the cautious reply.

'Will we be using sarge on this one, sir?'

Markham knew full well that as far as Doyle was concerned, his mentor Noakes would forever be 'sarge'. Burton was the same, and even Carruthers appeared to have accepted the unusual setup.

'I don't see why not,' he replied evenly, though well aware that Sidney could no doubt come up with any number of reasons for keeping Noakes at arm's length. Carefully, he added, 'Natalie Noakes is by way of having an entrée to the boutique . . . makeovers and so forth.' No need to expand on the bizarre 'self-marriage' scenario just yet. Or at least not until Noakes said he could share it with the team. 'So naturally I'll be wanting to explore that angle with Noakes.'

Naturally.

'Let's get an incident room set up here,' Markham instructed. 'Then we can work through some more background and line up interviews for tomorrow. . . you and me at the Confetti Club, Kate, and then ideally a meeting with Claudia Everard.'

He noticed that Carruthers and Doyle appeared somewhat crestfallen on hearing this.

'Don't worry, you'll get your chance,' he told them. 'Having a crack at the *Gazette*'s intrepid hack for one thing, then there's Messrs Harvison and Conteh along with the disgruntled ex-employees. . . Plenty to get your teeth into, believe me.'

In the meantime, though it was doubtless sexist and chauvinist and a whole load of 'isms' to boot, he needed Burton for the Gentle Touch — not the other two barging in with their size twelves.

Markham thought of Gino Everard's silver-blond bouffant, the powder-puff face horribly bloated and congested in death. And vowed to leave no stone unturned in bringing the killer to justice.

Now to tackle DCI Sidney and persuade him that George Noakes was indispensable to his enquiries . . .

Which meant careful negotiation of Sidney's sour-grapevine accompanied by lashings of flattery. Well, if he could secure his old friend for this one, the grovelling would be worth it.

Let the battle commence.

2. THE PERSONAL TOUCH

'Ginelli don' zackly look like love's young dream in these promo pics.'

Such was George Noakes's pronouncement as he sat with Markham in the staff room at Rosemount Retirement Home on the morning of Tuesday 5 April scrutinising brochures for the Confetti Club.

Despite the traumatic events of their previous investigation at Rosemount, Markham felt that the shadow hanging over the place had lifted. A new young administrator had greeted him cheerfully, and in no time at all the DI found himself installed cosily à deux with his old ally enjoying a surprisingly excellent coffee and a plate of amaretti biscuits.

Even the portrait of moustachioed General Charles Gordon, formerly Noakes's pet hate on the grounds that the picture gave him the heebie jeebies, seemed somehow more benignant than of yore, as though the nineteenth-century hero had accepted the new regime and was determined to make the best of it.

'Gino *Everard*,' Markham reminded his friend. 'Make sure you don't call him Ginelli to anyone else,' i.e. Sidney. He had a feeling the DCI wouldn't find the ice cream tutti frutti connotations particularly hilarious.

'Yeah, *whatever*,' Noakes grunted, his piggy eyes riveted on Everard's face. 'He's kinda puffy-faced, an' that quiff's flipping ridiculous.' Slightly shamefaced, he added, 'But I checked him out on YouTube when Nat started banging on about him. . . he didn't look quite so soft and flabby on there.'

'Ah, the wonders of clever lighting and makeup,' Markham retorted drily. 'The camera angles probably flattered him. . . whereas perhaps he rather looks his age in the PR glossies.'

Noakes scowled. 'He came across as a right ponce. . . waving his hands around like he were doing magic tricks.'

Markham grinned, imagining the dramatic gesticulation, with flowing fingers and easy wrists.

'That's his stock-in-trade, Noakesy. It's what people expect from a "royal" dress designer. The same with the accent. . . it's meant to hint at cosmopolitan connections and the crème de la crème—'

'Yeah, that got on my nerves an' all,' the other grouched. 'Like summat out of *Downton Abbey*.'

'Physically, Mr Everard was pretty unprepossessing,' Markham said. 'Quite small-boned actually. . . That larger-than-life stuff was all "smoke and mirrors".'

He recalled Everard's dead features, flesh slack and the strangely lidless eyes. He was somehow almost feminine in death. 'He was older than people thought. . . sixty-nine on his next birthday.'

Noakes was not to be appeased. 'So, what business did he have making eyes at young girls like my Nat?'

Markham suppressed a sigh. 'That's the whole point. He was like that with everyone. . . The cleaner who found him clearly thought he was marvellous, so he must have sprinkled some kind of stardust around the place.'

'What did you make of the setup?' Noakes enquired beadily. 'The missus had a gander and thought it were very flash. . . your Olivia too.'

Markham flinched slightly at the words 'your Olivia' but managed to laugh. 'It's what you'd call Quatorze the Fifteenth,' he hazarded.

'Oh aye, you mean like a tart's boudoir.'

'Well, lots of chintz and gilt, if that's what you're getting at. . . but quite tastefully done. It is a bridal shop after all. . . they want clients to feel they're stepping into a fantasy world.'

Noakes's gaze sought out bemedaled General Gordon brooding sternly above the fireplace, almost as though to elicit sympathy from the eminent Victorian, before returning to the man he still thought of as 'the boss'.

'They certainly got my Nat living in fantasy land,' he growled. 'First, all this self-marriage crip crap an' then Ginelli trying to talk her into offering some sideline in piercings.'

Markham was startled. 'Piercings?'

Noakes was highly gratified by the effect of this revelation.

'Yeah. According to Ginelli, getting yourself mutilated counts as,' here Noakes assumed an affected falsetto, '"empowerment". I kid you not. . . nipples an' noses done same time as you're shopping for the dress.'

'Well, well. . . I had no idea that body modification was breaking into the bridal market.'

'Nat says you get mums an' daughters asking about it these days. . . she says piercing parties — y'know, needles an' tattoos with a glass of bubbly — are gonna be the next big thing. An' price is no object, so it don' have to be scuzzy. . . you can have a diamond in your belly button if you want it.' Noakes was comically conflicted between feelings of repulsion on the one hand and pride in his girl's familiarity with the zeitgeist. 'Obviously the missus ain't up for that kind of caper,' he added hastily.

Fighting down a wave of hysterical mirth at the notion of Muriel Noakes opting for a navel barbell, Markham replied gravely. 'Presumably Mr Everard thought highly of Natalie's commercial acumen, otherwise he wouldn't have floated the idea.'

'Yeah, he were on to a good thing with Nat's wellbeing stuff. . . plus, she's got her finger on the pulse when it comes to fashion an' all that.'

Markham tried not to recall Olivia's acid remarks about Natalie's 'hooker wear' and its impact on susceptible young detectives at CID Christmas parties down the years, their eyes out on stalks at her décolletage ('all meat and no gravy,' as one wit put it). Since her engagement to Rick Jordan, however, Natalie had started dressing more conservatively, toning down the polyfilla-thick makeup and oompa-loompa tangerine tan. Ditching the Katie Price look had obviously paid dividends in terms of her working relationship with Gino Everard.

Or had it been more than a working relationship, the DI wondered.

Carefully, he asked, 'You weren't happy about Natalie working for Mr Everard, were you?'

'Your Liv said it were all right,' Noakes said reluctantly. 'An' there's no flies on *her*. . . so I reckoned everything had to be kosher. It's jus' the way Nat seemed so taken up with him and some other bloke with a weirdy Wop name . . .'

Markham ignored the unrepentant xenophobia. You had to make allowances for a worried father, and clearly there was something about the Confetti Club that had made Noakes uneasy.

'Careful,' he cautioned mildly. 'You mean Franco Santini, Mr Everard's deputy.'

'Thass the fella . . . He's in the background on one of them YouTube gigs. . . genuine Eyetie cos he's got the accent.'

'*Noakes*.' Markham was firmer now.

'Don' worry, I'll watch it round Burton.' Slyly, the other added, 'Got you all to herself today then, has she?'

Markham ignored the insinuendo.

'Custody of the tongue's important on this one, Noakesy. . . not just as a matter of respect for cultural diversity,' which he knew was for the birds as far as his friend was concerned, 'but because there's been a certain amount of ill feeling against the boutique in various quarters, so we need to tread extra carefully.'

'You mean the rent-a-mob lot . . . all high dudgeon an' dungarees.' Markham stifled a chuckle at this. 'Nat said the uni lefties, including some ex-boxer,' Noakes sounded disgusted, 'were stirring the pot.'

'Did Natalie see anything kick off at the boutique?'

'Nah . . . But there's been nasties in the *Gazette*.'

'Yes. . . not the kind of column inches Mr Everard was after. And apparently Mr Mark Harvison took exception to the way his daughter came across in some pilot for Bromgrove TV.'

'That twonk from the committee,' Noakes chortled. 'Loved the sound of his own voice an' bored everyone rigid.' As far as he was concerned, slag-gate was payback for all those hours of Harvison's grandstanding.

Markham's tone was flinty. 'Like you, he was concerned about his daughter, Noakes.'

'*All right, all right, boss*. . . Don' get all narked with me. . . *I were only saying*.' It was a time-honoured refrain, with a side-helping of injured innocence.

'Was Natalie aware of any tensions in the boutique . . . jealousies . . . grudges . . . that kind of thing?'

'She said it could be bitchy sometimes, but fashion's like that, innit?' Noakes scratched his chin. 'You can ask her yourself when you come round for your tea tomorrow,' he said, anxious lest Markham had forgotten Muriel's pressing invitation. ('*So* important that Gilbert doesn't *brood*.' Especially not over Olivia Mullen.) 'I'll tip Nat the wink that you're after the full low-down.' Suddenly the mastiff features brightened. 'What with the piercings palaver an' Ginelli's plans for pamper sessions or whatever they're called, at least it meant she'd kind of put the self-marriage thing on ice.'

'Natalie's insights will be very welcome,' Markham replied with cast-iron courtesy. Even at the price of Muriel's faux commiseration on his love life.

Noakes looked pleased, once more meeting General Gordon's eyes as though to say, 'The boss is one of *us*. . . the kind who gets things *done*.'

'So, what're you up to today then?' Noakes's voice was somewhat wistful.

'A shufti at our suspects with Kate. . . Somehow, I felt she'd be a safer bet than the other two.'

Noakes guffawed at the very notion of Doyle and Carruthers clodhopping amid sequins and lace.

'And then hopefully a visit to Claudia Everard, the ex-wife.'

Noakes's eyes gleamed. 'Oh *yeah*,' he said thoughtfully. 'Nat mentioned summat about that. She never met her, though, cos her an' Ginelli were daggers drawn.'

Shyly, he tufted his salt and pepper thatch into myriad little prongs in a sure sign that he wanted to say something but didn't know how to get the words out.

'Spit it out, Noakes,' Markham said kindly.

'Will you be, er . . . *needing* me at all on this one, boss. . . civilian consultant kind of thing?'

'As if you needed to ask! Of course, I will. I ran it past Sidney yesterday and he took it on the chin.'

Noakes grinned. 'He don' have one.'

Markham held up a forefinger in admonition.

Noakes reeled it back. '*Okay*, I get you. . . Custody of the tongue, right?'

Amused, the DI nodded.

'Quite.' He smiled. 'Rosemount's rubbing off on you, Noakes . . . And may I compliment you on the new wardrobe.'

In the startlingly loud mustard Harris Tweed suit, his former wingman resembled a down-at-heel gamekeeper (*Downton* on a budget), but overall, it was an infinitely more respectable look than the shockingly mismatched ganzies and combat trousers of his DS years, which had resulted in Sidney complaining loudly about the decline in standards of dress.

'I'm assuming you're settled here, Noakesy?' Markham prompted after an interval of bashful preening.

'Yeah, things are kushdi now the board's letting me tighten up on security. . . An' the missus likes how everything's dead. . . *genteel*.'

She would, the DI thought sardonically.

'But now an' again I kinda get itchy feet. . . like I should be out there getting scrotes off the street.' He shrugged.

Markham knew what he meant. Years previously, in collaboration with DI Chris Carstairs (Vice) for a dare, Noakes had penned a limerick for *Police Life* entitled 'And Plod Those Feet' which included the immortal lines: 'No time left to tackle toughs. Too weighed down with torch and cuffs. Get on *Crimewatch*. Study hard. Your two feet might make the Yard.' Sidney and the higher echelons were outraged by such lèse-majesté, but the troops loved it and belted out the Noakesian credo at many a black-tie bash:

Call for back-up from the Bill.
Or the Sweeney, that's a thrill.
PC-this and DC-that.
On the mobile for a chat.

'Glad to hear you're up for a challenge. That being the case, I believe I can help make your dreams come true,' Markham said deadpan. Then, more sombrely, 'There's something seriously out of whack at that boutique, Noakesy. . . I need to get a handle on it. *Fast.*'

'No worries, boss.' His friend was chipper now that he was assured of the inside track. 'Nat'll give you the gen on everyone at *Brides 'R Us* tomorrow.'

The two men wandered out to the Georgian mansion's porticoed entrance. Along the driveway, tall pines and cypresses waved gently, reminding Markham of the trees in St Chad's cemetery. Always mindful of the murdered dead, he endeavoured to believe that existence for everyone ended in new life beyond the grave.

As ever sensitive to 'the guvnor's' moods, Noakes said gruffly, 'Ginelli's gone, boss, but you'll make it right. . . then he can get stuck into the heavenly banquet an' all that, knowing everything's sorted down here.'

At times like this, Markham would have given much to emulate his former colleague's evangelical certitude. But even though he struggled with the eternal verities, just knowing that George Noakes was enlisted in his team's corner counted for much.

He flashed a smile at his old friend.

'I've got to get on top of this, Noakesy.' Then, almost inconsequentially, he added, 'What was it your old Sergeant Major told King Hussein of Jordan?'

He knew the answer (no doubt apocryphal) but needed to hear the other say it.

Noakes proudly stroked the regimental tie that he wore as a badge of honour.

'"If you do not get a grip of yourself, Mr King, Sir, we will have to report you to your people!"'

'Right, well, replace the Hashemite Kingdom with Superintendent Bretherton and his ilk, and you'll have some idea what I'm up against.'

'I'd back you against that shower any day of the week, sir.'

Markham couldn't say why this awkward admission should mean so much, but the assurance of Noakes's faith in him worked its usual magic. Suddenly he felt he was recovering his *true* self — the part not submerged by bureaucracy and politics — in the consciousness that he was with one who totally believed in it.

Strolling down the drive to his car, Markham smiled as he recalled the way his former sergeant's eyes had kept straying to the rather ugly painting of General Charles Gordon in Rosemount's staffroom. During their last investigation, Noakes had ferreted out some information about that epitome of heroic failure, concluding that it all boiled down to jealousy and Gordon was hung out to dry because the politicians resented his glamour. Now his wingman's words came back to him: 'Jealousy's one of the seven deadly sins an' that's what did for soldier boy in the end.'

One of the seven deadly sins . . .

Was jealousy at the root of Gino Everard's murder, as in so many homicides that Markham had investigated over the years?

Or was there some hidden transgression in Everard's past that lay behind the discovery of his obscenely posed corpse?

His mobile buzzed with a text message from Kate Burton.

His fellow DI was waiting for him at Queen for a Day, the bridal accessories store which adjoined the Confetti Club, Gino Everard's business being temporarily relocated there while the SOCOs carried out forensics at the crime scene.

Time for a first look at the suspects.

* * *

'Bloody hell, sir,' Burton said out of the corner of her mouth as they perched awkwardly on a flouncy sofa surrounded by cards and balloons and soft toys. 'Someone's gone out and raided the local Clintons. It's like the Ashley Dean case at Hope, remember?'

'How could I ever forget, Kate . . . I remember thinking then that a depressing number of people seem to think eternity consists of reading excruciatingly bad doggerel verse.'

She flashed him a puckish grin. 'Not to mention meeting Noddy and the entire cast of *Brambly Hedge*.' She glanced around at the cornucopia of tributes. 'Along with Winnie the Pooh, Piglet and Eeyore.'

'Just as well Noakesy's not here. This lot would be guaranteed to bring out his . . . subversive streak.'

'How's he doing out in the sticks, sir?' Burton invariably deferred to Markham as her superior officer, even though they were now equal in rank, and he had given up trying to dissuade her.

'Seems acclimatised to Rosemount,' Markham replied, 'but champing at the bit to have a look-in.'

They shared a conspiratorial smile.

'The DCI'll wear it, provided Noakes keeps a low profile,' Markham said, without disclosing that Sidney had only agreed to allocate 'expenses' so he intended to make up any shortfall from his own pocket.

'I'm not sure he knows what a "low profile" is, sir.'

'Oh, we'll keep him in order somehow between us, Kate.' *And out of Sidney's sight as far as possible.* 'Natalie's going to give me some intel on the setup here — personalities, rivalries, that kind of thing. . . by way of supplementing whatever we get today.'

Which in the end didn't turn out to be all that much.

Franco Santini was a well-preserved if slightly haggard man in his sixties who exuded chic in a well-cut dark suit. Wearing gold-rimmed spectacles that gleamed and glittered, and with dark wavy hair that glistened with a rich dressing, his courtly manners and accent were decidedly Mediterranean. Only a narrow nose, pinched sharp at the tip, detracted from the impression of personableness. He didn't appear to be prostrated by grief, but the detectives knew better than to draw any adverse conclusions from that, not least since Santini was now the man at the helm of Gino Everard's flagship enterprise and therefore obliged to keep a cool head.

They learned nothing from Everard's number two which shed any light on animosities past or present, the man raising well-groomed eyebrows when Markham raised the subject of disaffected employees, Joanna Osborne and Jamie O'Neill. 'They became, how do you put it, too big for their boots,' he confided. 'As for thinking that Gino felt threatened by Mr O'Neill. . . the very idea of a designer at the top of his game, in such demand by the media, having anything to fear from an *apprentice consultant* . . . It's simply too ludicrous for words.'

'What about Ms Osborne?' Burton pressed.

A theatrical gesture of the elegant hands. '*Pouf*. She misunderstood when Gino said her particular strengths lay in designing ready-to-wear dresses. There was no intention to offend . . . Like Mr O'Neill, she had her own way to make.' And a long way to go before attaining Everard's stellar heights, his tone implied.

Antonia Rambert and Lucille Chilton — Everard's senior consultant and PA — parroted the same line so glibly that it felt rehearsed.

The former was a whip-slim middle-aged woman with vulpine features and a mid-length platinum power bob. Her manner towards the police was ingratiating, but Markham received the impression that the staff feared her.

Lucille Chilton was a scrawny young redhead wearing an impossibly short black dress and stilettos, heavily made up and with hair streaming over her shoulders. Whereas Antonia Rambert's black pinstripe, shapely legs, looked classy, the youngster's appearance verged on tacky. Markham was surprised she got away with it, before reflecting that Gino Everard presumably liked the gymslip aesthetics. An overloud Estuary accent was in keeping with the brashness of her appearance. Rambert — whose own tones were upmarket northern — perceptibly winced as the decibel level rose. Reddened eyes indicated that the PA had been crying, whereas the older woman showed no sign of discomposure.

Two other women were introduced as Antonia Rambert's assistants.

Maria Hagan was an unthreatening looking bottle blonde in her forties. With her hair pulled somewhat incongruously into Pippi Longstocking braids, she had a kind, plain face, tree trunk legs, broad Lancashire accent and a nervous laugh.

Christina Skelthorne was more soigné. Slightly plump but attractive with a rounded face, long curly black hair and catlike eyes, she reminded Markham of a young Marie Helvin. She could almost have passed for a woman in her thirties, but on closer inspection he gauged that she was probably the same age as Rambert and Hagan. Judging by the approving look the senior consultant shot her, it was clear that she regarded Christina a far better advertisement for the boutique than Maria Hagan with her thrown-together boho look. And yet there was an easy camaraderie between Christina and Maria Hagan which suggested that they were probably allies behind the scenes.

Randall Fenton the young backroom supervisor — tall, shy and dark-haired with a slight stoop — very much deferred to Santini and Rambert, didn't have much to contribute beyond stammering awkwardly that he couldn't imagine how the Confetti Club would manage without Gino Everard. Glancing at the senior personnel's steely expressions, however, Markham figured that they considered themselves more than capable of taking the reins.

The question was, had they privately *wanted* a chance to shine, away from the perpetual shadow cast by Everard?

Such at any rate were the Confetti Club's key players. Certainly, as Everard's closest associates, they were the individuals of principal interest.

Notwithstanding which, Markham and Burton watched and listened politely as various others — seamstresses and outside hires — trotted to and fro, essentially repeating the same conventional platitudes, though the detectives detected genuine affection for their bouffant-haired boss. 'He was never too grand to speak to you,' as one youthful freelancer put it, unconsciously making Everard sound like royalty.

It would be interesting to learn Natalie Noakes's perspective on the working atmosphere that she had described as being occasionally bitchy.

In the meantime, however, it was a case of what her father would have called 'slim pickings'.

None of the principals had a strong alibi, though with the murder now confirmed by Dimples as having occurred just before midnight, this was hardly surprising.

Afterwards, adjourning to Waterstones for coffee, Burton glumly admitted as much. 'All of them on their lonesome and just Maria Hagan's husband to say where *she* was,' the DI grumbled. 'Worse than useless.' Then she straightened up self-consciously as though suddenly aware she was hardly demonstrating appropriate *esprit de corps*. 'But I've lined up

Danielle Rigsby at the *Gazette* for tomorrow morning, boss. Then there's Joanna Osborne and Jamie O'Neill—'

'Ah yes, the Young Pretenders,' Markham said somewhat listlessly. 'That should be illuminating.'

'They're due in to the station for interviews tomorrow afternoon . . . And I had a call from Claudia Everard who's back on *terra cotta.*'

Amused to note how his prim colleague had absorbed Noakes's Del Boy patois to the point that she now used it without thinking, Markham felt a surge of energy. It was still early days and hardly to be expected that the killer would just drop into his lap.

'Franco Santini talked about Everard being at the top of his game and in demand by the media,' Burton mused. 'But d'you reckon that was really true, sir? I mean, being proprietor of a provincial bridal shop's no big deal . . .'

'I get the feeling Mr Everard's star had waned and he was trading on past glories, Kate. Presumably the TV pilot thing was aimed at resurrecting his career . . . some sort of comeback.'

He paused, lost in thought, then smiled at his colleague.

'Right,' he said, 'after coffee, we'll see if Mrs Everard can shed any light on her ex's media prospects.'

Some fifty minutes later, they sat in Markham's car outside a large Victorian terrace in Wembley Gardens just off Bromgrove Rise.

'Well, *she* wasn't giving much away,' Burton lamented.

Markham mulled over his impressions of Gino Everard's ex-wife.

There had been something of the ice maiden about her, from the no-fuss swept-back silver hairstyle to the severe grey pinstripe suit teamed with a burgundy silk shirt. Coolly self-possessed, she confirmed that she had travelled by Eurostar to Paris for a business meeting on Sunday afternoon before returning to the UK the following day.

Another suspect without an alibi for Everard's murder on Saturday night.

Now Burton commented, 'She was right about her ex being quite the heartthrob when they were starting out. I looked up some of their early publicity shots online and he's like a young David Cassidy. . . all puppy-dog eyes and blow-dried hair. . .' She caught herself up hastily. 'If you like that kind of thing.'

Markham suppressed a smile at the thought of decidedly un-cute Professor Nathan Finlayson. This was followed by the familiar needle-sharp stab of pain at the remembrance of her engagement. However outwardly uncharismatic, Finlayson would be her husband . . .

Suddenly aware of Burton's eyes on him, he pulled himself back to assessing the Everards.

'Things began to sour when they became competitors as opposed to collaborators,' he said thoughtfully.

'It's weird,' Burton observed. '*Her* designs are the exact opposite of how she looks — all romantic and ethereal — almost like ballet costumes . . . Whereas *he* went in for more modern form-fitting stuff, which is how he got the gig for that granddaughter of the Duchess of Kent or whoever it was.'

'In terms of their partnership, Mrs Everard definitely felt that he'd claimed credit where it wasn't due,' Markham observed.

'That was a low blow when she said he was more like a canny self-promoter than any kind of serious creative talent,' Burton pointed out. 'And I don't reckon she was half as relaxed about the TV pilot as she wanted us to think . . . all that about it being tacky and vulgar, and how she couldn't believe they'd been taken in by Everard's blarney. Somehow it didn't ring true . . . I had the feeling she'd probably give her eye teeth for exposure like that.'

'Yes,' Markham concurred before adding, 'We need to dig deeper into Mrs Everard's career trajectory, Kate . . . find out more about the ups and downs.'

Burton nodded vigorously. Then, 'What did you think of her new bloke?' she asked. 'He's got to be quite a bit younger,' she added diffidently, clearly reluctant to make any allusion to 'cougars' (or 'jaguars', as Noakes had once described them in one of his more memorable malapropisms).

'Hmm. I believe Mrs Everard is seventy-one and her partner looked to be in his fifties . . . though he had the assurance of someone older.'

Slight, with the dark hair and eyes of a Cornishman, Claudia Everard's partner Martin Carthew had been cold but courteous, confirming that he had spent Saturday night with Claudia at Wembley Gardens then driven her to the train on Sunday before returning to collect her the following day. Declining to be drawn on Gino Everard, he told them his work as a lawyer meant he had nothing to do with the fashion industry. 'Which suits us both,' Claudia had added frigidly.

Neither of them had anything to say about the Confetti Club, though the superciliousness with which Mrs Everard referred to the boutique was of a piece with her overall affectation of inhabiting a different world. 'I'm sure customers had a . . . memorable experience,' she said. 'Gino was master of the personal touch.'

When it came to insinuendo, here was a practitioner to rival George Noakes.

'No shortage of funds,' Burton ruminated. 'Everything back there looked minimalist but high spec.' She pulled a wry face. 'No IKEA in sight.'

'Yes, she certainly appeared to be the epitome of a successful businesswoman,' Markham agreed. 'But I'd be interested to know what happened to her along the way.'

As he looked back at the house, an upstairs curtain twitched.

Someone was waiting for them to leave.

'Right, Kate,' Markham said. 'Let's check that the incident room's set up, and then we can turn our attention to some of the other people Mr Everard managed to alienate.'

He had the feeling it might turn out to be a sizeable roster.

3. ADVERSE REPORTS

'How's sarge getting on with General Custer then?'

It was the morning of Wednesday 6 April, and the team was gathered in Markham's office ready to compare notes.

Markham smiled at Doyle's question.

'General *Gordon*. Noakesy's got plenty of work on hand . . . what with sorting out Rosemount's security and the rest of it.'

'Is he coming on this case with us, boss?' Carruthers asked.

Markham realised that the new DS understood just what George Noakes meant to him and the team. And that there was no longer any need for subterfuge.

Sidney's spy or not, Roger Carruthers wasn't going to unsettle the dynamic that had worked so well down the years.

On the other hand, Markham still wasn't sure if Carruthers was truly 'his man' yet. He had found it difficult to bond with him, not being sure to start with if the newcomer possessed that all-important sense of humour. As Olivia had once mischievously observed, lack of GSOH didn't allow for the wind: either of change or dyspepsia.

But he had observed Burton and Doyle gradually warm to the new recruit and was determined to give Carruthers a chance, though there was no question of him ever filling the Noakes-sized hole left in Markham's unit.

Now, however, he was startled when Carruthers, flushing awkwardly said, 'Gino Everard wasn't the worst.'

Three heads swivelled his way.

'My girlfriend Kim went to the Confetti Club for a bridesmaid's dress. She's . . . well, plus-size . . . but Everard didn't make her feel uncomfortable.'

'Thank you, Sergeant,' Markham said simply. 'I appreciate your sharing this with us.'

Carruthers' prominent Adam's apple was undergoing all kinds of gyrations, but Markham just regarded him with kind reassurance. 'You know you're among friends here, Sergeant,' he said gently. 'Anything you tell us stays in this room.'

'Sorry, I should have said something earlier, boss . . . Somehow it felt difficult.'

'Of course.' Markham's steady regard never faltered. 'But we'd be very interested to know what Kim made of Mr Everard.'

Bloody hell, Doyle thought. *Maybe Carruthers was one of those blokes with a thing for fat girls.* Well aware of Markham's disapproval of prejudice, he maintained his expression of impenetrable solemnity, glad for once that Noakes wasn't there to undermine his efforts in that direction.

However, he couldn't help remembering the bizarre fetish sites they had come across during their investigation into murders at the Beautiful Bodies clinic, struggling to assimilate the idea that the uptight, almost prissy Carruthers could have a plus-size partner.

But then he noticed Markham's expression of gentle acceptance and felt ashamed of himself. The DI didn't have a problem with any of it, so why should he? And anyway, his ex-girlfriend Paula's obsession with looking like Twiggy had been a right pain at times. It might have been all to the good, he reflected darkly, if she had been able to let herself go once in a while and splurge on a cream cake. Suddenly aware that Burton's eyes were on him, Doyle stopped wool-gathering and adopted a look of alert interest.

'Kim said Everard was really nice,' Carruthers volunteered. 'There were smaller girls in there at the same time — perfect waist measurements and spray tans — but he treated her exactly the same as them.' The DS was squirming uncomfortably but determined to get his point across. 'People think girls like Kim sit at home scoffing cakes.' Doyle gave a guilty start at this. 'And watching stuff like Jeremy Kyle. But it's medical with her . . . She has thyroid problems and it's a minefield planning things. She always wants to map a route in her mind to get from A to B without attracting attention. . . won't even go shopping if there's a risk of getting a load of abuse from teenagers shouting about "chub-rubs".'

Doyle couldn't help himself. 'What's one of them?'

'When your legs rub together,' Carruthers replied, his pale face almost naked in its vulnerability. 'Being overweight can be terribly lonely, see.' With a proud defiance which made Markham warm to him as never before, he added, 'Kim's *gorgeous*, but she's got zero confidence. It took a lot for her to go to the Confetti Club rather than an outlet for . . . curvy women. She'd tried a few of those before and practically lost the will to live . . . Well anyway, Gino Everard didn't bat an eyelid. And he didn't behave as if she was invisible below the neck either. She actually *bought* an outfit in the end . . . and what's more, it really suited her.'

Markham nodded encouragingly. There was a risk of them viewing Mr Everard like some kind of pantomime dame on account of his flamboyant personality and backstory, so it was good to hear someone praise him.

Burton cleared her throat. 'What did Kim make of the rest of them in there?' she asked.

'Polite enough,' Carruthers replied, shrugging, 'but Everard really went out of his way to be charming, even though brides are supposed to be the main event and she was only getting a bridesmaid's dress. She had the feeling some of the sales staff could be quite overbearing, not nasty or anything like that . . . more like manipulating shoppers' emotions so they'd sign on the dotted line. But Everard told people not to rush and said they should take a day or two to think about things if they needed it. His voice and mannerisms were over the top all right, but underneath it all she felt he was a regular guy . . . pretty authentic.'

'Interesting,' Markham said. 'Did she notice anything else?'

'While she was in there, some TV bloke came in — at least she thinks that's who he was. She only overheard snippets because they were in Everard's office most of the time. But when they were wandering round the shop, Everard got quite wound up about not liking the kind of show which ramped up the drama by pitting people against each other — you know, encouraging brides and their mothers to fall out over revealing dresses and that type of thing, or getting bridesmaids who are bitter about not getting married to have a bitch-fest and stick it to the bride.'

Doyle was somewhat bemused. 'But isn't that the whole point of reality telly?' he enquired before adding hastily, 'Not that I watch much of it, but Kelly,' the new girlfriend, 'says that's the fun part, when the "entourage",' he air quoted ironically, 'don't get along.'

Carruthers screwed up his features, evidently remembering Kim's thoughts.

'Kim said Everard didn't sound like he was going to be pushed around. . . told mister hotshot producer or whoever he was that he didn't like confrontational stuff and preferred to focus on the creative side . . . designs and fittings. . . He said you could extract plenty of drama out of last-minute panics.' Self-consciously, Carruthers added, 'Like when a bride loses tons of weight so dresses suddenly have to be taken in. Or someone changes her mind about bling, so the backroom crew have to do on the spot alterations . . . whipping off straps and sequins. . . shortening trains and all the rest of it. . .'

'Not as much fun as a cat-fight,' Doyle demurred, ignoring Burton's frown.

'Well, Kim said Everard's number two was trying to talk him round, saying stuff about needing to exaggerate and send things up a bit for the cameras.'

'Franco Santini?' Burton asked eagerly.

'Yes, that's right. Odd really. . .' Carruthers said.

'What is?' Doyle prompted.

'Well, you'd think Everard would be the one up for a spot of play-acting seeing as he was so theatrical and OTT . . . But Kim said it was *Santini* who talked about how it made commercial sense to spice things up, sort of role reversal. . .'

The subject of television came up again when Markham betook himself to the DCI's office.

On arrival in the inner sanctum, he could not help his gaze wandering to the Hall of Fame, as the photomontage which took up the whole of one wall was irreverently known. Yep, there was a new picture of Sidney's Brunhilde-like wife hobnobbing with his all-time favourite royal the Countess of Wessex and other assorted notables. When it came to scary millinery, Mrs S easily trumped Muriel Noakes . . .

Sidney himself looked reasonably good, the executive buzz cut, clean-shaven jaw (goatee long gone) and sharp tailoring — together with the new addition of professorial spectacles — combining with his 'paperless office' and acres of polished mahogany desk to give the impression of a man at the top of his game.

Olivia had never been able to stand 'Judas Iscariot' as she called him, and it was true that Sidney's resentment of Markham's Oxbridge credentials, handsome looks (the thick dark hair being a particular grievance) and wunderkind reputation had in the past caused difficulties between them. Not to mention Sidney's antipathy towards Noakes whose slobbishness and renowned subversiveness literally induced an allergic reaction (his eczema had noticeably abated since Noakes's departure).

But now, with the prospect of retirement moving closer, Sidney was inclined to be less territorial and abrasive. Olivia had said, 'You wait and see, Gil, he's desperate to get his phiz on TV — reinvent himself as some sort of police pundit or a consultant on those creepy crime documentaries for Channel Five. God, can you just imagine it . . . Sidney doing Jack the Ripper!'

And the ignoble thought *had* crossed his mind that Sidney's affability might not be unconnected with Gino Everard's status as a pseudo celebrity (or what passed for one in Bromgrove) and television's interest in the Confetti Club.

It turned out that Sidney's niece — on Brunhilde's side — had got married the previous year and called on Everard's services. To Markham's surprise, the DCI confided, 'We would have liked a daughter . . . Not that we aren't extremely proud of the boys, of course.' And he was off, holding forth about his stellar offspring, paying particular attention to the eldest, Jake, who was currently doing officer training at Sandhurst. All things considered, Markham thought wryly, it was just as well Noakes wasn't there to puncture Sidney's balloon with allusions to barrack-room bad lads and his favourite army jokes, liberally sprinkled with colourful Saxon expletives on the subject of 'crap-hats' and 'jankers'. He suppressed a grin as he thought of the last time CID had hosted the Royal Military Police, when Noakes had assumed the duties of unofficial toastmaster in a manner that none of those present was ever likely to forget.

Possibly something in Markham's expression reminded Sidney of those Top-Table-Terrors, because the DCI abruptly terminated his raptures on the subject of army life. 'Well, as I was saying, we've no daughters to marry off.' Markham rather suspected that, given the DCI's notoriously parsimonious streak, he didn't particularly object to dodging the financial obligations that belonged to Father of the Bride. But he was nonetheless touched by the wistfulness in Sidney's voice, more evidence of the man behind the corporate mask.

'What was your niece's experience of the Confetti Club, sir?' the DI asked.

'Oh, everything was entirely satisfactory I think, the dress and so forth. . . a halter neck. . . very, er, *daring* according to Mrs Sidney.' From which it might be deduced that the DCI's formidable wife hadn't approved the choice of outfit. Certainly, his boss's squeamish expression indicated a degree of discomfort around the subject of the family nuptials.

'Did Mrs Sidney see much of Mr Everard herself?' Markham continued.

'She'd been into the boutique once or twice,' the other said vaguely, careful not to use the word 'shop' with its overtones of the lower orders. 'And of course, Everard was a regular on the charity circuit. Very charming by all accounts.' It occurred to Markham that Noakes and Sidney were probably as one in their assessment of Everard's charm.

Markham briskly took his boss through the rollcall of suspects, with Sidney clearly hoping someone from the shop floor or 'sewing side' could take the top spot, rather than that (horror of horrors) anyone from the *Gazette* or university. . . or, even worse, the ex-wife or Mark Harvison, scourge of Bromgrove CID, should assume pole position.

'Are we looking at an inside job, Inspector?' the DCI honked in the strident bray that always affected his subordinate like nails scraping down a chalkboard.

'I think Mr Everard arranged to meet his killer by appointment, sir—'

'But why would he be on the premises at that time on a Saturday night?' Sidney interrupted impatiently. 'I mean, isn't that somewhat *bizarre?*'

'I think it would appeal to Mr Everard's sense of drama, his persona . . . enjoyment of intrigue, if you like,' Markham replied calmly. 'From what I've learned of him, cloak and dagger would have been right up his street.'

'CCTV?' Sidney enquired.

'The system was being upgraded at the weekend, sir . . . Everyone knew the score, so it offered the perfect opportunity for those who were aware of that.'

Now the DCI was revolving scenarios in his head.

'Could the killer have known that Everard was planning to come in late at night and then lain in wait for him . . . planned some kind of *ambush*?' Sidney speculated.

'The senior staff had their own key fobs for getting into the centre and knew the shop's eight-character alarm code which was changed monthly,' Markham said. 'A master set of keys apparently went missing a few weeks ago, but they didn't bother to change the locks. I suspect there was a pretty laissez-faire attitude to the alarm code as well, with people jotting it down on post-its or giving it out willy-nilly, though of course they all swear blind nothing like that ever happened . . . An ambush is obviously one possibility, sir, but I'd say a pre-arranged rendezvous is more likely. Plus, the pathologist tells me Mr Everard had taken a large glass of Chablis not long before he died, which is one reason why his defences were down when he was attacked. Apparently, he always kept a few bottles in the fridge in his office for special visitors. The staff can't say for sure if a bottle's missing, but I'm inclined to think he and his assailant shared a drink . . . According to their cleaner, Everard's drinks cabinet is missing two glasses, which most likely points to the killer removing them after-wards. In terms of forensics, cross-contamination means we need a suspect in the frame before raising our hopes.'

Sidney's face bore the look of one far from accustomed to getting his hopes up.

'And where does George Noakes fit in to this investiga-tion,' he enquired with a rapier thrust.

'Well of course Noakes sees himself very much in the . . . boiler room when it comes to helping us out,' Markham improvised hastily thinking, *Boiler room, that'll be the day!* 'He's currently busy reassessing Rosemount's security needs and doing risk assessments.' *Yeah, for Bingo.* He could almost hear Noakes's scornful Greek chorus as he uttered this reassurance. 'I believe Natalie may have some useful insights in terms of the boutique's working environment seeing as she offers var-ious, um, *holistic* services to clients. In fact, I'll be seeing her about that shortly.' No need to mention that he would be

44

dining chez Noakes. Nor that his former wingman suspected Gino Everard of having nefarious designs on the fair Natalie.

'Well, if you're sure that Noakes can be trusted to remain in the background. . .'

'Absolutely, sir. . . completely in the engine room for this one.'

What was it with Ordeal-by-Sidney that he found himself spouting the most awful tripe . . . boiler and engine rooms?

But the DCI seemed to buy it, appearing mollified by this depiction of Noakes as the proverbial shy violet.

Some cordial conversation followed concerning the progress of Kate Burton whom Sidney, a fellow psychology graduate, clearly regarded as a kindred spirit. Markham suppressed a grin as he recalled one occasion when the DCI and Burton got on to the burning philosophical question of whether religious belief had been superseded by evolutionary science. Asked where he stood on heaven and hell, unconsciously parodying Jane Eyre, Noakes solemnly cautioned Sidney, 'You wanna be careful an' don' ever die!' After that, the DCI made sure to keep off Richard Dawkins and similar subjects when Markham's lumbering number two was around.

Having assured Sidney that DI Burton would liaise with Professor Finlayson on psychological profiling (no doubt his eager beaver colleague was already on it) and promised 'utmost discretion' in respect of 'prominent people', Markham at last salaamed himself out of the office. A brief exchange with the current dragon who guarded Sidney's domain — an intimidatingly efficient woman who, like the DCI, had shed few tears at Noakes's departure — and he was free.

Right, time to tackle Danielle Rigsby over at the *Gazette*. He'd take Doyle along for that — see what effect his vaunted 'boyish charm' would have on a cynical hack. Then Doyle and Carruthers could sit in on the interviews with Joanna Osborne and Jamie O'Neill. Meanwhile, Burton could check out background information on the TV people once she and

Carruthers had processed Everard's flat in Dunbabin Mews. He considered it unlikely that Everard had been murdered for anything to do with 'creative differences', but the television pilot was another element in the mix.

The DI's spirits lifted at a successful outcome (more or less) to his meeting with Sidney who had *finally* stopped telegraphing clumsy sympathy for the split with Olivia. Any more of those comments about Markham looking 'peaky' (*cringe*), or unsubtle reminders that 'his door was always open' (*pass the sick bucket*), and it wouldn't just be Noakesy cashing in his chips!

* * *

Danielle Rigsby at the *Gazette* seemed cheerfully unconcerned about featuring on their list of suspects. A chunky woman with a shaggy blonde perm and big jam-jar glasses, she clearly didn't give two hoots about her appearance, sporting a mismatched sweatshirt, and baggy combat trousers reminiscent of Noakes's pre-Rosemount wardrobe.

Despite showing no signs of succumbing to Doyle's ingenuous charm, she seemed easy-going and friendly, chatting affably about her early days as a cub reporter working on Marriages and Deaths.

'Cue major hysterics when things go wrong,' she chuckled. 'I remember there was a huge fuss a couple of years back over some headstone which said: As the years roll onwards, And memories grow dim, We promise that, forever, We shall remember *her* . . . And there was this other time when Veronica Williams — you know, Bromgrove's first female councillor of colour who did all that outreach for sex workers — died and some dickhead curate announced at her funeral that the choir would sing the old Negro Spiritual *Carry me back to Old Virginity* . . . God, the row over *that* went on for ages.' She winked at the two detectives. 'Mind you, we got the biggest postbag ever.'

Doyle sniggered appreciatively but, at an imperceptible sign from Markham, moved on to the subject of Gino Everard.

'You weren't a fan of Mr Everard,' the DS prompted her. 'Criticised him in the paper, right?'

'Look, the man was so OTT he practically *invited* us to take the piss,' she retorted, rolling her eyes. 'All those airs and graces and waving his hands around. . . I met him at this charity bash, and he was like some condescending aristo assuring members of the great unwashed, "There's no need to call me Sir, my good man."'

Doyle grinned. He'd already sorted a file of press cuttings for the guvnor to read later, greatly enjoying the journalist's sarkiness about the 'embourgeoisement' of Everard and the designer's enthusiasm for tippexing his working-class antecedents.

'There was no great malice in any of it,' the journalist insisted. 'We stayed just the right side of libel.'

'What about Mr Everard's TV pilot?' Doyle asked silkily. 'He threatened to sue over that piece you wrote about him being some gigolo and rumours about him plying the mums with complimentary Prosecco so they'd lose their inhibitions and kick off . . . and it'd boost ratings.'

'Look, I did a follow-up to put things right,' she said. 'Explained how that customer — the one who slapped the senior woman with the French surname — was on medication, which is why she lost it and—'

'Turned tired and emotional?' Doyle suggested helpfully.

The journalist nodded vigorously. 'Precisely. And anyway, that barney never made it into the programme.'

'In fact,' Markham interposed, 'I have it on good authority that Mr Everard was apparently strongly averse to anything that looked like staged melodrama.'

Carruthers's girlfriend had said nothing about alcohol being pressed on customers, though Markham could easily imagine Everard offering fizz to favoured clients.

'If anything,' the DI continued, 'it was apparently his deputy Franco Santini and not Everard who favoured that kind of approach.'

Danielle Rigsby's expression was highly sceptical, as though she found it difficult to imagine Everard taking the moral high ground.

Doyle ploughed on. 'There was that section where you said every wedding planner in the country would be up in arms about the way he encouraged his staff to treat them like total charlatans.'

'Again, I clarified that in the follow-up.' And now Markham fancied the woman sounded distinctly nettled, her earlier friendliness evaporating. 'I said Everard was just anxious that brides shouldn't feel they were under pressure or at risk of their big day being hijacked.' With a clear note of exasperation in her voice, she added, 'To be honest, I was more interested in how Everard's social media accounts didn't do much to support women who struggled with their body image . . . reinforced discriminatory stereotypes, that kind of thing.'

'Ah yes,' Markham interjected smoothly. 'Your interview with Mr Shay Conteh.'

'That's right.' Now the journalist was undeniably defensive. 'It wasn't a case of inciting people to go out and picket Everard's shop or anything like that. But at different times he *had* been outspoken about obesity. He did that awful quote about plus-size brides being the "Buntys of Bulimia all puke-u-like and mess" . . . well, him or some smart-alec PR type were looking to get him some attention.'

After they had left the *Gazette*'s offices, Doyle turned to Markham, 'Strange what Carruthers said about Everard being so nice to his girlfriend and then hearing the journo tell us that about him taking pot shots at fat girls. . . I mean women with body problems,' he amended hastily, well aware of Markham's dislike of pejorative language but inwardly thinking it was getting ridiculous the way you had to police every bloody word, especially when it came to women's issues

. . . Like Noakesy said, any day now they'd be talking about the pigging *Peopleopause*.

'I seem to recall Ms Rigsby's career stalled after all the fuss with Everard, so she never made it to senior features writer,' Markham observed.

'Yeah, it would give her a reason to hate him.'

'Her and quite a few other people by the sound of it,' the DI sighed. 'I think this murder was possibly an "inside job", but we'll need to check Everard's customer records and look into any incidents of shoppers' rage.'

'Not to mention wedding planners', sir.'

'Indeed.'

The list of to-dos was growing longer by the minute, Markham reflected wearily.

'Okay,' he said, 'let's see if Joanna Osborne and Jamie O' Neill have anything for us.'

* * *

In the event, they didn't.

Joanna Osborne was a very pretty young woman with laughing hazel eyes and shoulder-length honey-streaked hair, worn slightly long over one eye so Markham wondered how it didn't drive her mad. However, with an inward shrug, he supposed this was the fashion nowadays and he was too old to appreciate such artful dishevelment.

She had come straight from her job as a buyer for fashion chain Zara and was wearing a lime green crochet knit dress teamed with a blazer and trainers, a look that flattered her athletic figure. The DI was amused to note how both Doyle and Carruthers sat up straighter when they saw her.

'I'm sorry Gino's dead, of course I am,' she said in a soft clipped tones that reminded Markham of Princess Diana's Sloaney voice. 'And to be murdered . . . just *awful*.'

The DI wasted no time getting to the heart of the matter.

'You left the Confetti Club on bad terms,' he said levelly.

She bit her lip but answered readily enough. 'Yes, Gino sneered on TV about my being this ready-to-wear designer — made it sound like I was some little nobody. The truth was, I'd worked with him on some couture items, only he never gave me any credit for it. And I had a couple of commissions in the pipeline from clients who'd seen my sketches . . . It sounds big-headed to say so, but I think he was jealous and insecure. And the others didn't like me—'

'Why not?' Doyle asked, though he had a feeling as he looked at their doe-eyed interviewee that her colleagues' reaction had to be down to jealousy too.

'I think they felt I should have stayed more in the background. But the TV people wanted me in shot and I couldn't exactly say no.'

'Who's "they"?' Carruthers followed up. 'Do you mean the sales team?'

'Oh, pretty much everyone, I think,' she said vaguely. 'It was just this sense I had that they all thought I was pushing myself forward, hogging the limelight.'

There was something of the wide-eyed ingenue about her, Markham thought, but that didn't mean it was necessarily false or put-on; more like a demeanour she had somehow assimilated so that it became a part of her character. She appeared to be happy and successful in her new position, admitting that while it was a sideways move away from designing, she still had her freelance work and was optimistic about her chances of breaking back into the bridal market.

'Did you reckon later you might've overreacted a bit about the TV pilot?' Carruthers asked as she got up to leave.

'Well, Gino practically bit my hand off when I gave him my resignation,' she replied frankly. 'Couldn't wait to accept it.'

'If she *does* regret how things turned out, she's doing a good job of hiding it,' Doyle said afterwards. 'Plus, she seemed pretty philosophical about Everard.'

Markham wasn't so sure about that, with the words 'some little nobody' reverberating in his ear.

Jamie O'Neill, tall, blond and languid with well-cut features and a slight transatlantic accent, made no bones about the reason for his dismissal.

'Everard said I was too slow. Apparently, I let appointments overrun . . . wasted too much time on chit-chat . . . said I didn't understand it was all about making money dah-di-dah.'

'Was that why he fired you then?' Doyle demanded bullishly.

'*Was it heck!*' O'Neill smiled, but to Markham his expression looked somewhat strained. 'He just didn't like me sweet-talking the mothers and Bridezillas. That was supposed to be *his* forte. And then after the pilot thing, some reporter talked about me being the boutique's Prince Charming, which didn't help.'

Markham could well imagine how Danielle Rigsby enjoyed *that* little bit of mischief-making.

'As for my airtime, it was a case of blink-and-you'd-miss-it,' O'Neill continued. 'I was smart enough to know Everard wouldn't want me muscling in, so I tried to stay well out of the way . . . And I saw the sour faces when the TV lot wanted to use Jo. I congratulated myself on dodging a bullet . . . but,' with some bitterness, 'the cameras caught me anyway.'

'You didn't think about taking Everard to a tribunal?' Carruthers pressed.

'I had grounds all right, but in this industry if you're seen as a troublemaker and make waves, then you're *dead*.' An awkward laugh. 'Sorry, not the best choice of words.'

After O'Neill's departure, Markham announced. 'Right, I think I need to see this infamous TV pilot and then I'm off for a consultation with Natalie Noakes.'

His two young subordinates shared a look that said eloquently, *Rather You Than Me.*

'Do some more digging on Ms Osborne and Mr O'Neill,' Markham instructed. 'Superficially, *he* seems to have the more obvious grudge against Everard seeing as he's currently out of work,' the DI continued. Which in itself was somewhat odd given the man's good looks. 'But I don't want to jump to any conclusions. The more background we have, the better. . . And see if you can schedule Shay Conteh and Mark Harvison for tomorrow.'

'On it, boss,' they chorused in unison.

Having skipped lunch, Markham found he was looking forward to getting his supper at Noakes's.

But first, time to immerse himself in the world of . . . what had O'Neill called them? Oh yes, the *Bridezillas!*

4. THE FABRIC OF CRIME

Markham felt reasonably sure that supper chez Noakes didn't normally feature a chicken liver pâté starter, Duck à l'Orange and sherry trifle, but he was nonetheless touched by the trouble Muriel had taken — as though she considered her 'superior' cuisine balm for a wounded heart and guaranteed to expunge painful memories of Olivia.

Mrs Noakes was wearing one of her fearsomely floral tea dresses, with her blonde bouffant lacquered within an inch of its life. Very Margaret Thatcher, Olivia would have said.

The two women didn't get on, though Olivia somehow never had the heart to disabuse Noakes of his fond notion that she and his womenfolk had gradually become the best of friends.

'I hate the way Muriel's so arch with you while giving me these snide looks — as though I'm something she's stepped in,' was his ex's regular plaint. 'And there's the way she elongates her vowels and does the whole highfalutin elocution thing whenever she sees you. . . like some weird psychodrama where she's playing Professor Higgins and Eliza Dolittle at the same time.'

But Muriel, clinging to social niceties in the barracks of gentility, existed in 3D for Markham in a way that she never did for Olivia.

'Noakesy's this Yorkshireman who just sticks two fingers up with one hand even as he's forelock-tugging with the other (not that there's too much of that),' he had told his partner. 'He doesn't give a stuff about whether he's working or middle class. But with Muriel, it's much more complex. . . I think somewhere along the line she's developed a bad case of social anxiety . . . internalised some sort of chronic class insecurity, which weirdly means she puts "upper-class" behaviour on a pedestal precisely because of its *exclusivity* — the fact that the likes of her don't get to be part of it . . . Then she replicates that dynamic by categorising folk as Other People and deciding whether or not they're "respectable"—'

'You mean she gets off on looking down her nose because it makes her feel better about herself,' Olivia groused.

'I'm not sure if that's the right way to put it,' he said. 'It's more that her obsession with correct behaviour gives her a chance to recalibrate the social scales in her own favour.'

'Whatever goes on in that woman's head, it's beyond me. Whenever we visit them, it's like some gruesome remake of *Abigail's Party*.'

Despite the memory of Olivia's jaundiced commentary, now as he looked as Noakes's wife, Markham somehow found her poignant. She might have internalised respectability from her backcombed hair to the classic shoes (Sole Bliss, as worn by the Duchess of Cornwall), but he sensed that she adopted her protective camouflage of middle-class pretension to keep herself safe from being on the outside looking in. Whereas Olivia disdained this attitude as 'small-souled petty-mindedness', *he* understood and sympathised, seeing the flipside of Muriel's snobbery and social climbing — the fear that went with it . . . the lurking worry that she somehow wasn't good enough. Markham had come to admire her resilience and pragmatism — you could almost call it gallantry — in the way she deployed 'middle-classness' to keep her sense of identity and core beliefs (prejudices) intact. Listening to her over coffee and chocolate truffles (Fortnum & Mason) as she extolled the performance of Bette Davis in the previous night's offering on Film4 (no doubt mentally reassigning the role of Jezebel to Olivia), he suspected his hostess found comfort in the reflection that even beautiful rich women occasionally hit rock bottom . . . one respect at least in which that shimmering exclusivity became accessible.

Poor, dear Gilbert, Muriel thought as she chatted brightly about culture (receiving precious little help from her husband or Natalie), it was so obvious from the intensity of his gaze that he was starved for *gracious living* and some *elegant* conversation. Olivia Mullen with her penchant for takeaways and clever clogs intellectualising — *showing off*, to be honest — was not at all the right partner for a man like that. Quiet, unflashy refinement was what he required . . . and she flattered herself that, blessed with so many inner resources, she knew how to provide it. Really, it was all a question of *breeding*, but so many people nowadays had no clue when it came to social savoir-faire. At least *she* would never be found wanting in that department.

Natalie, meanwhile, felt she had never done so many eye rolls as during the course of this meal.

Mum always got herself dressed up like a dog's dinner whenever Gilbert Markham came calling. It was dead obvious she thought the sun shone out of his backside and was seriously chuffed he had split from Olivia.

As for herself, well she wasn't Olivia's biggest fan — always felt the other woman was laughing up her sleeve at them — but she couldn't help feeling sorry for Markham's ex who had looked properly miserable that day when she came into the Confetti Club to pick up some brochures for a friend. Olivia had lost tons of weight — when she already looked like a toothpick to start with — and had bags under her eyes. In fact, she looked so bad that, for the first time in their acquaintance, Natalie felt herself to have the upper hand. There were stories about her stepping out with Mathew

Sullivan, the Deputy Head from Hope, but she didn't believe it. . . I mean, *seriously*, who'd want that nerdy long drink of water after *Markham*, and anyway wasn't he supposed to be gay!

Okay, so the DI was an older man, but he definitely still had it, like Jeremy Irons or that bloke from *X-Files* with the peculiar surname . . . something about the haunted eyes and that air of being a wounded dreamer. . .

Muriel had banned shop talk while they were eating, on the basis that a skilled hostess never allowed conversation to become heavy or depressing, but over coffee they finally turned to the burning topic of the Confetti Club murder.

Even Olivia had been forced to concede that Muriel, for all her love of police gossip, was invariably tight-lipped about CID investigations outside their own immediate circle. So Markham was able to discuss victim and suspects freely.

'Gino Everard seems to have been a "like him or loathe him" kind of character,' he said. 'The ex-wife Claudia and her lawyer toyboy clearly hated his guts. On the other hand, his PA Lucille Chilton seemed pretty upset—'

'Cos she had the hots for him,' Natalie interjected, ignoring her mother's frown. 'Always prancing round in skirts so short you can practically see what she's had for breakfast.'

Markham suppressed a smile as he recalled Natalie's own wardrobe in her pre-Rick Jordan epoch. There was none so puritanical as a reformed party girl who these days preferred 'nun chic' to in-your-face glamour (though the eye makeup and false eyelashes were startling as ever).

'Indeed,' he said with his trademark grave courtesy. 'Lucille certainly struck me as having a more . . . *informal* approach than Antonia Rambert.' He looked enquiringly at Natalie, who was more than happy to dish the dirt on the senior sales consultant.

'Oh, that one's a real *witch*.' The film talk had clearly lit a flame. 'Have you ever seen *The Devil Wears Prada?*' she asked Markham.

He shook his head with a charming expression of regret.

'Well, there's this character, total piece of work played by Meryl Streep . . . dead mean and snaky, like Anna Wintour. . . you know, the editor from *Vogue?*' she added hopefully.

'Right, I'm with you now,' Markham nodded. 'The anorexic-looking woman who always wears sunglasses even when she's indoors?'

'Yeah, that's her. Thinks she's better than everyone else. . . wore sunglasses to meet the Queen.'

Muriel's lips thinned with disapproval at this.

'And Rambert's just the same,' Natalie continued. 'She really knows how to make people squirm. Good at her job, mind . . . kind of *frightens* customers into choosing something and ponying up.' Clearly Natalie admired the hardnosed side of the senior consultant. 'Even Gino was scared of her.'

'What about Franco Santini?' Markham asked, aware of Noakes's louring expression.

Natalie simpered. 'Oh, he's such a *sweetheart* . . . You can talk to him about *anything* and it's like he can read your mind or something.'

Noakes's expression darkened still further at this suggestion of Svengali-like powers, but he comforted himself by abstracting another truffle while Muriel's attention was distracted.

Markham hadn't exactly received the impression that Santini was a particularly 'cuddly' personality, but clearly he had some kind of charisma where women were concerned.

'Franco understands the media side,' Natalie continued, with an air of worldly wisdom that amused Markham. 'Knows you have to give them what they want — drama, fireworks, people falling out, that kind of thing.' She pursed her lips. 'Gino wasn't happy about that, but he was starting to come round to the idea, knew it made sense.'

'What were your impressions of the junior staff?' Markham asked.

'Maria Hagan's dead nice, kind of motherly and cosy. . . good at calming everything down if it gets stressy.'

Ah, the Bridezilla phenomenon, Markham thought. Aloud, he asked, 'Do you ever have men visiting the boutique?'

'Nah. It's usually just GBFs.'

'*GBFs?*'

'Gay Best Friends,' she translated with an air of kind forbearance.

'Right.' Markham decided to return to safer ground. 'And how did you find the other salespeople?'

'They're okay. Chrissy Skelthorne and Maria pretty much stick together . . . safety in numbers kind of thing.' Grudgingly, she added, 'Chrissy's quite glamorous but,' somehow Markham just *knew* there would be a qualification, 'a bit up herself. She puts on airs and graces for customers . . . bit OTT if you ask me.'

'The backroom lad, Randall Fenton didn't have much to say for himself,' Markham observed.

'Oh, he's nice but really shy.' Markham could well imagine pneumatic Natalie Noakes terrifying the living daylights out of Fenton. 'Hero-worshipped Gino. Trailed round after him like a puppy dog.'

It didn't sound as though any of Everard's employees had it in for him. 'So, you'd say that on balance the boutique was a happy ship then?' Markham pressed Natalie.

'Gino was the tops.' Suddenly she looked woebegone. 'Him and Franco were dead understanding about me wanting a ceremony thing so I could draw a line under Rick . . . have *closure.*'

And get the cash register ringing, Noakes thought.

With a wary glance at Muriel, she continued, 'They were really keen about moving into body art.' Her mother's expression strongly suggested she considered 'piercings' an unsuitable topic for coffee and truffles. '*Physical ornamentation*,' she amended hastily, 'to express your personality.'

Markham smiled warmly. 'How very interesting, Natalie. I believe there's a specialist module offered by the university as part of its MA in Performance Studies. They'd probably bite your hand off if you fancied some teaching.'

Natalie looked pleased as punch at this.

'I got interested in costumes and makeup and stuff after that poisoning case at Carton Hall,' she said. Ducking her head shyly towards Noakes, 'Dad got me some books out of the library.' Almost defensively, she added, 'He knows so much about history and all that, I said he should do a degree or something.'

Muriel looked gratified, having considerable respect for academic study as some sort of moral enterprise, regularly boasting of Noakes's extracurricular interests in the same way as a proud parent might flaunt their child's achievements in the high jump.

'I always felt GCSEs and A levels seemed practically *designed* to stop youngsters like Natalie — Talented Late Developers' (Markham could hear the capital letters as Muriel said this) — 'from fulfilling their potential at school.' Oddly enough, it was an observation he had heard many times from Olivia's lips, too. Muriel bridled. 'But I've always said you can't beat the University of Life' (more capitals). Her beringed hand waved as though brandishing an invisible scroll, for all the world like Neville Chamberlain returning from Munich with his piece of paper. Markham felt a strong compulsion to laugh but managed to maintain his expression of polite complaisance.

Notwithstanding his amusement, he never failed to be moved by these glimpses of Muriel's inner life, though he knew his ex would have scoffed at the rooted prejudices that ran through her like a stick of Blackpool rock (Mrs Noakes would not have cared for that comparison on account of its vulgarity).

'D'you reckon the TV lot will want to go ahead with something about the boutique after all of this . . . the murder and everything?' Natalie asked wistfully. She hadn't been in the shop the day they filmed the pilot, and anyway she figured they'd have wanted to focus on the brides and dresses. But who knew, maybe they could do a follow-up . . . kind of like a tribute to Gino . . . with a look at the spin-offs he was developing. . . on the *cosmetic* side . . .

Again, Markham felt his heartstrings plucked by the transparency of her comment.

'They might well want to do a feature at some point, Natalie,' he said, while privately reflecting that there was nothing like ghoulish notoriety for bumping up ratings. 'I'll be looking to see if there were any production issues, but so far there don't appear to have been any disagreements which turned nasty.'

'That Jo Osborne,' Natalie said suddenly with a little hiss, 'and Jamie O'Neill imagined the pilot was gonna make them into stars. I heard the two of them were *posing* like mad — trying to catch the producer's eye.' Annoyance gave her normally pretty features a sulky, discontented look. 'It wasn't my day for doing treatments, but one of the girls in repairs told me all about it . . . can't say I was surprised.'

'They didn't get all that much camera time in the end, though,' Markham said thoughtfully.

Judging by Natalie's expression, it wasn't for want of trying.

'I take it *you* found them pushy,' he observed mildly.

'*And then some*! Talk about thinking you're "God's gift" . . . Franco always said Gino spoiled them and *that's* why they got so conceited.' She looked as though she was wrestling with herself whether to be indiscreet or not. Natalie being Natalie, the inner conflict lasted a matter of seconds. 'I reckon Jamie fancied Gino but got knocked back,' she said.

'Mr O'Neill is gay?'

'He didn't come right out and say it, but you could *tell*.' It was clear from the knowing air that Natalie considered her gaydar to be pretty infallible.

'What about Mr Everard. . . did you know about any romantic attachments . . . any boyfriends?' Markham asked. He had drawn a blank on this during the interview with Danielle Rigsby, who was quick to point out that she had confined herself to hinting that Everard's sexuality was 'fluid' and had never named names.

Natalie scowled, and Muriel looked like she was sucking a lemon.

'That stuff in the *Gazette* was a pile of *crap*,' she said vehemently, the lack of any tut-tutting from Muriel eloquent testimony to the fact that mother and daughter were singing from the same hymn sheet. 'I never saw *anything* like that . . . I mean, the way he behaved round customers and the mums, it was obvious he was a hundred per cent straight. And anyway, if you ask me, I reckon he was so *scarred* from the divorce that he didn't want to get into anything romantic for the rest of forever.'

From the way Noakes was shuffling his feet, it was obvious he didn't care for the subject of Gino Everard's sexuality. But he said nothing, preferring on such occasions to give his wife and daughter the floor.

'Did you see the incident where Ms Rambert ended up getting slapped by a distraught bride who'd been plied with drink?' Markham enquired, deftly changing the subject.

'*Nah.*' Natalie was clearly disappointed to have missed this Bridezilla moment. 'But I know it wasn't anything to do with Prosecco,' she said smugly, having clearly been briefed by her spies on the ground. 'The daft cow had taken too many chill pills . . . So, when Rambert made a snippy comment about needing to be "realistic" — cos she was three sizes too big for the look she wanted — she totally lost it . . . apologised afterwards, mind you, so Rambert was able to guilt-trip her into buying something way over budget.' Natalie clearly rather admired how the senior consultant had turned things round. 'Gino was well upset when the *Gazette* ran that piece about him trying to get customers pissed.' *Ahem* from Muriel, but Natalie was oblivious. 'He only brought out the booze at Christmas and New Year, or if it was a customer's birthday . . . said it was all about giving people a Rolls Royce experience . . . nothing to do with winding them up. He didn't like aggro or arguments.'

'And yet he parted company with Ms Osborne and Mr O'Neill,' Markham demurred.

'*She* was a pathetic attention-seeker . . . flounced out cos Gino didn't make enough fuss of her. And O'Neill just couldn't cut it. Maria Hagan said he was so laid-back he was practically horizontal — did everything in slo-mo — and it was driving everyone nuts. *That's* why he had to go.' Fiercely she added, 'They were bigheads, the pair of them. They didn't seem to realise it was *Gino's* gig and they were fricking nobodies.'

At this juncture, Muriel deftly removed the Pinot Grigio from Natalie's elbow and ushered them into the 'drawing room' for the inevitable Richard Clayderman.

All in all, it had been an illuminating evening, Markham reflected as he walked back to his apartment in The Sweepstakes.

Natalie hadn't been able to shed any light on Mark Harvison and his daughter — how her eyes had gleamed when Markham mentioned slag-gate! — but she had given him plenty to think about in relation to the other suspects. Tomorrow he and Carruthers would beard Shay Conteh at the university, and hopefully after that Mark Harvison back at the station. Then on Friday he would catch-up with Noakes at Doggie Dickerson's boxing gym in Marsh Lane before his appointment with Gino Everard's solicitor.

He thought about his researches earlier that day. Nothing had jumped out at him from the TV pilot, which came across as fairly anodyne — though there was the possibility of juicier segments having ended up on the cutting room floor.

Now that Burton had inducted him into the mysteries of bridal reality TV, Markham felt he had a better appreciation of the genre, evaluating the slick superficiality of the half hour pilot as typical of the desired formula for such programmes. He hadn't detected any overt signs of tension among the boutique's personnel, nor had there been any bust-ups between brides and their 'entourages' aside from some fairly good-natured bickering about styles and 'silhouettes'. There was no sign of Prosecco being quaffed, though it could have taken place off camera.

Reviewing what Natalie had told him, he thought about her insistence that the proprietor of the Confetti Club hadn't liked aggro or arguments. Which chimed with what Carruthers' girlfriend Kim said about Everard's aversion to the idea of staged catfights for TV.

On the other hand, if Kim was right, Franco Santini wasn't against the idea of engineering displays of temperament on the basis that it was good box-office. . .

When it came to the file of press cuttings assembled by Doyle, again there was nothing that really stood out . . . other than Danielle Rigsby's skill when it came to sly malice.

Suddenly tired, Markham decided to forget about bridal stores and tantrums for the time being. Hopefully tomorrow's visit to Bromgrove University would give him and Carruthers something useful to chew on.

* * *

The Sports Science Centre at Bromgrove University was one of those edifices whose brutalist architecture King Charles must surely have had in mind when he spoke of 'monstrous carbuncles' — so Markham thought as he and Carruthers contemplated the rhombus-shaped black steel and glass main building.

'God, it's ugly,' Carruthers said fervently. 'Most likely cost a fortune too.'

The DI nodded agreement. Despite Thursday morning being mild and dry, nothing could soften the centre's uncompromising angles. A group of sculpted figures in the main forecourt, presumably meant to depict genderless athletes, put him more in mind of Easter Island monoliths than heroic Olympians. Raised beds around the perimeter of the forecourt were conspicuously devoid of flowers, featuring shrubs whose uncompromising sturdiness was of a piece with the stark geometric complex. In front of the sculptures was a rectangular raised pool with a granite javelin thrower (at least this one being recognisably human) in the centre.

Shay Conteh had arranged to meet them in the centre's coffee shop on the ground floor, so the detectives duly headed in and settled themselves with two flat whites.

Noakes had emailed Markham some items from the *Gazette*, and Markham had been surprised to see that Conteh didn't resemble his idea of an ex-boxer, being a tall thin man with light red hair and beard and features that narrowly missed being handsome due to an expression of fretful tetchiness. 'Conteh were a featherweight,' Noakes explained in his accompanying phone call. 'Not plug ugly like some of the others, a good mover round the ring. Did pretty well but broke his hand which meant curtains for his career. Took A levels an' became a poster boy for the uni. Jumps on every bandwagon going. Between you an' me, guv,' — that was always the prelude to something deeply derogatory, Markham knew — 'he's a sanctimonious twat. Plus, he looks jus' like that pervy writer your Liv likes. . . the one who did the Lady Chatterley book.'

And now as Conteh made his way to their table, Markham had to admit he could see what Noakes meant. The former boxer with his famished good looks undoubtedly bore a certain resemblance to D.H. Lawrence, though Conteh's vaunted puritanical streak presumably ruled out extracurricular erotic high jinks.

In conversation, however, he appeared amenable with nothing to hide, though the temperature dropped several degrees when Carruthers touched on rumours that had featured in the *Gazette*'s 'Confidential Correspondent' column.

'There's this story that Gino Everard called you a D-lister desperate to be relevant. . . something about taking a mickey mouse degree at a tinpot university. That had to have hurt, right?' Carruthers pressed. 'And then, apparently, he said you were — what was it — oh yes, a pretend male feminist spouting the liberal lefty line because it was a way to get publicity . . .? After that, you really cranked up the rhetoric about how designers like him were taking women back to the dark ages with their "size discrimination".'

Conteh didn't rise to the bait, though there was an edge to his pleasant Northern tones as he shrugged: 'I didn't know the man, and the papers will say anything these days. I just wanted to help some of the plus-size bloggers share their stuff on social media . . . they saw Gino Everard as being part of the problem, frankly. And *they* were the ones who got the bandwagon rolling.'

But it was *Conteh* whom Everard had allegedly singled out for ridicule.

'What did you make of him, boss?' Carruthers asked after Conteh terminated the conversation on the grounds that he was late for a lecture.

'Self-contained, difficult to read. No love lost there and no alibi . . .'

'Same as the rest of them,' Carruthers groaned. Then, brightening, 'Harvison's bound to give us something, though, what with Everard showing his daughter up like that.'

'I wouldn't count on it, Sergeant.' Markham's thoughts turned to Harvison, an unattractive specimen of manhood with his broken-veined nose and thinning slicked-back hair. 'The Harvisons went through an acrimonious divorce not long ago, so I reckon the "outrage" over his daughter was pretty much confected and a way of getting back at his ex. The TV pilot didn't flatter the young lady, but that's because she's a big girl and the camera adds around ten pounds. Plus, the makeup was laid on with a trowel. But it was the same with practically everyone — including Harvison's ex-wife and half the staff.' Markham shook his head. 'Everard was ultra-respectful, so there were no grounds for saying the daughter was portrayed as some kind of slapper . . . Now that Daddy Dearest has had time to think about it, I'm reasonably sure he'll backpedal fast.'

And so it transpired, Mark Harvison proving extremely keen to distance himself from everything to do with the Confetti Club, though — through all the backslapping bonhomie — Markham detected the embers of a smouldering resentment against Gino Everard. It struck him that

Harvison was the kind of man who regarded the women in his family as chattels — his possessions — and that the mere notion of other men encroaching on his preserve was liable to trigger a violently irrational response. The combination of the divorce and his daughter's nuptials — in which, by his own admission, he was accorded only a walk-on role — had clearly inspired a seething hostility to all things bridal. In addition to which, the pilot showed Gino Everard doing his usual hand-kissing troubadour-ish routine with mother and daughter in a manner bound to inflame Harvison.

The question being, had all of this been the breeding ground for murder?

As Markham sat in his office pondering the conundrum, Kate Burton burst through the door in a state of high agitation.

The DI half rose.

'What is it, Kate?'

'There's been another one, sir. Another murder.'

5. FASHION VICTIM

'All right, Markham . . . Going by the lividity, I'd say we're looking at around nine o'clock yesterday evening,' Dimples said as they stood in the living room of a terraced house on Bromgrove Rise.

Nine o'clock. The very time that he was enjoying coffee and truffles with the Noakeses, Markham thought grimly.

The pathologist cleared his throat.

'You're dealing with a proper sicko here,' he said, shaken out of his usual dry composure as he regarded the figure in the armchair. 'I mean, what with the Miss Havisham getup and everything . . .'

Dimples' consternation arose from the fact that Antonia Rambert's corpse was grotesquely attired in a billowing 'princess' wedding dress and voluminous tulle veil which cruelly accentuated the bony emaciation of her frame. One might have thought a corsage of crimson roses bloomed on the sequinned bodice were it not for steel dressmaker's scissors protruding from the dead woman's chest.

It seemed that Dimples could not tear his eyes away from the spectacle.

'That poor woman,' he said finally, and there was anger in his voice. 'Not content with murder, they had to make a mockery of her.'

Markham too felt his insides contract with pity as he looked at the darkly flushed face whose empurpled hue clashed so horribly with the white of the veil. The eyes were fathomless pools of horror while a trail of congealed saliva bisected her sagging chin like the sticky trail of a slug or snail.

'Will you be able to get her out of here with reasonable dignity, Doug?' Markham asked. Somehow this felt very important.

'Leave it to me,' the other said, clicking his fingers to summon the hovering paramedics who waited with screens. 'Between us we'll see her right.'

Markham nodded and moved into the hallway where his colleagues were waiting.

Initially he said nothing, appearing to observe the paper-suited SOCOs as they swarmed through the property. But his gaze was remote as though he were somewhere else entirely.

Carruthers watched his boss curiously. Doyle had explained that the guvnor sometimes 'went off on one'. Something to do with him being RC and majorly into old churches and statues (which seemed rather a non sequitur). 'He's big on respect for the dead,' the young DS had confided. 'Chose his flat cos it's smack next door to a cemetery . . . Got a thing about monuments and memorials and all that. Carstairs asked him about it once and he started spouting stuff from the Bible about iron bars and bronze gates.'

As he stood there, it wasn't biblical verses running through Markham's mind but some lines from one of Olivia's favourite poems: 'Life is real! Life is earnest! And the grave is not its goal; Dust thou art, to dust returnest, Was not spoken of the soul.' With the image of Antonia Rambert's desecrated remains seared on his retina, he needed to believe that she was destined ultimately for a very different kind of raiment.

In that instant, he wished desperately that his former wingman was there, even though much of what passed between them was as wordless as a windy sky. It was just that the two of them shared some mysterious affinity at times like this. Noakes offered no insights or smart answers, but

Markham knew that his sorrow was somehow safe because the other man shared it.

With an effort, he roused himself. He had a good team, and it was encouraging to see the way Carruthers had gelled with Doyle and Burton. Now they had to hammer out a plan of action.

'Let's leave Dimples and the SOCOs to it,' he said. Then, turning to Burton, 'Where are we up to?'

'Uniform are dealing with the press and gawkers,' she told him. 'Then they'll be on house-to-house.'

'Who found her?'

'One of the backroom girls from the Confetti Club, Tracey Gould. Franco Santini got worried when Antonia didn't come into work this morning — normally you can set your watch by her apparently. She doesn't have a land line, but he kept trying her mobile only there was no answer. Finally, he decided to send someone over. The neighbour Mrs Carmichael has a spare set of keys, so she let Tracey in . . . The poor kid nearly passed out when she found the body. . . Says she didn't touch anything, just legged it as fast as she could. She's next door now getting a cup of tea.'

'We need to check out the boutique staff right away,' Markham instructed. 'See about alibis. . . But more importantly, establish all of Ms Rambert's movements and interactions yesterday, find out how she seemed. Did she appear bothered about anything or have any run-ins . . .'

'They're still based at Queen for a Day seeing as the third floor at the shopping centre is closed off till next week.'

'Okay, I want Doyle and Carruthers down there taking statements from everyone, including following up any clients or visitors who came in. In the meantime, Kate, I'd like you to handle Tracey and then process Ms Rambert's house.'

'It was her mother's house, sir, that's why the furniture's so dated.' Burton anticipated his next question. 'The parents are dead and there's only a brother. Mrs Carmichael says they weren't close, and he emigrated to Australia about ten years back . . . Family liaison are going to check it out.'

'I'm surprised Ms Rambert didn't gut this place. . . put her own stamp on it,' Markham said looking round.

'Her mother only died three months ago — according to Mrs Carmichael, Antonia planned to sell the house once probate was sorted and invest in somewhere smarter. She'd been renting in town before moving out here, so most likely she had her eye on a flat in one of the new developments.'

Markham felt immeasurably sad as he inhaled the drab little property's airless shut-in scent of shabby gentility. Antonia Rambert had been poised to escape her past when a murderer caught up with her.

'I'll just take a quick look around, Kate,' he said quietly. 'Then I need to brief Sidney and,' he grimaced at the thought of the *Gazette*, 'issue a news bulletin to appease the ravening hordes. Let's have a team meeting later this afternoon at four-ish, and then we can compare notes.'

The décor throughout was monumentally depressing, with an abundance of 1950s beige moquette pervaded by a musty odour reminiscent of boiled fish. The front bedroom overlooking the street contained Antonia Rambert's things, but there was no sense of her presence apart from a penguin edition of Giacomo Leopardi's *Dialogue between Fashion and Death* on the bedside table. The front cover's illustration of a beautiful Pre-Raphaelite heroine kissing a skull seemed like a ghastly commentary on the tableau in the living room below. An exercise book contained some scribbled notes whose headings — 'Corsets and the Pleasure-Pain Principle', 'Conspicuous Display', 'Hobbleskirts and Shackling the Legs' — suggested a quasi-feminist academic interest in the evolution of fashion that was intriguingly at odds with the idea of Antonia Rambert being some kind of hard-nosed capitalist harridan and workaday tyrant. He felt a sharp pang at this evidence of an intellectual hinterland that doubtless went unsuspected by her colleagues.

There was no sign of a mobile or computer. Presumably the killer had made sure to remove anything that might contain a clue to their identity.

He was startled by the sound of a minor commotion in the street below.

Twitching aside the heavy net curtains, he saw Noakes's bête noire Gavin Conors being restrained by Carruthers of all people. Clearly the *Gazette*'s most intrepid reptile had somehow circumvented the crime scene cordon and decided to chance his arm in hopes of snagging some appropriately salacious nuggets.

Markham grinned as he watched Carruthers and Doyle frogmarch Conors along the pavement. He would personally ensure that any protests from that quarter about 'police brutality' fell on deaf ears. Noakesy for one would be delighted to learn that Carruthers was showing distinct signs of promise when it came to the lost art of muscular persuasion.

* * *

Friday morning was always a quiet time at Doggie Dickerson's gym in Marsh Lane, which meant Markham and Noakes had the 'premium locker room' — so called by virtue of being marginally more salubrious than the other changing room, with showers that emitted something stronger than a lukewarm dribble — to themselves.

Doggie was delighted to welcome his 'fav'rite 'spector' and the former sergeant whose un-PC worldview so closely corresponded to his own.

Nobody was sure how Doggie had come by his infamous moniker (best not to ask), but the proprietor's seedy appearance was Exhibit A in DCI Sidney's bill of indictment against him, his customary attire being an extraordinary horsehair wig, eyepatch and dingy black frock coat, with the overall effect less Johnny Depp in *Pirates of the Caribbean* and more Blind Pew or some other notorious reprobate. A reek of Johnnie Walker and mothballs generally enveloped him, while tombstone yellow teeth and a Fagin-like cackle were apt to unnerve the uninitiated.

Sidney and the 'gold braid mob' also strongly objected to the fact that patrons of Doggie's Bromgrove Police Boxing

Club included local criminals who benefited from an extraordinary amnesty whereby they and Bromgrove's finest slugged it out in the ring alongside each other before both sides reverted to their usual roles of pursuer and pursued once safely off the premises.

And then there were the recurring battles with Environmental Health officials whom Doggie somehow always managed to outwit in spite of all.

The gym was the absolute antithesis of what Noakes called 'Lycraland' — realm of those utterly sanitary but synthetic and soulless outfits such as Fitness Mission and The Reshape Lounge. Despite the trenchant disapproval of Sidney and their superiors, Markham and Noakes relished the proprietor's unreconstructed awfulness and the sweaty authenticity of his little kingdom. Plus, there was something endearing about the man, for all that he was suspected of complicity in any number of dodges.

Being now respectably (more or less) affianced to one Evelyn (Marlene of bingo hall fame but a distant memory), Doggie had smartened up somewhat and sported a double-breasted black suit which, although old-fashioned and looking like something Leonid Brezhnev might have worn, was a considerable improvement on the dressing gown-cum-overcoat of yesteryear (unfortunately, there was nothing to be done about the wig and teeth). Exchanging greetings, Markham was amused to note that the old villain and Noakes were eyeing each other's wardrobe overhaul with an air of considerable complacency as though trying to decide who was the sartorial frontrunner.

As with Muriel (though she would doubtless have been mortally affronted by the comparison), Markham was able to speak freely in front of Doggie (What's Said Here Stays Here, Mr Markham) who, along with Noakes, was fascinated to learn about developments in the current case.

'Evie went into that Gino Everard's shop a while back,' he confided. 'Wanted to get some ideas about dresses an' stuff . . . I didn't go with her, it's not my kind of thing.'

Markham was careful not to meet Noakes's eye. The notion of Doggie Dickerson checking out bridal accessories added a whole new dimension to the term 'Groomzilla'. Whenever the nuptials with his intended took place, it would require a rare breed of wedding planner to get Doggie up the aisle in such a condition as not to traumatise the couple's guests.

'What did your lass reckon to Gino Ginelli then?' Noakes enquired.

Doggie guffawed by way of demonstrating his appreciation of the nickname.

'He was a bit . . . greasy. Laying it on thick kind of thing . . . making puppy-dog eyes at her.'

Noakes nodded darkly on hearing this.

'But she said there was no great harm in him. He was nice and didn't give it the hard sell or anything like that, but there was this right snotty cow who looked like she didn't think Evie had any right to be in there. When her money's as good as anyone else's,' he added indignantly. Suddenly Doggie checked himself, somewhat crestfallen. 'Sorry, she's the one who got murdered, right?'

'Correct, Dogs.' Markham smiled reassuringly.

'Togged out like a wedding doll,' Noakes pointed out. 'In the dress an' veil an' everything.'

Doggie looked queasy. 'Gotta be a sex maniac to do that, Mr Noakes.' The rheumy eyes squinted in thought. 'I saw a documentary about it once. . . There's these blokes get off on all the white frilly stuff . . . you know,' his voice dropped to a shifty whisper, 'the lin-ger-ie an' garters an' stilettoes. Got a thing about women in white being pure an' innocent, a cut above the rest, see.' Doggie warmed to this theme. 'Sometimes they even dress up in it themselves. There's all these fetish sites an' no one blinks an eyelid.'

Noakes grinned at Markham's expression. 'Too much information, Dogs,' he chuckled, remembering their nightmarish exposure to fetishism in the Beautiful Bodies investigation.

'No that's okay, Doggie,' Markham said weakly. 'You could be right, but I'm more inclined to think there's a personal vendetta at the back of this. . . that Mr Everard was murdered because of a grudge then somehow Ms Rambert became a threat to the killer, so they had to silence her—'

'An' they played dress-up to throw sand in your eyes,' Noakes suggested grimly. 'Make it look like this were some random sex thing.'

'Or simply because they enjoyed humiliating Ms Rambert,' Markham observed quietly, remembering the hideous tableau at her flat.

Doggie preserved a respectful silence as he digested this.

'Well, gents, you're the experts,' he said, including Noakes in a deferential bow. 'Either away, they're a right sicko.' It was nice the way Markham never stood on ceremony or came over all haughty, he thought complacently. Always ready to have a pleasant chat about police procedure. 'I s'pose all of 'em at the shop have got alibis then?' he enquired interestedly.

'Not so that you'd notice,' Markham sighed. 'All virtuously at home in the bosom of their families or chilling out in blissful solitude . . . worthless from our point of view.'

'No joy with the neighbours?' Doggie asked hopefully. 'No curtain-twitchers able to help?'

''Fraid not, Dogs. Nobody saw a thing. . . glued to the TV — some football match or other.'

'How'd they get into the house?' the other wanted to know.

Markham grimaced. 'Spare key under the doormat.'

'With it being her old mum's gaff, she felt safe,' Noakes explained. 'Got careless. . . prob'ly knackered after everything that had happened with Everard an' all the rest of it, so she conked out in the front room. Didn't hear a thing until it was too late.'

'Ms Rambert was what you'd call a skinny malink, Dogs,' Markham went on. 'If she was groggy and taken by surprise, the attack would have been over in minutes. Kitting her out in the bridal gear would have been relatively easy.' And probably intensely pleasurable, he thought with an internal shudder at the image of a faceless intruder gloating over their task. 'They cleaned up after themselves pretty thoroughly, too, so clearly they're forensically aware.' And anyway, he thought, secondary transfer would account for any DNA in the property, especially given that the weapon used to stab her turned out to have been taken from the Confetti Club, he thought glumly. As for the bridal wear, they hadn't been able to trace it to any outlet in Bromgrove and it didn't belong to Antonia Rambert, so the killer must have sourced it themselves.

Doggie shook his head mournfully.

'To think of 'em sneaking in an' out like that an' no one seeing a thing.'

'A combination of luck and cunning,' Markham told him.

Doggie cleared his throat with a noise reminiscent of a cappuccino maker starting up.

'The one who's dead . . . she wasn't zackly popular, right?' he asked carefully.

'Correct,' Markham said. 'By the sound of it, she was a perfectionist. Very intense . . . very focused.' Remembering that little exercise book next to her bed, he added, 'A self-improver.'

'Men friends?' Doggie pressed, his mind still running on bridal fetishism. 'Her working in a place like that'd be a turn-on for weirdos. . . Maybe some creep had a thing about her and Everard. Hey,' in a burst of phlegmy inspiration, 'maybe the three of 'em were involved in some kind of romantic triangle and it's a whatchamacallit . . . a crime of passion.'

'You could be right,' Markham agreed solemnly. 'As things stand, everything's on the table.'

After Doggie had shuffled away to let them get changed, Noakes grunted, 'Bit of a stretch, ain't it? The idea of Everard an' Rambert in some kind of threesome?'

In one fluid movement, Markham's shirt was off, causing the other to wonder crossly how come he had to battle middle-aged spread, whereas the guvnor was buff enough to star in a Calvin Klein ad. It just wasn't fair. Here he was watching what he ate (most of the time) and making sure to exercise, and he still had this flabby 'dad bod' at the end of it. Nat said it was all about bench presses and lateral pull downs these days and he should think of getting a personal trainer if he couldn't face proper gym sessions (which he couldn't, seeing as he looked like this big red tomato next to all the Tom Cruise lookalikes). But he reckoned that stuff was for blokes who used moisturiser . . . not a graduate of Stand By Your Beds military training.

Markham glanced at his friend indulgently, having a shrewd idea what he was thinking. But all he said was, 'I don't see Everard and Antonia Rambert as being involved in some sort of shared romantic intrigue. But as things stand, we've got nothing.'

'How about Shippers an' the criminal profiling side?' Noakes asked with a wicked grin. 'Bet him an' Burton had their noses in that creepy book she carts around before you could say "Ted Bundy".'

Markham laughed. 'I'm not sure the Diagnostic and Statistical Manual of Mental Disorders has got much to offer us at the moment. But yes, Nathan's onside, if only to satisfy Sidney that we're covering all the bases.'

Noakes winked at him. 'An' ruling out anyone important, any big wigs.' He knew the DCI of old. 'Much better if it turns out to be some old bridal fetishist escaped from the loony bin.'

Markham sighed again. 'God forbid, Noakesy. No, this has to be personal.'

'What did you mean about that poor cow being a self-improver, boss?'

'Just that I found some notes she'd made on the history of fashion . . . with a feminist slant.'

'P'raps she were on a course at the university,' Noakes hazarded. 'Or wanted a job there instead of flogging her guts out selling frocks to stroppy madams.'

'Good point. I'll get Kate to check it out.'

'The rent-a-mob crowd are planning a demo at the shopping centre tomorrow, boss,' his friend continued, tapping the side of his bulbous nose. 'If you're down that way, happen we could run into each other . . . accidentally on purpose, like.'

'Don't see why not, Noakesy.' Markham was thoughtful. 'What kind of a demo is it?'

'It's meant to be a protest against sexual violence towards women . . . reclaiming the streets kind of thing.' Noakes scowled. 'You can bet your life Shay Conteh'll be along for some free publicity. Now there's two deaths connected with Everard's gaff, he'll milk that for all he's worth.'

'I'm withholding details of how we found Ms Rambert,' Markham said. 'If people knew about the wedding dress and all the rest of it, there'd be hell to pay.'

Noakes nodded, morosely contemplating Markham's athletic figure.

'Come on, Noakesy,' Markham admonished. 'Get changed and meet me in the ring. I've got a hot date with Everard's solicitor after this and I need to work off some aggro first.' And with that, he headed out of the changing room.

Noakes tugged off his George boots, a smile slowly spreading across the battered features. Okay, so he might not look like a Calvin Klein ad but that didn't mean he couldn't put his ex-guvnor on the ropes.

* * *

Two hours later, Markham sat opposite Kate Burton in Waterstones, having met her there after his visit to Trathen Solicitors just around the corner on the high street.

'Where did you hear this about Mr Everard's funeral, Kate?' he asked.

'Chris Carstairs got it from Superintendent Bretherton, sir,' she replied. 'Apparently it's down for Monday twelve noon at St Mary of the Angels, that church the other side of Old Carton.' She sipped her soy macchiato daintily before continuing. 'Word is, Claudia Everard wanted it sooner rather than later. . . she's struggling to get commissions, so it'll be good PR.'

Markham's lips thinned at the image this conjured up of the not-so-desolate widow exploiting Everard's obsequies for commercial gain.

Burton looked apologetic. 'Now that the PM's been squared away, Franco Santini okayed it.'

'Gino Everard left the Confetti Club to Mr Santini,' Markham said heavily. 'So, I imagine Santini won't exactly be averse to some sympathetic press coverage. That and the frisson of notoriety from the boutique being the backdrop to murder should bring the punters flocking in,' he added with distaste.

His fellow DI digested this information.

'Stands to reason he gave the business to Santini,' she said. 'What with them being best friends.' Then, 'What about his flat?'

'That too,' Markham replied. 'Santini gets the lot — lock, stock and barrel, well, more or less. . . There were a few minor bequests. The PA is in line for a couple of thousand and one or two other people were left small sums . . . nothing to get excited about.'

'Dunbabin Mews is the pricey end of town and it looked like Everard had some decent antiques,' Burton mused. 'So Santini getting the lion's share gives him a motive—' Seeing Markham's doubtful expression, she broke off. 'You're ruling out financial gain, sir?'

'Well, he was sitting pretty as things were, Kate. It's difficult to see him murdering Everard to get his hands on that inheritance unless he wanted an early payday because he needed money, or unless there was some reason for him to think Everard intended to change his will. . .'

'How did it go with the solicitor?' she asked.

Markham thought about the froglike, expensively dressed senior partner with his chilly, exophthalmic gaze.

'He made no difficulty of telling me about the will, which sounded completely straightforward.' The DI's voice hardened. 'I'd say he positively enjoyed telling me I should rule out filthy lucre as a motive.'

'Keen to vouch for Santini?'

'Almost indecently so,' was the dry response. 'But then, the prospect of a long and profitable association no doubt played some part in his calculations.'

Burton smiled at the barely repressed cynicism, but then her attention was caught by something on the other side of the first-floor café.

Seeing her freeze, Markham followed his colleague's gaze.

Olivia and Mat Sullivan stood together by the Arts section, their heads almost touching as they examined a glossy coffee table tome. They looked very cosy, Olivia's bell-like laughter suddenly ringing out at some witticism. Though noticeably thinner, the green eyes as she looked up at her lanky colleague were still big and starry. As for Sullivan, his normally sardonic expression was openly admiring, even tender.

Oblivious to their surroundings, they hadn't noticed Markham and Burton.

And he was keen to keep it that way.

His colleague was already on her feet, tactfully murmuring something about needing to check in with the others. Despite a tight, bitter feeling in his chest, as though he had been running hard, Markham also rose. 'I think I've recovered from that workout with Noakesy,' he said in an attempt at lightness. 'Time for a catch-up back at the station.'

He knew he hadn't fooled Burton, but at least his pride was intact.

There was no time to repine over his lost love.

Not with a murderer to catch.

6. KILLER FACTS

Markham slept badly that night, which was a regular occurrence with him during a murder enquiry.

Instead of the oblivion for which he longed, he was back in one of the bedrooms at Carton Hall, the mansion that had featured in a recent investigation. He could recognise the crimson silk panelled walls, massive Jacobean furniture and canopied bed with its intricately carved posts. Next door was the little dressing room with antique wallpaper of pheasants and flowers and the Chippendale vanity table over by the window . . .

There was a cinematic dissolve, a shift in focus, and suddenly he was looking down at himself from the coffered ceiling, the surroundings like a set made of cardboard.

He watched himself move from the bedroom into the dressing room, stopping next to a massive mahogany wardrobe.

A man's voice — he didn't know whose — said, 'You can hear mice scratching all night long somewhere behind the plaster.'

Instinctively he knew it wasn't mice.

Then a hole appeared in the wall next to the wardrobe, small at first then gradually widening via some sinister necrosis like the mouth of a secret vault.

As he watched, a skeleton in a wedding dress and veil toppled forward from the gaping recess, crumbling to ash as it hit the wooden floorboards.

'She must have gone in there alive,' the voice said again. 'Scratching and scratching to get out. She was trapped, and no one came. Screamed herself hoarse and still no one came.'

And now he was unable to breathe, lungs burning as though being eaten away by acid.

Markham knew this was just a movie — celluloid footage — and he was the director. He was the one in charge.

But with the hallucinatory quality of a Pathé newsreel, before his eyes the heap of ash became a dust storm which resolved into a veiled figure holding a bridal bouquet of roses.

The figure lifted its veil.

Olivia.

Her green eyes glittered feverishly in a white sunken face that bore an expression of sardonic amusement, but she said nothing.

He wanted to move towards her, but he was rooted to the spot, unable to advance a single step.

Regarding him steadily, she began plucking petals from the flowers like some nightmarish reincarnation of Ophelia.

'Why are you playing games with me, Liv?' he finally managed to whisper through dry lips. 'What's got into you?'

Her lips curled. 'Their name is Legion,' she sneered.

And . . . cut.

The screen went black.

Markham woke clammy and damp with sweat.

With the voice that he felt to be his own — the voice that was fighting with other voices from the dream — he told himself this was merely a subconscious reaction to the peculiarities of the Confetti Club investigation and the stress triggered by his glimpse of Olivia with Mathew Sullivan.

He forced himself up and made strong black coffee which he took into his study, gazing out at the neighbouring burial ground with thoughts of coffins and shrouds and skeletons going round and round in his head.

He knew that he had the reputation of a ghoul in CID. Knew too that only Olivia and Noakes truly understood how the apartment's proximity to the municipal cemetery somehow helped him to keep his murdered dead close.

As dawn stole over graves and monuments, the faces of stone cherubs were disclosed, celestially smooth and unwrinkled — pain and suffering to them just a distant dream, guessed at but never endured. He felt that until he avenged the deaths of those who met violent ends — dragged them up from the failure pit — they could never be like the angels and find true peace . . . could never transcend the terrible story of betrayal and pain until he turned the tables on their murderers.

The archway over the gateway to the cemetery bore the legend: Death is swallowed up in victory. Sculpted seraphs with flaming swords stood sentinel on either side, the very personification of ultimate triumph.

It was up to him to fulfil that promise in the here and now. But as things stood, he had no leads. Nothing.

His thoughts wandered irresistibly to Olivia. What was she playing at with Sullivan? Was there anything to it? Was she simply trying to get back at him for his closeness to Kate Burton? What should his next move be?

He had offered her marriage, but she didn't believe he was genuine and thought he was just humouring her.

He knew she had always liked Sullivan and that they were good friends as well as colleagues. Was it possible that liking could have turned to love or that the deputy head could envision an alternative happy ending from the one Markham had always pictured for him?

Markham's head ached from all the questions.

Time to face the day.

Perhaps he would learn something from the demonstration down at the shopping centre. Or Bromgrove TV might throw up something.

A last look at those fiery divine messengers poised on their winged heels, then he got to his feet and headed for the shower.

* * *

'Conteh's got a face like a smacked arse,' Noakes said with considerable satisfaction as he and Markham stood outside Bromgrove Shopping Centre watching the Women Together protest, which looked to be something of a non-event. He scowled portentously, his Ivan the Terrible face causing a group of female students from the university to back away in consternation. 'An' anyway, the bloke's got a chuffing nerve banging on about "Toxic Masculinity" after all them stories about him slapping girlfriends around.'

'He's a reformed character these days, Noakesy,' Markham replied patiently.

'Yeah, and that type's always bleeding irritating, if you ask me.'

It was an overcast grey day, the steady drizzle putting a decided damper on proceedings.

'Where's the others?' Noakes asked peering round suspiciously. 'Oh don' tell me,' with heavy sarcasm, 'Burton's off with Shippers doing summat intelleckshual . . . an' Doyle's saving hisself for the footie on Sky.' Momentarily stumped when it came to Carruthers, he swiftly rallied. 'An' old SpeckyFourEyes is holed up thinking about his next spy mission for Slimy Sid.'

'Don't be such an old grouch,' Markham chided. 'I gave them today off.' With a grin, he added, 'Burton's down at the art gallery taking a look at that exhibition on foot binding in the Tang Dynasty . . . Nathan cried off.'

'Don' blame him,' Noakes said with a heartfelt shudder. Then, curiously, he enquired, 'What's got her into that?'

'I think it's this investigation . . . all the corsets and flummery in the boutique. It started her wondering about the dangers of fashion . . .'

'Yeah . . . Hey boss, d'you remember in the Beautiful Bodies case finding out about folks' bums exploding from too much Botox?'

'Thank you for the reminder, Noakes.' It was not an image the DI cared to recall, having learned enough about cosmetic procedures during their previous investigation to last him a lifetime.

Noakes's thoughts turned to Imperial China.

'Barbaric the way they broke lasses' feet,' he ruminated. 'I remember, me an' the missus watched this documentary about it. . . how they wanted 'em to have golden lotus wotsits and take itsy bitsy steps. It happened in Europe too. . . posh folk stacked their toes on top of each other so they could squeeze into titchy shoes. Not as bad as China, mind . . . they tried to change kids' bone structure to make it look like they came from a better class an' didn't have to schlep around. Did it to six-year-olds. . . tried to make the toes fold under—'

'Yes well,' Markham said hastily, anxious to move on from mangled metatarsals. 'Kate's got hooked on the lethal aspects of fashion. She told me the other day that crinolines — you know, those vast petticoats Victorian women wore — caused lots of deaths because they made dresses stick out, so if you passed a fire there was a risk of being set alight.'

'Handy for dealing with sex pests, though,' Noakes pronounced. 'I mean, pervs couldn't get near enough to cop a feel.'

Markham burst out laughing. 'Indeed . . . A perfect example of women claiming their space,' he exclaimed. 'We'll make a feminist of you yet, Noakesy!'

Much gratified, Noakes's pouchy features relaxed into a smile.

'Burton's bound to get all PC an' preachy about bridal stuff,' he predicted. 'You know what she's like. . . No peacocks were used in the making of this hat kind of thing. God, when she an' Shippers finally tie the knot, it'll probably be all New Agey with them two dressed up like Druids in hemp sacks or summat.'

Markham's lips quirked. 'Somehow I don't see Nathan as a Druid . . . reckon he'll at least want to go the conventional route.' Again, there was that sense of a blade slipping between his ribs at the thought of Kate Burton making the ultimate commitment.

Noakes returned to his original grievance. 'Bet I'm right about Doyle an' Carruthers,' he griped.

'And there was me thinking that Carruthers was growing on you, Noakes.'

'Well, I guess Roger the Dodger ain't so bad,' his friend conceded. 'Leastways, so long as he don' go snitching to Sidney. Doyle told me about his girlfriend being plus-size . . . Like Doggie said, there's some blokes prefer women with a bit more meat on their bones an' bloody good luck to 'em,' he added magnanimously.

'Well, there you go . . . important to remember redeeming features,' Markham exhorted.

'Even so,' Noakes pointed out sententiously, 'it's a bleeding murder investigation.'

'Don't I know it. Look, they're only getting today off, Noakesy, then it's back into the station tomorrow.' Slyly, Markham added, 'By the way, you're welcome to tag along with me this afternoon.'

He suppressed a smile at the way the shaggy head came up, like a Saint Bernard scenting Bonios.

'Oh aye, what you got planned then?'

'A visit to Bromgrove TV . . . see what they have to say about the atmosphere in the Confetti Club when they were filming that pilot.'

Noakes suddenly looked cheerier. 'Well, it's gotta be better than listening to the comrades sticking it to one half of the population. I mean, guv, I know there's bad apples,' he said plaintively, 'but we ain't all bad. My missus says she's glad we didn't have sons cos it's no picnic being a man these days with all the Julie Burchill types out to get you . . . Ackshually,' Markham braced himself, 'it's amazing we ain't all got whopping inferiority complexes with everyone saying we're bullies an' pervs an' all that. That luvvie Benedict Cucumber was at it the other day . . . should've stuck to Sherlock Holmes, if you ask me.'

'Ah, I believe Mr Cumberbatch joined the debate because he was keen to distinguish his latest film role from the kind of misogyny that's so prevalent today. And besides,' Markham fixed his friend with a quizzical eye, 'I'd say your ego is sturdy enough to withstand any amount of feminist denunciation.'

Ignoring the latter part of Markham's remark, the other retorted. 'Yeah, he's playing some badass cowboy but still wants the carey-sharey brigade to fancy him.' Drawing himself up, 'Give me John Wayne any day . . . Hey up,' he nudged the DI, 'ain't that Ginelli's number two over there at the top of the steps?' Learning that Franco Santini was the principal beneficiary under Everard's will had intensified Noakes's mistrust of the man. 'Hmm . . . him an' Conteh look pretty cosy. Ugh,' Noakes's expression became one of concentrated disgust, 'Look at the two of 'em posing for that spotty Herbert from the *Gazette*. You'd think they were bezzie mates the way they're puckering up. . .'

'Keep your hair on,' Markham murmured. 'It's probably a slow news day . . . and anyway, some photos of "Trotskyites" fraternising with Mr Santini and the Everard contingent should go down well with Sidney, by way of reassurance that the university isn't going to give us any aggro.'

But Noakes was clearly thinking of Natalie. 'Santini gives me the creeps,' he muttered, 'but the rest look harmless enough. That middle-aged one with her hair in them daft pigtails, she's got a kind face at least.' He scanned the little group. 'You can tell the pretty lass next to her — the one with the continental looks cringing at the back — don' want to be there.'

'Those are Ms Rambert's assistants, Maria Hagan and Christina Skelthorne,' Markham informed him.

'What about the redhead. Is she the one our Nat said fancied Ginelli?'

'Yes . . . Lucille Chilton, his PA.'

'Looks like she forgot to put her skirt on,' was the laconic rejoinder.

'I imagine it's what they call a fashion statement,' Markham temporised.

'Looks dead tacky from where I'm standing. Plus, I reckon she could do with a square meal . . . Him an' all,' Noakes said as his gaze alighted on Randall Fenton. 'Looks all of twelve, that one.'

'Appearances are deceptive. Mr Fenton's in charge of the repairs and alterations team.'

'The lad Nat said were always following Ginelli around like his blinking shadow?'

'The very same.'

'Him an' Lucy look proper upset,' Noakes observed.

'*Lucille.*'

'Same difference.' He yawned. 'Them women in the overalls look bored rigid.'

Markham was inclined to agree with Noakes's verdict. 'They're the seamstresses and people who work behind the scenes . . . the others cover the shop floor.' The Confetti Box's backroom team did look decidedly fed up. He presumed Franco Santini had dragged the boutique's personnel out for a photo op . . . perhaps by way of counterpoint to the police bulletin about Antonia Rambert's death. Despite sticking to the usual formula — 'sudden death . . . unexplained circumstances . . . request for press restraint (some hope!) . . . respect for family's privacy, etcetera' — Markham had little doubt that innuendo and speculation would be swirling through Bromgrove, the rumours growing more lurid with each retelling. In the circumstances, it was understandable if Santini desired a show of professional unity.

Now Shay Conteh was speaking.

Markham had to admit that the man had a certain presence and spoke well, his rhetoric about the 'erosion of feminine identity' and 'need to retake control' for the most part avoiding inflammatory flourishes or provocative comments about the bridal industry's contribution to body fascism. It was the standard spiel but delivered with quiet sincerity. Whatever Shay Conteh's mortification at the size of his audience, the university's new messiah let none of this show once he took the megaphone.

'Looks like some of 'em have had enough,' Noakes declared as Conteh wound up amid a smattering of applause and some of the assembly began to disperse. 'Can't say I blame em,' he muttered balefully as a bovver-booted woman with a buzzcut began limbering up in the background. 'Don' seem like there's going to be any chanting or fisticuffs or owt like that.'

'You sound almost disappointed,' was Markham's dry response.

'Nah, I jus' thought. . . if it's school letting out time, happen we could grab a bite to eat before visiting the TV folk.'

'Quite like the old days,' the DI said amicably. 'But I absolutely draw the line at a grease-fest, Noakesy. . . don't want to turn up there smelling of Big Mac.'

'How about Pret?' was the hopeful enquiry.

Markham smiled. 'That sounds like a fair compromise,' he said. 'And in the meantime, we can think about how best to broach the subject of Joanna Osborne and Jamie O'Neill.'

Discreetly, the two men melted away.

* * *

Bromgrove TV's features department had all the impersonality of a call centre, while the harassed-looking commissioning editor Mark Harris — a tall bullet-headed man who bore an uncanny physical resemblance to DCI Sidney — appeared less than thrilled to see them. One could hardly blame him for that, in light of all the flak from the Beautiful Bodies investigation.

Harris's office wasn't particularly grand, with its utilitarian gunmetal filing cabinets and functional office furniture.

All eco-friendly no doubt, Markham thought wryly, recalling their last visit and the earnest conversation about 'ethical sourcing'. A glance at Noakes told him his former wingman was remembering it too, 'tree-huggers' and 'Swampy types' ranking high in his pantheon of PC deplorables.

Whatever the editor's private feelings, he dispatched an icily glamorous blonde for coffee and biscuits, engaging in desultory chit-chat before they got down to business. Harris appeared unfazed by Noakes's latest incarnation as a 'CID consultant', which was all to the good, as was the fact that the editor hadn't wheeled in any HR or legal honchos to guard his back.

'How can I help you, Inspector?' he enquired once the door had closed behind his colleague.

'I'm after your impressions of the Confetti Club,' Markham said without preamble. 'Essentially anything that will help our investigation into two murders.'

'So this second death is definitely murder then?' Harris asked in a deep guttural rumble.

'Obviously what I'm telling you isn't for general consumption.' Markham paused meaningfully to let this sink in. 'But yes, Antonia Rambert was murdered in a particularly sadistic manner.'

'Are you linking it to Gino Everard's murder?'

'Yes, but again, that piece of information doesn't leave this room,' Markham replied.

Harris registered the steely tone. Word on the grapevine was, you didn't want to get on the wrong side of CID's wunderkind. Looking at the tall dark figure with the implacable expression, he could well believe it. Interesting that he had the dishevelled sidekick in tow, almost like some kind of personal bodyguard. The backstory between these two polar opposites — Peter Wimsey and Bunter, as he'd heard them called in the newsroom — would make for fascinating television, especially in light of their formidable clearance rate. But apparently nobody ever got past first base when it came to Markham.

The set-up with Noakes seemed downright bizarre, given the inspector's Oxbridge polish and the other's reputation as a real bruiser who would probably have been booted off the force years ago were it not for Markham's point-blank refusal to part with him. The bloke kept turning up like a bad penny even after he retired, most recently in that weird business at Carton Hall . . .

Yes, Harris thought, he'd give a great deal to know what secrets bound these two men together. 'Markham doesn't care diddly-squat about fame or publicity,' the head of current affairs had told him exasperatedly. 'He's one of those bookish, religious types. . . so God knows what he sees in Bunter. The girlfriend's an English teacher, though they're not together right now.' *Probably sick of playing second fiddle to the job.*

He became aware that Noakes was watching him with beady-eyed suspicion. Markham had mentioned something about coming from a student demonstration and looked the part in chinos, rollneck sweater and tweed jacket. His rottweiler, on the other hand, must have stood out like a sore thumb in that military camouflage getup, all red, florid and menacing like some psychopathic paramilitary.

A gleam in Markham's eyes brought Harris up short. Almost as though the detective knew exactly what he was thinking.

'Nothing out of the ordinary happened with the TV pilot,' he said. 'Basically, it just ran to a formula, like all those reality TV programmes . . . Gino Everard was a local celebrity, so we planned to capitalise on that.'

Noakes leaned forward. 'Did anyone try to spice things up?' he demanded. 'You know, make it a bit more edgy . . . get 'em ripping chunks off each other?'

'Well, it's not bear-baiting, you know.' Harris sounded genuinely affronted. 'I certainly wasn't aware of anything like that. But don't take my word for it,' he pressed a buzzer on his desk, 'let me get the producer in — he can set your minds at rest on that point.'

The programme's producer Andy Cosgrave — geeky-looking with the look of a young Elvis Costello — was duly summoned. Perfectly affable, he seemed on the level, frankly admitting that he hadn't been averse to ramping up tensions on set but backed off when Everard wouldn't wear it. 'His number two seemed more persuadable,' Cosgrave shrugged, 'but ultimately it was Everard's party and we needed him to play along.'

'What about stuff behind the scenes?' Noakes pressed. 'Staff argy-bargy?'

'As in pushy behaviour.' Markham prompted. 'Any divas?'

'Oh right, I'm with you now,' Cosgrave said. 'There was one young lad, Jamie O'Neill. . . I suppose you could say he was a bit full of himself, but he was great eye candy. Perfect for a soft-focus mid-afternoon slot like Phil Schofield or Dan Walker. . . and he knew it too—'

'But folk didn't want him stealing Everard's thunder?' Noakes jumped in.

'Well, as I remember it, Mr Santini had a tactful word with O'Neill. . . said something about *Gino* being the leading man. He was nice about it though . . . didn't try to make the youngster look small or anything like that.'

Interesting that O'Neill hadn't mentioned anything about Franco Santini's intervention, the DI thought.

'Were you aware of any exchange between O'Neill and Mr Everard?' he asked.

'Not that I noticed,' Cosgrave replied. 'Which isn't to say that it might not have happened, but I was focused on getting something in the can,' he admitted.

'Do you recall a woman called Joanna Osborne?' Markham continued. 'She worked on the design side.'

'Yes,' the producer answered promptly. 'Very photogenic. . . She wasn't the only pretty kid there, but the camera loved her—'

'An' the rest of 'em didn't,' Noakes put in.

Cosgrave grinned ruefully. 'A few noses were put out of joint,' he agreed. 'But we took the hint and pulled back. . . No point curdling the atmosphere.'

'Not even to spice things up?' Noakes challenged pugnaciously.

The producer appeared unperturbed. 'Touché,' he laughed. 'Sometimes viewers like it if they get to see sales-people being a bit bitchy with each other, but this was only a pilot. . . early days for showing staff at each other's throats.' He thought for a moment. 'And anyway, Everard wanted to give this impression of them being one big happy family.'

Sadly ironic in light of subsequent events, Markham thought grimly.

'Were you aware of Ms Osborne being upset with Everard?' he asked.

'No, nothing like that,' Cosgrave assured him. 'He seemed quite gracious and said something about her doing ready-to-wear collections . . . I presumed she was some sort of rising star and he was giving her a plug.'

And yet Joanna Osborne had insisted this was a put-down.

Feeling that they were going round in circles and aware of the TV men's restlessness, Markham brought things to a conclusion having received Cosgrave's promise to send him an unedited version of the pilot which, he assured them with some regret, hadn't included any alcohol-fuelled tantrums. Shortly afterwards, Mark Harris showed the DI and Noakes out of the building with false cordiality and ill-concealed relief.

'D'you reckon they'll go ahead with a show about the boutique then, guv?' Noakes asked as they made their way to Markham's car.

'Who knows,' Markham replied slowly. 'Being the back-drop to murder has to be an added draw,' he said with an air of repugnance.

'There's other bridal shops in Bromgrove,' Noakes pointed out. 'The one with that soppy name for starters . . . Happy Ever After?'

'Oh yes, I remember, in the Medway shopping centre.'

'Happen the telly folk'll try somewhere else,' the other mused. 'Ginelli ain't the only game in town.'

Markham had a sudden acute sense of foreboding.

Whatever game was afoot, he thought, somewhere out there was a killer preparing their next move.

7. AN UNSUITABLE CONNECTION

Sunday 10 April was peaceful in CID, and Markham's team looked all the better for having taken Saturday off.

Markham was amused that Doyle and Carruthers appeared almost to be vying with each other in assuming Noakes's responsibilities for commissary, the former turning up with croissants and hot drinks from his local deli while Roger the Dodger shyly produced some homemade brownies baked by his girlfriend. Kate Burton's vegan muesli cookies really couldn't compete, though the DI nobly took one to be polite. The other two looked askance when she whipped out her Tupperware of wholesome goodies, but a stern glance from Markham discouraged any witticisms about bird droppings.

They were interested, however, in her account of Empress Dowager Cixi and other notables of the Tang dynasty, especially their ingenuity in devising punishments such as the bastinado, or death by a thousand cuts, which involved beating miscreants to death with long wooden bats, and the cangue, a heavy wooden yoke which sat on the criminal's neck and shoulders, in some cases for ever. They were less enthralled by the subject of foot binding and deformed feet, but enjoyed hearing about eunuchs, harems and palace intrigue. Seeing their eyes glaze over when Burton got on to Chinese calligraphy, Markham judged it expedient to bring the conversation round to the current investigation.

His fellow DI promptly snapped into professional mode.

'I checked with the university yesterday,' she said. 'A woman in HR was helpful. Turns out that Antonia Rambert attended an Open Day for mature applicants and she went along to a few student fashion shows.' Even the treasures of the fabled Tang Dynasty hadn't kept Burton, with her bloodhound tenacity, from following the trail.

'Any connection between Rambert and Conteh?' Doyle asked eagerly.

'Not that anyone's aware of,' Burton replied. 'At least, there's no official record of their paths having crossed.' She sighed. 'And nobody from the Confetti Club is admitting to anything untoward having happened on the shop floor. . . apart from that woman who had a go at Rambert.'

'What do we know about her?' Markham asked.

'Mental health issues galore, guv, but not enough smarts to have done the murders. Reading between the lines, she floats around in a haze most of the time while her family pick up the slack.'

He trusted Burton's judgement, so it looked like Antonia Rambert's assailant could be ruled out. And anyway, he was convinced these two murders were connected and the saleswoman had been killed on account of some secret knowledge that made her dangerous.

But what was it that Antonia Rambert knew?

Carruthers interrupted Markham's thoughts. 'Santini inheriting the loot has to put him in the running,' he suggested.

'Not unless there was a falling-out with Everard or he was in some sort of financial hole,' Markham pointed out. 'And we've no evidence to support either of those scenarios.'

'The manager at Queen for a Day, Mr Khan, mentioned some kind of unpleasantness involving Santini and a female customer a while back,' Burton resumed. 'He and Santini are friendly, so I figure he decided to mention it in case tongues started clacking and someone tried to finger Santini as a letch.'

'Or Santini primed Khan to get it in before anybody else did,' Doyle observed cynically.

'What kind of unpleasantness?' Markham asked quickly, thinking of Natalie Noakes and her father's misgivings.

She shrugged. 'Something and nothing really. The woman's boyfriend came round shouting the odds after deciding that she and Santini were a bit too cosy for comfort. He apologised later once he'd calmed down.'

'Santini's a bit of a lounge lizard,' Doyle said censoriously. 'With all those nubile lovelies on the premises, you could imagine him thinking he was in with a chance.'

'*I* couldn't,' Burton said disapprovingly. 'And Mr Khan was positive the whole thing was rubbish. He's got daughters of his own . . . said Santini's kind of, well, fatherly.'

'I thought he looked like a mafia hood,' Carruthers joined in. 'What about all that hair oil!'

'You shouldn't judge a book by its cover,' Burton said repressively. 'And anyway, I checked it out. Mister macho man had biceps bigger than his IQ. According to the girlfriend, it wasn't the first time he'd come over all paranoid and possessive.'

'And going by what people said, *Everard* was the ladies' man, not Santini,' Carruthers mused.

'The *Gazette* hinted he swung both ways,' Doyle countered.

'When you did the interviews, was there anything to show Mr Everard might have been romantically interested in one of his employees?' Markham asked.

'Nothing like that, boss,' Doyle said. 'Whatever he got up to, it doesn't look like he messed with the help.'

'How about Jamie O'Neill?' Markham asked, remembering Natalie Noakes's conviction that the young salesman had got 'knocked back' by Everard.

Doyle and Carruthers shook their heads in unison.

'What do we know about Mr O'Neill's CV?' Markham persisted.

'Before coming to the Confetti Club, he'd had quite a few jobs which only lasted a few months,' Burton said. 'But that's not unusual for the industry. The same goes for Joanna Osborne, Randall Fenton, Christina Skelthorne and several of the backroom staff.' She checked the ubiquitous notebook. 'None of the CVs threw up any red flags.'

'What about Maria Hagan?' Markham wanted to know.

'She and Antonia Rambert were the old-timers, guv,' Burton told him. 'Twelve years between them.'

'And before that?' the DI pressed.

'Hagan leased a unit at the Artisan Centre in Old Carton, called Bride on a Budget. But it struggled. Everard called in there when she was on her ups . . . must've seen something he liked, because he offered her a job on the spot.'

'She's a nice lady,' Carruthers said. 'When Everard's PA kept blubbing, she sorted a cup of tea and calmed her down . . . Otherwise, we wouldn't have got any sense out of the kid.'

Markham had overlooked Lucille Chilton. 'What do we know about Ms Chilton's background?'

'Came to the Confetti Club straight from uni,' Doyle replied. 'HND in business, so not as ditsy as she looks.'

'Any problems, any bust-ups with Everard or Ms Rambert?' Markham pressed.

'No. She seems decent enough,' Carruthers replied. 'Thought the sun shone out of Everard's backside by all accounts.' There's no accounting for tastes, his expression said.

'Could she have made a play for him and got slapped down?' Markham demanded.

Carruthers thought for a moment. 'I reckon it was more a crush sort of thing,' he replied finally. 'The others teased her about it. But she's got a boyfriend. I heard her banging on to Chrissie whatsername about him, saying she wanted to get engaged . . . a load of stuff about the nesting instinct.' He and Doyle exchanged sardonic glances, from which it might be deduced that their sympathies in this scenario lay with the hapless male.

'She should get a cat,' Doyle said authoritatively. 'That'd sort her out.'

A glance at Burton's stony expression suggested the advisability of moving on from the subject of prescriptions for domestic bliss. 'Regarding the accusation that Mr Santini had been over-familiar towards a customer, did it cause any problems between him and Gino Everard?' Markham asked.

'Mr Khan said Everard was relaxed about it,' Burton informed them. 'Joked about it being an occupational hazard.'

Markham got up and walked to the window, by way of suppressing the urge to be doing something. Rarely had he felt such a sense of impotence during the early stages of an investigation. But with the Confetti Club murders, he was struggling to identify a motive.

Beyond his office window, gentle sunshine bathed the leylandii, an occasional pedestrian picking up speed as they passed Bromgrove Police Station, almost as though to outpace the long arm of the law.

Whose reach, on this occasion, fell seriously short, Markham silently lamented.

As he turned back to face the troops, a knock at the door disclosed the burly station sergeant on an errand that was clearly too important to be left to one of the civilian staff.

Markham's antennae twitched. 'What is it, Bert?' he asked.

'Vandalism at that bridal shop you're investigating, sir. Looks like some hooligan's had a go at the dresses.'

His colleagues were on their feet.

'We're on it,' Markham said tersely, the detectives moving as one towards the door.

* * *

'Bloody hell, this footage is worse than useless,' Doyle groaned as the team pored over CCTV angles in the operations room at the shopping centre ten minutes later.

'They knew to look out for the cameras,' the weekend security manager, Mr Nelson said defensively. 'That's why they kept their hood up.'

Stout, balding and high-complexioned, the man didn't look, Doyle sarcastically observed later, as if he'd be much use in a high-speed pursuit. Nor did his assistant Mr Carter, similarly paunchy with the rolling gait of one more used to puttering about on a bowling green than chasing ne'er-do-wells, give them much joy. 'I was out back by the bins, taking a breather,' he told them. In other words, having a crafty cigarette. 'Didn't notice anyone hanging around.'

'We're not glued to the monitors, you know,' Mr Nelson pointed out huffily. 'Unless an alarm goes off, there's no reason to think we've got intruders. It was only when Carter did foot patrol this morning that we realised something was amiss.'

'Columbo and his sidekick couldn't find their way out of a paper bag,' Carruthers snorted disgustedly as the dynamic duo left the detectives alone to review the situation.

'You sound more like Noakesy every day,' Doyle grinned before turning serious. 'There's no way of telling who it is from the video.'

Burton mulled it over. 'With all those layers and the hood up, it could be anyone,' she said dispiritedly. 'All you can really tell is, they're average height.'

'But at least we know it's got to be an inside job, cos even if they snuck in without Batman and Robin noticing,' Doyle's tone was withering, 'they must've had a fob and had the access sequence to get into the shop.'

It didn't help, Burton frowningly recalled, that the shopping centre's facilities manager hadn't got round to recalling all passkeys and changing the entry codes after Gino Everard's murder.

'The Confetti Club lot are careless about security,' Carruthers pointed out. 'Nothing to say someone didn't leave a fob lying around or give out the code. In which case, one of Shay Conteh's groupies could've got in,' he added darkly. 'Could've wangled a passkey and the rest of it. . . who knows, maybe they had a mate on the inside who helped, one of the youngsters, and then they got stuck in, all fired up to strike a blow for the cause . . .' he paused. 'Whatever it is,' he added dubiously.

Doyle considered this theory. 'If you're right about it being one of that crowd, then maybe Conteh put them up to it himself,' the DS said. 'Publicity for his anti-capitalist bandwagon plus another plug in the *Gazette*.'

But Burton wasn't so sure. 'There's easier ways of going about it,' she said. 'And this just means he ends up with us on his back. Plus, I don't see anyone in the shop being in on it or lending lanyards and what have you . . . not with a serial killer on the loose.'

Serial killer. The words hung in the air.

'I'm inclined to agree with you, Kate,' Markham said after an uneasy pause. 'There's something very personal about the way those mannequins were slashed about,' he said. 'Something that adds up to more than vindictive yobbery.'

'Weird the way they hacked the arms off,' Doyle mused. He winked at Carruthers behind Burton's back. 'Maybe it's one of those paraphilias, ma'am. You know, some kind of identity disorder . . . like the ones Professor Finlayson covered in his seminar last week.'

Finlayson certainly knew how to hold his jaded CID audience, Markham reflected wryly, remembering how the younger attendees had sat up wide-eyed once the university profiler got started on killers with a thing for amputees.

Before Burton could launch into Acrotomophilia or any other bizarre fetish, he said firmly, 'It wasn't just mutilation of the dummies. Daubing the dresses with those red hearts and arrows seemed like some sort of ritual they felt compelled to act out—'

'Almost like they were leaving their signature?' Doyle suggested.

'Exactly like that,' Markham said approvingly, sending the young DS into the seventh heaven of delight with this endorsement.

Carruthers didn't want to miss out.

'The symbol thingies *did* make it look like it was personal,' he said with a judicious air. But reluctant to look like he was currying favour, Doyle's fellow DS continued to play devil's advocate. 'It could still be some kind of feminist protest slogan, though,' he pointed out. 'Last year on Valentine's Day, they painted graffiti like that on the tax office.' He frowned. 'Dead creepy till you clocked it was paint and not blood.'

'Typical Guardianistas,' Doyle muttered, then registering Burton's thunderous expression, 'Sorry, ma'am, no offence.'

Ignoring him, the DI turned to Markham. 'By the way, guv, I meant to tell you before we had the call-out, Danielle Rigsby got in touch yesterday and told me — "full disclosure"—', Burton air quoted ironically, 'she'd heard that Claudia Everard had put feelers out to Franco Santini . . . Apparently Mrs Everard was interested in some kind of partnership with him.'

Markham considered this, thinking that it looked as if the cards were stacking up against Gino Everard's deputy.

'Did Ms Rigsby say whether Gino Everard knew about this?' he asked.

'All very secret squirrel apparently, guv. But she's positive Mrs Everard was keen as mustard about it.'

Markham looked back again at the grainy, profoundly unsatisfactory CCTV footage.

'Well, whoever our intruder is, they kept their head turned well away,' he sighed. 'Too savvy to get caught.'

'They had a key fob and knew the access code,' Doyle returned to his original starting point. 'So, if we're ruling out protesters or nutcases, then it's got to be one of the staff,' he reiterated portentously.

'Those little bags in the changing cubicles were freaky,' Carruthers said, his thoughts returning to the scene that had greeted them in the Confetti Club.

'That's another factor which to my mind strengthens the case for its being an inside job,' Markham observed. 'The wedding favours were beautifully put together. And while I doubt we'll be able to track down whoever ordered those silk bags with the charms, little scented candles, bride and groom dolls and all the rest of it, such attention to detail makes me feel sure that the person we're looking for has a serious hang-up around everything to do with marriage ceremonies.'

'Yeah, that kind of figures, seeing as the CCTV has them rocking up at seven but not leaving till half past eight,' Doyle agreed. 'Which means they wanted to spin it out.'

'Maybe they were jilted at the altar or something weird like that,' Carruthers hazarded.

Burton looked sceptical. 'All our suspects are either in stable relationships or happily single, as far as we know . . . no dramas that I've been able to uncover,' she said doubtfully.

'So, what've we got then?' Doyle demanded. 'Either one of the shop lot has a screw loose or some nutter managed to worm their way in and stage an Izzy Wizzy moment while no one was looking.'

Markham knew only too well that the nutter option would be far more palatable to DCI Sidney than any other theory. In the past, he had been profoundly irritated by Sidney's tendency to blame everything on 'mentalists', junkies, dropouts and his beloved 'Bushy Haired Stranger'. But now he was inclined to think his boss secretly feared the idea of respectable citizens — those with whom he happily rubbed shoulders — harbouring deviant impulses beneath a smiling exterior. Easier to suppress all such thoughts than to conceive of Jekyll and Hyde at large in Bromgrove. . .

Carruthers broke into the DI's reflections.

'Whoever it is, they're a cool customer,' he observed with reluctant admiration. 'I mean, hanging around for an hour and a half . . . it was taking quite a risk.' With a sardonic lift of the eyebrows, he added, 'Nothing to say Nelson or Carter wouldn't have spoiled the party if they swung by on, er, foot patrol.'

'Somehow I think the killer planned for every eventuality,' Burton commented. 'But in any event, it looks like those two are creatures of habit,' she added, gesturing to a noticeboard. 'Foot patrols every three hours at the weekend . . . Saturdays it's six, nine and midnight.'

'And probably everyone who works in this place knows the drill,' Carruthers commented.

'Not to mention anyone passing by the office,' Doyle grimaced.

Burton ruffled her bob distractedly. 'At least they didn't run amok in the stock room as opposed to vandalising the displays,' she said.

'Perhaps they couldn't bear to wreck the really expensive stuff,' Doyle suggested.

Which was another argument in favour of this being an industry insider, Markham thought.

His mobile buzzed.

Then, having briefly responded, he addressed Burton.

'I'd like you to finish up here please, Kate,' he said without vouchsafing the identity of his caller. 'It's a pain, but we need to check alibis for Saturday evening.'

'No worries, sir,' was Burton's crisp response. 'I'll get on to Danielle Rigsby too . . . see what else she can tell us about Mrs Everard's proposal to Franco Santini.'

'Thanks, Kate.' He knew he could count on her to go through everything with a fine-tooth comb. 'I feel these murders have their roots in "ancient history". Whatever it is, I'm afraid so far we've managed to miss some vital connection.'

'Leave it with me, boss,' she said levelly.

And Markham knew that so far as it lay within Kate Burton's power to sift the boutique's personnel and local whack-jobs, she would do so.

Driving back to the station, he reflected on the latest developments of the case.

Something told him they were dealing with a profoundly disturbed killer whose psychosis, if that is what it was, centred upon the bridal industry. But nothing in the profiles assimilated to date pointed to a dysfunctional killer of the type sought.

Back at the station, he checked in with the desk sergeant.

'Where've you put her, Bert?'

'In your office, guv. Didn't seem right to use an interview room.'

'Thanks . . . Any chance of some tea and biscuits?'

Bert nodded. 'Coming right up.'

* * *

Mrs Noakes, as ever, was dressed for a garden party at Buckingham Palace, this time in a shiny navy-blue taffeta creation printed with large pink and green cabbage roses that accentuated her abundant bosom and rear. The helmet of stiffly sprayed blonde hair looked as though she had just come straight from the hairdresser's (as indeed she had), while court shoes, black patent handbag and pearls all proclaimed her middle-class credentials to the world.

It occurred to Markham, as he murmured the conventional pleasantries, that Muriel's fear of unpleasantness was not unlike the DCI's antipathy to anything that threatened his concept of the natural order.

He had a shrewd idea about the kind of unpleasantness that might be in question on this particular occasion but made no attempt to rush his friend's wife, treating her with the old-world gallantry that she took to be her due and loved to receive from him.

Tea and biscuits were deposited with a smart salute by the desk sergeant, this acknowledgement of the visitor's V.I.P. status further reinforcing her amour propre.

Despite being in the middle of what might be his most complex murder investigation ever, Markham's patience and courtesy never faltered, not even when Muriel archly compassionated his newfound bachelordom and dropped none-too-subtle hints to the effect that he was wasted on uppity schoolmarms.

Showing kindness and chivalry towards Muriel was part of the debt of honour that Markham owed to his old friend and ally. He still smiled at the memory of their convoluted theological discussions during the Theresian Club case. When the subject of papal infallibility came up, Noakes promptly offered a definition. 'It means the Pope can't make a mistake,' he pronounced. On Doyle protesting that it was impossible to say someone couldn't make a mistake, the old warhorse shot back. 'Why not? My missus don't.' And this after all the travails of the Bluebell case! Truly, Markham felt as if the intricacies of the Noakeses' union must forever be a mystery to him.

Now, having gently batted away all offers of consolation, ranging from hotpots to honey cake ('So important to keep your strength up, Gilbert. . . Now more than ever') and received innumerable coquettish glances without in the least knowing what to do with them, he gradually brought the conversation round to Natalie.

This unlocked the floodgates, as he knew it would.

'Oh Gilbert, we do wish she wouldn't have anything to do with that bridal boutique.' Even in the midst of her distress, Markham noticed that not for worlds would Muriel have said 'shop'.

'Is it the self-marriage scheme?' he probed gently. 'Is she still wanting to organise some sort of ceremony by way of, er, closure after the breakup with Mr Jordan?'

'Oh, that's pretty much gone on the backburner for now,' Muriel told him, her voice dropping an octave as she added in a whisper, 'with its not being totally seemly in the middle of murder.' A sense of her irritation with Natalie's pet project began to revive. 'But I ask you. . . all that nonsense about making vows to herself. It's just not dignified. . . Though I suppose it could be worse. George told me about some dreadful new age trend for marrying trees.' Her eyes widened. 'Would you believe!'

Markham suppressed a grin as he remembered his friend's outrage over the widely reported story of the woman who married a tree and then changed her name to Elder.

'I mean, *Sologamy*,' Muriel paused impressively to underline her extensive vocabulary, 'well it's simply ridiculous and not the way people like us behave.'

Markham smiled encouragingly, suppressing the urge to ask whether self-marrieds went on honeymoon. Best to let her get this out of her system, he thought, and she'll come to the point eventually.

The point, it transpired five minutes later after some further huffing and puffing about undignified carryings-on — 'shamans, chakras, nonsense about ancestors and the four elements' — was Natalie's association with Franco Santini.

And at this point the affectation and archness that gave Markham a sensation of being light-headed dropped away, and Muriel Noakes said anxiously, 'I don't know the ins and outs of Natalie's dealings with that man, but somehow he makes her unsettled, dissatisfied with home and with me and her father. . . as if,' and here the heavily lipsticked lower lip trembled, 'we're not good enough.' This was Mrs Noakes's deepest fear. 'It's not just that, though. Suddenly she's anti everything she liked up till now. . . anti having a nice boy-friend and a church wedding, anti everything she says is "conventional" and "stuffy" . . . She's obsessed with being cutting edge and different and I just know it's all down to *him*.'

There was a dreadful irony about Muriel Noakes complaining that her daughter had turned into some kind of crashing snob who regarded her parents as not being good enough, but Markham's expression of tranquil sympathy never wavered.

'It's like she has this bitterness and, well, contempt for us,' Muriel concluded. 'And it's just not her true character at all.'

Markham suspected that Olivia would have had something to say about the fond parent's image of her daughter as the epitome of girlish softness, but luckily she wasn't there to catch his eye.

It was interesting, though, to hear about the flipside of what Mr Khan had called Franco Santini's 'fatherliness' . . . the possibility of its screening more sinister traits.

'Has there ever been any impropriety that you're aware of, Muriel?' he asked delicately. 'Any question of Mr Santini behaving inappropriately towards Natalie . . . perhaps being over-familiar or intimating a wish that they become romantically involved?'

He was relieved to see that she looked startled.

'No, nothing like that.' Mrs Noakes's lips formed her 'prunes and prism' expression, as though she was casting around for a becoming demeanour. 'I mean, he's more than twice her age . . . quite unsuitable.'

Over the years, Markham had become familiar with Muriel Noakes's partiality for a certain type of older man (most recently Dr Nariman of Beautiful Bodies notoriety); what Olivia mischievously termed her 'crushettes' on avuncular smoothies in their sixties and seventies — professional men with a certain standing in the community whose intellectual and other talents she regarded with awe. Always platonic, though suffused with an element of rose-tinted fantasy, such harmless infatuations made no difference at all to Muriel's devotion to Noakes and raised barely a ripple in the current of their married life.

Unusually, Mrs Noakes was impervious to Franco Santini's well-honed allure, though he was precisely the type of man for whom she would normally have fallen hook, line and sinker . . .

After she had left his office with reassurances that he would keep a watchful eye on Mr Santini, Markham asked himself if Muriel — so often shrewd and intuitive through all the silliness — had sensed something that spelled danger, something that he himself had missed.

There was without a doubt something of the masked actor about Franco Santini. And now it seemed possible he was guilty of double-dealing towards Everard.

Yes, Everard's number two merited closer attention.

Tomorrow was Gino Everard's funeral which Noakes had offered to attend (mercifully, Muriel's reading group could not do without her). With all the suspects together, there would surely be an opportunity to make discoveries . . .

8. SENSELESS MESSENGER

St Mary of the Angels was a long sandstone church built in the Pugin Gothic style and dating back to the late nineteenth century. The building had been funded by a shipping magnate, which might have accounted for the solidly unpretentious exterior with its low-pitched roof, modest gabled wings, arched porch and rose window.

Inside was a different story, however, with fittings that seemed designed to bring Renaissance Italy to Bromgrove. Two rows of colonnaded pink-hued marble arches lined the walls on each side of a single-naved interior, with crimson-carpeted steps leading to the apse and an altar of black marble flanked by more columns and mosaics. Behind the altar, a vast gilt-framed painting formed an impressive backdrop that glowed mysteriously in the dim vaulted recess. Below the crimson steps, white stone rails separated the sanctuary from the main body of the church with its chequered marble floor, plain oak pews and a more modest communion table — albeit with richly embroidered frontal — which served worshippers' daily needs. The overall effect was at once ornate and intimate, but Markham decided that he liked it, glad that he and Noakes had arrived early to sample the unusual ambience.

Noakes was more ambivalent, scanning one of the little leaflets on the history of the building. 'Looks like Mrs Big Cheese might've fancied joining your lot,' he sniffed. Despite Muriel's recent flirtation with Catholicism, and the fact that Noakes himself had proved to be unexpectedly receptive to its mysteries during their investigation at the Theresian Club, he was always vociferously mistrustful of 'too much Rome'. Markham was a lapsed Catholic, but most of the time Noakes didn't hold this against him. Now and again, however, his Anti-Papistical prejudice reared its head.

'Well, this church is High Anglican,' Markham pointed out mildly. Looking round, he added, 'And if Mr Santini is to be believed, Gino Everard liked dropping in here from time to time.'

'Yeah, he's the sort who'd get off on smells an' bells.'

Markham opened the little wrought iron gate in the centre of the altar rails and the two men moved towards the huge painting behind the high altar, gazing up at it with keen interest.

Noakes alighted on a point of interest in the little pamphlet. 'It says here the painting shows the Archangel Raphael an' Sarah.'

Markham turned enquiringly towards his friend, awaiting an explanation of this gnomic pronouncement, aware that Noakes enjoyed nothing so much as a trawl through biblical stories from his Sunday school days.

'She'd had seven husbands but there was this demon got jealous an' killed each of 'em on the wedding night, so God sent Raphael to help out.' Noakes gave another of his eloquent sniffs as he scrutinised the youthful looking seraph. 'Not that the lad looks much like an archangel in that skimpy tunic an' them wings ain't up to much. . . Raphael's big league, so by rights he should have whopping ones an' a fiery sword. Anyway, he's killed the demon — that's the dragon — an' now he's tying it up.'

'Presumably the rather anaemic young couple in medieval wedding finery kneeling next to that four poster are meant to be Sarah and prospective bridegroom number eight?'

'Yeah, thass Tobias an' he's her last chance. . . though with his whey face an' the girlie hair she's gotta be *desperate*.'

Markham smiled. 'I like all the little cherubs crawling over the bed.'

'Me an' all. They're the best thing in it. . . them an' the dog,' Noakes conceded, squinting at a forlorn canine in the foreground. 'Says here that Raphael's the patron saint of marriage an' the painting's a copy of some Dutch Old Master.'

'Perhaps the connection with the patron saint of marriage is why this church appealed to Gino Everard,' Markham said thoughtfully.

'That an' the fact that it's seriously OTT with all the marble an' mosaics an' everything . . . Right up Ginelli's street,' Noakes retorted. Then with the magnanimous air of one making concessions, 'At least they eased up on the stained glass,' he said pointing to the plain glazed domed windows high above the colonnaded arches. He turned back to the sanctuary mosaics. 'An' they've got some proper looking angels on them picture tiles.' The pug nose was once more buried in his little pamphlet. 'There's the Archangel Michael telling Adam an' Eve to clear out of Eden. . . an',' with lip-smacking relish, 'hunting Old Nick.'

Markham suddenly felt sharp discomfort at the reference to Satan, as though some cloven-hooved creature from a medieval bestiary had capered onto the sanctuary and was watching them, hot red eyes gleaming wickedly in the gloom with unholy amusement.

At least that devil had horns and a tail as distinguishing traits.

No such sign would mark out a killer who assumed the protective camouflage of a mourner, hiding in plain sight.

Notwithstanding the reason for their visit, Noakes had clearly begun to enjoy himself.

'There's more angels in these little cubbyholes,' he said, examining niches in the stone reredos underneath the Sarah and Tobias painting. 'Says here the important ones have more twiddles. . . those rosette thingies. The second-class ones don'

111

get as much fuss.' As an ex-soldier, he entirely approved the distinctions of rank when it came to the celestial hierarchy. 'Saint Mary don' get much of a look-in, mind. . .'

'She's up there in the rose window,' Markham said, pointing. 'Washing Christ's feet with her hair.'

'She looks even more drippy than Sarah,' was the tart response. 'An' Jesus looks well fed up when he's supposed to be dead chuffed about it.'

Markham chuckled. 'You're a hard man to please, Noakesy.'

The two men left the sanctuary and did a circuit of the building, weaving between the barley-sugar columns and further examples of rococo art. Noakes expressed distaste for the aquamarine-tinted walls. 'Too bright. . . should be summat dignified an' serious.' But sundry war memorial tablets with curlicued coats of arms and the complicated oak engravings of biblical scenes, writhing with carved whorls and positively swarming with fantastical creatures, pleased him as being orthodox.

For his part, Markham liked the unexpectedness of stepping into a Primavera blue-green world; it felt somehow soothing after the massiveness of the sanctuary with its strange mythical canvas.

At the back of the church, he was momentarily discomposed, however, when they came upon another painting — a framed reproduction of William Blake's *Parable of the Wise and Foolish Virgins*, the famous depiction of Christ's parable comparing the spiritually unready to bridesmaids who turned up late to a wedding feast. While Noakes muttered disapprovingly over the bridesmaids' diaphanous draperies, Markham reflected uneasily that there seemed no getting away from the theme of Blighted Marriage, right down to the trumpeting angel flying overhead as a harbinger of doom. Disconcertingly, all the wavy-haired damsels had a look of Joanna Osborne, while the stormy landscape made him think once more of demons and the forces of darkness. That such a picture should look down on the murdered designer's funeral struck him as the eeriest of coincidences. It also set him to wondering again about the character of the killer they hunted, a killer he believed had ripped those wedding dresses to shreds and wrenched the arms off harmless shop dummies.

Was it Gino Everard who had tipped the murderer into madness or what he represented?

Stealing a sidelong glance at the guvnor's sensitive, well-moulded profile, it was apparent to Noakes that the boss had 'gone off on one' as was his wont in churches. Not that he particularly objected, being rather proud of the affinity that allowed him to partake of Markham's cultural interests.

Waiting for the DI to emerge from his abstraction, he reflected that as churches went, this one wasn't at all bad, especially the carvings of griffins and monkeys and lions. He didn't like the engraving he'd spotted by the porch, though . . . the one with a cat holding a little lizard-like creature in its jaws, surrounded by the corpses of dead mice and birds. No, that one gave him the creeps. Too sneaky and stealthy for words. Maybe it was something to do with the Garden of Eden and all the animals.

Suddenly a line from Sunday school came back to him. Something about cats clothing themselves with cruelty.

Cruelty.

And like Markham on the high altar, he shivered, as though someone had walked over his grave.

'C'mon, Noakesy.' The guvnor's voice broke into his thoughts. 'Let's collect our Orders of Service from the porch and park ourselves somewhere near the back. That way, we'll have a grandstand view of our suspects. Mischievously he added, 'And by the way, may I compliment you on the suit.'

Noakes's funeral-wear was pure Politburo, but infinitely preferable to what he used to disinter for such occasions from the back of his wardrobe.

'Cheers, guv,' was the gruff response. 'The missus reckons it makes me look slimmer.'

Markham privately reckoned this was beyond the power of artifice but nodded gravely, leading the way to a bench on the left-hand side.

* * *

It wasn't long before the other three joined them, the men wearing well-cut dark suits while his fellow DI looked unexpectedly striking in a belted cashmere pencil dress and two-tone stilettos. Nathan Finlayson had never exactly struck him as a style guru, but there was no denying that Burton had rebooted her fashion mojo since his arrival on the scene. The realisation gave Markham a brief pang before he chastised himself for failing to be glad at his colleague's emergence from her chrysalis.

He was grateful that neither DCI Sidney nor Superintendent Bretherton proposed to grace the proceedings due to prior commitments. The memory of their scandalised reactions to Noakes's lusty rendition of 'See the hosts of Hell advancing, Satan at their head' during a previous church service still had the power to bring him out in a cold sweat, so it was a relief to be spared.

Subdued organ music from the loft above them now accompanied mourners as they arrived in their various groups. It was a large, well-dressed congregation, but Markham only had eyes for Gino Everard's colleagues from the Confetti Club, alert for anything that might offer a clue to their killer's identity.

Maria Hagan, Christina Skelthorne and Lucille Chilton were escorted by Franco Santini, with Randall Fenton bringing up the rear. Maria looked somewhat dishevelled, with her peroxide hair straggling from its untidy chignon and the hem of a smock-like midi dress hanging down. Her companions, by contrast, looked well-groomed in flattering charcoal suits, with hair twisted into neat French pleats and minimal jewellery. Lucille Chilton, still swollen-eyed, had a somewhat glassy far-away look but Christina was swift to slip a guiding hand under her elbow. Randall Fenton looked more confident — less stoop-shouldered — than when Markham had seen him last, while Santini was elegant as ever in a superbly cut pinstripe. He and Fenton were solicitous of their female colleagues, but Maria Hagan seemed uncomfortable with the attention, slipping into a bench halfway down the church alongside some of the backroom staff and ignoring Santini when he beckoned her to come to the front.

The organist segued into 'Sheep May Safely Graze' as the church continued to fill up, and Markham's attention drifted to the Order of Service. There was certainly plenty to satisfy Noakes, he thought in amusement: solidly traditional hymns and readings from the Book of Common Prayer, with lots of references to souls struggling from miry clay to realms of celestial bliss. The black and white studio portrait of Gino Everard on the front of the booklet struck a somewhat incongruous note in that he looked like rock royalty or a celebrity hairdresser, but it wasn't overly vulgar or flamboyant. No doubt they had Franco Santini to thank for that.

Some lines halfway down the second page caught his eye: 'Those who have done good deeds will go forth to the resurrection of life; those who have done evil will go forth to the resurrection of judgement.'

The resurrection of judgement.

Whatever awaited the killer of Gino Everard and Antonia Rambert in the hereafter, Markham wished he could feel sure they would suffer earthly punishment. But as yet, he failed to discern the narrative behind these murders. . .

Suddenly Noakes nudged the DI and he looked up to see Maria Hagan twisting round in her seat and staring towards the porch with an agitated expression.

Quietly, Markham left his bench and slipped into the glassed-in entrance vestibule where he found Joanna Osborne and Jamie O'Neill standing awkwardly together as if debating where they should sit. The pair looked almost as though they could have stepped out of the pages of a mail order catalogue with their preppy, All-American good looks, but a muted air of defiance suggested they were ill at ease with the situation.

Before the DI had a chance to say anything, Maria Hagan was upon them.

''Who do you think you are turning up like this?' she hissed. 'After the way you behaved to Gino.'

'The way we behaved—,' Osborne began, but O'Neill laid a restraining hand on her arm.

'Look, Maria, we're not out to make waves or offend anyone,' he said with low-voiced sincerity. 'We just wanted to be here. . . for Gino and Antonia.'

'Antonia couldn't stand you either.' Hagan practically spat the words. As she did so, Markham caught a wave of cheap scent mixed with acrid body odour and something else — gin perhaps? — and couldn't help recoiling slightly.

Now Christina Skelthorne had joined them. 'Gino wouldn't want a scene in church, Maria,' she said gently. 'Decorum mattered to him. You know that.' There was a respectful deference about her manner that had its effect on the other woman. Without another word, she turned on her heel and walked back into the church. Christina shot the other two a hostile look, her gentle features hardening with something close to venom. But 'You shouldn't have come,' was all she said before following her colleague.

Now Joanna Osborne was looking embarrassed and self-conscious, though with an air of brazening it out. O'Neill seemed calm, but a muscle leaping at the corner of his jaw gave the lie to his apparently unruffled demeanour. 'If you'll excuse us, Inspector,' he said, ushering Joanna firmly before him.

A dry laugh came from behind Markham, and he turned to find Danielle Rigsby observing him with malicious amusement. 'Normally the Confetti Club lot are a closed little corporation, but today the cracks are certainly starting to show,' she said.

'Here to cover proceedings for the *Gazette*. . . and pay your respects?' Markham enquired with an ironic inflection.

He could tell that he had hit a nerve when the journalist replied, 'Oh I'm not pukka enough for that. . . There'll be people from *Hello!* waiting to write it up and catch all the. . . action.' And with that Parthian shot, she disappeared into the church.

The DI could only hope the journalist's acid reference to 'action' was merely designed to rattle him. So far there was no sign of Shay Conteh, Mark Harvison or any other malcontent turning up to make trouble, but of course the wake in the council's banqueting suite was still to come. . .

A polite cough from one of the undertakers alerted him to the arrival of the hearse, so without further ado he rejoined the congregation.

'What were all that about?' Noakes enquired.

'Just a misunderstanding.' And then some.

'What's Osborne an' O'Neill doing here? I mean, it ain't zackly tactful,' his friend commented having clocked their arrival. 'I guess they want the exposure,' he added cynically. Markham suspected there was a fair amount of truth in the observation.

And now Everard's coffin was being borne towards the trestles that had been set up in front of the smaller altar, tall arrangements of lilies on either side. Claudia Everard, platinum bob set off by a black fascinator with discreet veil, followed behind the coffin with Martin Carthew, their expressions fixed and unreadable. Mrs Everard's progress was enveloped in an aura of heady, expensive perfume — as different as possible from Maria Hagan's choice of scent — that was no doubt erotically named and produced in Paris. She gave no especial acknowledgement of Franco Santini beyond a frigid bow in the general direction of the boutique contingent.

The vicar was sandy-haired, young and nervous looking, like a sepulchral toastmaster, but he possessed a good, clear voice that did justice to the ringing prose of the funeral service. Markham was intrigued and touched by a sermon which took angels for its theme (no doubt partly in compliment to

117

the venue) and focused specifically on the role of Michael the Archangel in accompanying souls to heaven. A sidelong glance at Noakes suggested he was pleased at the choice of Michael as angelic escort, even if such a martial intercessor seemed an unlikely companion for Gino Everard.

'In Greek, *angelos* means senseless messengers,' the young clergyman concluded. 'But Christian belief tells us their influence extends way beyond space and time and they can act upon our souls without the need to speak. So, we pray that, led by Saint Michael, the angelic host has guided our brother Gino through the gateway of welcome that awaits all believers.'

Markham felt a lump in his throat at this image, thoughts of his dead mother and the brother lost to drink and drugs inspiring a fervent prayer that the gate to paradise had swung open for them too.

Antonia Rambert was not forgotten, though she was referred to only as 'our deceased sister' and Franco Santini in his bland eulogy omitted any allusion to violent death.

And now the organist was striking up a vigorous recessional, with Burton, Doyle and Carruthers predictably cringing as Noakes bellowed out verses about rising to God on winged heels and soaring heavenwards wreathed in clouds of healing balm.

'Hymns like that make you want to do away with yourself,' Doyle muttered as the chief mourners followed the coffin out to the forecourt and the waiting cars. Carruthers nodded in fervent agreement. 'Bloody awful,' he said as Burton shot them a hard look and pointed out that being a funeral, it was supposed to be sad.

'What's happening now?' Carruthers asked.

'Cremation at the north municipal cemetery,' Burton said crisply, well briefed as ever.

'We don't have to go there, do we?' Doyle sounded distinctly unenthused by the prospect, which was hardly surprising given the number of pinched suburban send-offs the team had attended in chapels which had all the character of an airport departure lounge or factory reception area. For all her dutifulness, Burton had no appetite for the final antiseptic, somehow retail, clipboard formalities which invariably left her feeling thoroughly depressed as opposed to uplifted or prayerful. The crematorium's memorial gardens were not without their charm, but she was glad to be spared the closing mundanities.

'Relax,' she said drily. 'That's just for family and close friends. Everyone else is invited back to the council offices for a buffet or some such.'

Noakes was gratified to learn there would be a 'funeral feed', saying piously, 'At least they're giving Ginelli a decent send-off. . . only right an' proper seeing as he's such a big noise round here.'

'Getting any vibes, guv?' Carruthers asked Markham, seeing the boss's forehead furrowed in concentration.

'Not a one, Sergeant,' Markham sighed. 'Apart from Mrs Everard giving us the unfriendly-look treatment, nothing else really stood out.'

'*She's* in a bad way, though,' Noakes said, pointing to Maria Hagan who sat slumped and white in her bench as Lucille Chilton and Christina Skelthorne hovered helplessly in the aisle beside her.

'Upset at seeing Joanna Osborne and Jamie O'Neill,' Markham replied.

'Weird those two turning up,' Doyle mused.

'They'll be looking out for anyone likely to give them a leg up,' Carruthers said sagely. 'Takes some brass neck, though. No wonder the boutique crowd were blanking them.'

'Not Santini, though,' Burton put in. 'He gave them a nod.'

'Well, it was really Everard who had a gripe with them,' Carruthers pointed out. 'So maybe Santini's happy to build bridges.'

'Could be,' she said thoughtfully.

The church was emptying fast, the sound of cars crunching on gravel reaching the team as they waited for the remaining mourners to leave.

As Doyle and Carruthers wandered up to the front to scrutinise the painting that had so intrigued their boss, Burton turned to the DI.

'I heard someone laugh,' she said flatly.

'You what?' Now she had Noakes's attention too.

'Well, I suppose it was more like a snicker . . . but I'm sure I heard it.'

'The padre didn't crack any jokes,' Noakes ruminated before adding with a reminiscent chuckle, 'Not unless you count that one he said Everard told him . . . about the bloke who said women were all childish an' whenever him an' his missus quarrelled she went an' hid his teddy. That were good.'

Burton's boot-faced expression strongly suggested she considered this was an example of misplaced levity.

Hastily, Noakes continued. 'Who was it then?'

And now Burton looked uncertain. 'I don't know,' she admitted.

'Could it have been nerves getting to someone?' Markham suggested. 'That can happen sometimes at funerals.'

Noakes returned to the attack. 'When did you hear it?'

'Right at the end when the vicar said that prayer about flights of angels leading Everard to paradise.' Self-consciously she cleared her throat. 'It reminded me of that time in the chapel at Sherwin College when the killer hissed.'

'Yeah, but we never knew that for a fact,' Noakes challenged, thinking about their investigation in Oxford. 'We just decided afterwards that it must've been them.'

Markham contemplated his fellow DI. Like him, she was sensitive to atmosphere and had picked up on something off-key. . . the same feeling he had experienced in front of the church's high altar when it seemed as if the devil had slipped the Archangel's leash and slithered down to join them. Maybe that too was an emanation from the killer — a sign that they were near at hand.

'Look, it could've been a psychological projection,' Burton suggested. 'Something conjured up by my unconscious due to thinking so much about the case.'

A spasm of pain or something very similar crossed Noakes's face.

God, no. That's all they bleeding well needed. Once Burton got started on '"isms", she'd never stop. All that stuff was meat and drink to her and the guvnor. Now they'd be nattering till the cows came home about Freud and Jung and all the other weirdos. And by the time they got to the council offices, the best of the grub would be gone. Come to think of it, a sausage roll would hit the spot nicely after all that caterwauling. . .

Markham watched Noakes out of the corner of his eye. He knew very well the direction of his former wingman's thoughts.

'It seems incredible to me,' DCI Sidney had once remarked acidly, 'that your team always seem to arrive for work clutching cartons from fast-food outlets.' He managed to inject considerable disdain into the last three words. 'Hardly professional in my opinion.' His expression had become more wintry still when, on querying Noakes's enthusiasm for attending wakes, the latter told him sententiously that 'Jesus were big on eating out. Plus, he said heaven would be like a banquet with plenty of wine an' everyone welcome.' Markham supposed he should just be thankful that Noakes hadn't gone on to make any quasi-blasphemous observations about the Elect getting pissed.

But it was true that eating and drinking were prime bonding experiences for his subordinates, and he had never discouraged it, however much it detracted from charisma of the CSI variety. He had been touched when Doyle said recently that he thought it was great, confiding that the new girlfriend Kelly, a secondary school teacher, said her lot always had 'cake days' and took them really seriously. With a stab of pain, he recalled Olivia saying something similar and chuckling over the internecine rivalry occasioned by such occasions at Hope Academy. . .

'Perhaps we should get moving,' he suggested signalling to Doyle and Carruthers, pleased to see that the two young sergeants were laughing conspiratorially.

'Whass the joke?' Noakes demanded.

'I was just telling Doyle about my mate who got married last month, sarge. . . They'd asked for the theme tune from Robin Hood for when the bride came up the aisle, all romantic and soaring. . . But the organist misunderstood and played that song from the fifties TV series with the cheesy lyrics.' Careful not to catch Burton's eye, he broke into song:

Robin Hood, Robin Hood, riding through the glen
Robin Hood, Robin Hood, with his band of men
Feared by the bad, loved by the good
Robin Hood! Robin Hood! Robin Hood!

'Sounds a bit cracked like everyone's jigging round a maypole or something. . . So anyway, they're expecting dreamy music from *Robin Hood: Prince of Thieves* but the old git gives 'em this Merrie England jingle like it's some kind of nutty acid trip. His missus never shut up about it all the way through their honeymoon.'

Noakes sniggered and even Burton cracked a smile, though seeing a verger coming towards them, she swiftly rearranged her features. 'Beautiful service,' she said. 'We're just on our way now.'

Under his watchful gaze, they headed for the exit.

* * *

The 'funeral feed' on the third floor at Bromgrove Town Hall Extension was sufficiently generous for Noakes to award it full marks, with the 'memorial menu' featuring quiches, wraps, canapés, blinis, sausage rolls, tartlets and platters of other assorted finger food. Desserts were not wanting either, two trolleys bearing a selection of gateaux, trifles and homemade cakes. After helping themselves from the buffet, mourners sat down at long tables adorned with snowy linen tablecloths and tasteful floral arrangements. Uniformed waitresses circulated offering hot drinks, along with wine for those who felt the need of something stronger.

Markham noted wryly that there was no great rush to join himself and the team after they had paid their respects to the principal mourners, though this was hardly surprising in the circumstances.

Unabashed, Noakes got stuck in with gusto.

'One of them lasses told me Santini organised everything,' he said having made short work of the sausage rolls on his plate. 'I'd have thought he'd be one for olives an' salami an' weirdy cheeses, but fair play to him, he steered clear of all that.'

The words 'foreign muck' remained unspoken, so clearly all those diversity courses hadn't been entirely wasted on Noakes, Markham thought wryly. Just in time for his retirement.

His eyes scanned the throng for signs of unusual tension, but everyone was behaving well, Claudia Everard and Franco Santini on their return from the crematorium acting as hosts (while giving the police a wide berth). That being so, and with Burton casually patrolling the room, the DI sipped his coffee which was excellent and did his best to look unobtrusive, something of a challenge given Noakes's bravura performance as gannet-in-chief.

But while apparently oblivious to everything except the food, his shrewd former wingman missed very little.

'Lucy an' the uptight one don' seem to be getting along too well,' he told Markham through a mouthful of chocolate cake, directing the DI's attention towards Lucille Chilton and Maria Hagan whose set expression gave her an appearance of lockjaw. It looked as though Christina Skelthorne was attempting to shield the pair from notice, so clearly something was up.

'Hagan's probably itching to have another go at Osborne and O'Neill,' Carruthers commented, pointing to Everard's former employees who were now deep in conversation with Danielle Rigsby and a brittle looking blonde who Markham guessed was a correspondent from one of the glossies. 'They're a right pair of opportunists those two.'

'Santini's being civilised, though,' Doyle said. 'So, if he's okay with it, maybe Hagan should wind her neck in.'

Burton overheard this remark as she rejoined their table.

'I reckon Maria's moved on from griping about Joanna and Jamie,' she murmured. 'I think now she's having a rant about the way people treated Antonia Rambert,' she murmured. 'I'm pretty sure I heard her say something about its being all very well to pull long faces once the woman was dead but how about showing some loyalty when she was alive.'

'Nice way with words,' Doyle observed.

'Well, something's definitely bugging her,' Burton said. 'And I think she may have been on the sauce before coming out. I heard Skelthorne tell one of the other girls they needed to get some coffee down her before she embarrassed everyone.'

Carruthers raised his eyebrows. 'Santini and the grieving widow won't like a scene.'

'I think I saw Mark Harvison downstairs when we arrived,' Burton said looking troubled. 'But as a councillor, he's got every right to be in the building.'

'You don't think he's planning anything, Kate?' Markham asked.

'Not by the look of things, sir, but I tipped the caterers off just in case he decides to have a pop at Santini.'

'Good thinking.'

'There's a university sub-committee having a meeting downstairs in one of the conference rooms . . . on diversity and inclusion,' she continued. 'Which means Shay Conteh and his rabble-rousers might be somewhere around. The food and drink people are going to keep an eye out for him too.'

'God, it's meant to be a wake,' Doyle said. 'You'd think they could give it a rest for one day.'

'At the demo, Conteh an' Santini looked like they'd called some sort of truce,' Noakes pointed out. 'They won't want any argy-bargy.'

Markham felt increasingly uneasy, the tension building up behind his eyeballs similar to the kind he got before a thunderstorm, but he couldn't put his finger on what was wrong.

'Another ten minutes and then we should get back to base,' he told the team before adding, with a sardonic glance at his neighbour: 'Time to eat up, Noakesy. I'll drop you off at Rosemount en route.'

Outside it had started to rain, wan trees shedding showers of water on to the town centre's pavements.

The DI looked back at the distinctively geometric and blocky building with its vertical reddish coloured concrete panels, feeling a curious reluctance to leave. But they needed to review what they had (cue hollow laughter) and formulate some kind of plan going forward including another press release.

They had been back in Markham's office barely two hours, heads bent over witness statements, when there was a sharp knock.

The DCI stood framed in the doorway as the three junior officers leaped to their feet.

Sidney looked pale, almost ill.

Before he uttered a word, the DI knew what was coming.

The murderer had struck again.

9. VANISHING FOOTPRINTS

'We left her right here,' Lucille Chilton said in bewilderment to the detectives as they stood outside the ladies' cloakroom along the corridor from the council's banqueting suite.

'Did you go in with her?' Burton asked.

'We just took a quick look,' Lucille said. 'Nobody else was in there. . . there's spaces under the doors, so we could tell.'

Markham interrupted. 'Did you actually check inside each cubicle?'

The woman was flustered. 'There wasn't any need. Like I said, it was obvious the place was empty.'

He nodded to his fellow DI to continue the questioning.

'Then what did you do?' she asked.

Burton's cool, methodical manner kept Lucille from losing it.

'She was that upset, we figured she needed some time on her own. . . So we said we'd come back in ten minutes or so.'

'Did you actually see her go inside a cubicle?'

Christina Skelthorne looked equally stricken. 'Yes. She shut the door and put her bag against the bottom. . .'

'Did she lock the door?'

'I think so . . . not a hundred per cent sure, though,' was the hesitant reply. 'We definitely heard it slam shut.'

'Where did you go after that?' Burton asked.

'We wandered back to the buffet—'

'What time was this?' Markham interposed swiftly, his voice steady and reassuring.

The two girls exchanged looks, clearly embarrassed.

'It was just after three,' Lucille said. 'We were the last ones. . . the caterers were clearing up round us. But they were ever so nice and said there was no rush.'

'Franco gave us the day off,' Christina explained. 'So we didn't have to dash back to the boutique or anything like that.' She chewed her lip, clearly wondering how much to tell.

'You're doing really well,' Markham said. 'The best thing you can do for your friend now is to tell us what you remember so we can catch whoever did this.'

'She'd had a bit too much to drink,' Christina said slowly.

'You mean before the funeral?' Doyle asked.

'She's not an alkie or anything like that,' Lucille took over quickly, poignantly using the present tense. 'She most likely needed something. . . just to get her through the funeral. And then when she had a couple of glasses of red on top . . .' Her voice trailed away.

'It wasn't just the funeral,' Christina cut in. 'Something else was bothering her. She was a bit off with us in the church and she wouldn't sit up at the front. Then later on, she got angry over nothing.'

Markham sensed an evasion, but there would be time later to probe witnesses' accounts.

'We thought if we waited till the end, then no one would notice there was anything wrong,' Christina continued.

'It didn't go on all that long,' Lucille said, before adding with a trace of bitterness. 'People only stayed to stuff their faces . . . or suck up to that woman from the *Gazette* and those other reporters.'

'It was awkward with what happened to Antonia. Everyone was on edge,' her friend said in a tone of mild reproof. 'There were so many rumours.'

Clearly news of the ghastly manner in which Antonia Rambert's body was posed had leaked out, Markham thought grimly. Reports of a third murder could easily trigger panic unless they somehow muzzled the press. In the circumstances, however, it was unlikely that Gavin Conors and his cohorts would play ball.

'Think carefully,' the DI said to the two scared women. 'You said you were the last ones to leave and the caterers were clearing up, correct?'

'That's right,' Christina said uncertainly. 'There was quite a lot of food left over, and one of them said it was a shame to see it go to waste . . . they asked if we wanted to take some of the leftovers. . .'

Lucille continued, 'Then this other woman who was packing stuff up said why not take your mate off to the loos, then she can get herself together while you have a cuppa.' Crestfallen, she added, 'It seemed like a good idea. My feet were killing me and I fancied some peace and quiet after all the dramas.'

Markham nodded understandingly.

'This woman from the caterers who suggested taking Maria to the loos, would you be able to point her out?' Burton asked.

'I think so,' Lucille replied. 'I think she just wanted to help.'

'Was anyone else in the vicinity while you were chatting about what to do?' Markham asked.

'I s'pose there could've been,' Lucille conceded. 'The waitress who asked if we wanted a cuppa was nice but dead loud . . . kinda shouty.'

Markham looked enquiringly towards Lucille's colleague. 'She did have one of those voices,' Christina admitted. 'The sort you can hear a mile off.'

'Do you recall anyone hanging around . . . eavesdropping on your conversation?' the DI persisted.

'All I remember is folk drifting towards the door,' she said. 'And then suddenly it was like we were the only ones left.'

Which didn't preclude the killer hovering, stalking their prey, watching and waiting for the chance to separate her from the rest of the pack, Markham thought darkly. And security arrangements at the Town Hall Extension worked in their favour, seeing as visitors were required to sign in but did not have to sign out again. 'Too much of a bottleneck when you have all these functions finishing at the same time,' he had been told at reception. It was scant satisfaction to reflect that the council's protocols would now be subject to an urgent review.

'Were the two of you together the whole time?' Burton asked carefully.

Lucille shook her head. 'I needed a fag,' she said looking shifty. 'Just nipped down to the courtyard on the ground floor.'

'Did anyone see you?'

'No, it's only bins out there and— hey,' suddenly she was indignant, 'what are you driving at? D'you think I did it?'

'We're just trying to establish everyone's movements by way of getting a clear picture,' was Burton's smooth reply.

'Luce was only gone five minutes,' Christina confirmed. 'And then when she got back, we had a cup of tea.' Guiltily she added, 'Perhaps we lost track of time a bit. . . left it longer than we should have before checking the loos. I remember looking at my watch and it was half three when we made a move.'

Markham decided that further questioning could wait, detailing Doyle and Carruthers to look after the two women and ensure that the premises were fully secured.

Then he and Burton re-entered the cloakroom where Dimples Davidson was waiting.

'Strangled with her own scarf,' the pathologist said succinctly gesturing to Maria Hagan, propped like a broken marionette against the side of the toilet cubicle, her complexion hideously congested and the eyes filmed over. A trickle of dried blood zigzagged down the woman's chin while her swollen tongue protruded obscenely from the corner of her mouth.

'I reckon they were already in here waiting,' Dimples advised them. 'Hiding in that end cubicle with all the cleaning products. . . the mops and buckets and the rest of it.'

'It's the only one where you can't see under the door because it goes right down to the floor,' Burton said slowly. 'And that notice "Staff Only" means her mates wouldn't think to worry about it. They were easy about leaving her . . .' She frowned. 'But how did the killer get at her?'

'Ms Skelthorne wasn't sure that Maria actually locked herself in,' Markham pointed out. 'She said the door slammed shut and they saw her bag plonked on the floor. . . no sign of it now, of course.'

'If the door wasn't locked, they could easily have forced their way in,' Burton concluded.

'Or she might've done her business and come out of the cubicle then over to the basin to have a wash or touch up her makeup,' Dimples suggested. 'Which gave them the chance to surprise her from behind. . . There's severe bruising to the back of the head indicating she received a heavy blow before being strangled.' Dimples cast a quick glance round the cramped surroundings. 'Hell of a risk to attack her here, though. . . They couldn't be sure someone wouldn't walk in and catch them at it.'

Markham recalled how Carruthers had called their quarry a 'cool customer' and felt a chill at his heart.

'Mind you, if he whacked her hard enough and moved like the clappers. . . dragged her into a cubicle and finished her off in there, it could all have been over in minutes,' the pathologist ruminated.

Markham shot him a searching glance. 'So, you think it's a he, then, Doug?'

'Hmm . . . I shouldn't be jumping to conclusions, inspector. A woman could have managed it, given that the victim was,' he paused delicately, 'tired and emotional . . . mellow—'

'As a newt.' Burton blushed crimson as she realised what she had said, but the medic merely grinned. 'A remark worthy of George Noakes, m'dear. Exactly so.'

'I'm sorry, sir,' Burton stammered awkwardly, shooting an embarrassed glance at Markham, fully aware of the guvnor's fastidious insistence on according victims the utmost respect, his tongue-lashings of hapless subordinates he considered deficient in this regard having passed into legend.

But Markham's response was surprisingly mild. 'Relax, Kate,' he said. 'You're absolutely right. Maria's defences were down, making her vulnerable.'

The pathologist looked from one to the other as though he saw something that greatly amused him before returning his attention to their victim.

'I'll stick my neck out here, Markham, and say she was knocked unconscious over at the sink,' he said. 'And then the murderer yanked her into this cubicle. There was no time for her to react.' Bluff features sombre, he added, 'No time for her to feel anything except oblivion.'

'I have a feeling forensics will confirm your scenario, Doug,' Markham said slowly.

Burton moved across to the end cubicle.

'There's one of those "cleaning in progress" cones in here,' she told them. 'They could have stuck that outside just to be on the safe side so people wouldn't bother with these loos . . .'

'And the killer could be sure of no interruptions,' Markham concluded stonily. 'Yes, that would make perfect sense.'

The trio contemplated Maria Hagan's pitiful sagging corpse, stocky legs splayed.

'Was there any interference, Doug?' Markham asked.

'No, nothing like that, no sexual assault from what I can see. For what it's worth, I'd say this was all about expediency . . . disposing of a problem.'

Like drowning a kitten or wringing a chicken's neck, thought Markham looking at the inoffensive, kindly woman whose mere existence threatened to expose a killer's secrets.

'Let's get her moved,' Dimples said gently. 'She must have died around half three this afternoon, so at least time of death is straightforward.'

Even if nothing else was.

Maria Hagan exited the building on a sheeted gurney fifteen minutes later, SOCOs and uniforms bowing their heads respectfully as she passed.

'We'll have to do a press conference right away, Kate,' Markham told his colleague. 'Before uninformed speculation gains traction.' *And Sidney has a conniption.*

'How much are we going tell them, guv?'

'The bare minimum.' Markham's lips were compressed tightly, and the finely chiselled nostrils flared with distaste. 'We can't get away with flannelling about suspicious circumstances this time round, so we'll have to come clean about Maria's death being linked to Everard and Ms Rambert. But if we give it the full *Crimewatch* — talk about doing a reconstruction at the council, ask for witnesses, float the idea of someone having a grudge against entrepreneurs etcetera — we can hopefully steer them away from all-out hysteria about bridal shops or mad talk about a "wedding day killer".'

'God, that's all we need,' his colleague said with feeling. Then, 'Did you get the feeling that Lucille and Christina were holding out on us about what went on at the wake, boss? It sounded to me like Maria maybe had a bone to pick with the two of them.'

'Yes, there was definitely something they weren't telling us. But whether it ties in with the other deaths . . . well, that's another matter.'

'They're not alibied for this one, guv.'

'That fact hadn't escaped my notice, Kate,' he said dryly. 'Lucille's fag break gave her enough time to do the deed—'

'And meanwhile, Christina was on her own having a cuppa in the banqueting suite . . . Which means that either of them had an opportunity to cut along to the loos and ambush Maria.'

Consternation was etched on Burton's gamine features.

'D'you see either of them for this, boss?' she asked finally. 'They seemed pretty shell-shocked to me. And I just can't imagine them having the nerve to pull it off.'

'But they were holding something back,' Markham reminded her quietly. 'However, I know what you mean about nerve. There's something rabbit-in-headlights about the pair of them which doesn't seem to fit this killer's modus operandi.'

'The same goes for pretty much everyone else too, guv,' she said resignedly. 'No obvious fit.'

'But all of them had the chance, Kate. . . People were milling around and nobody was paying much heed to who went where—'

'Including Mark Harvison and Shay Conteh . . . assuming they were somewhere on the premises today.'

'Indeed.' He sighed. 'So, we nail down alibis as far as possible. I want to know where all of them were between three and four. Anyone who can't be accounted for goes right on our—'

'Shit list.'

A smile illuminated the aquiline features. 'Dimples was right, Kate. You're becoming more like Noakesy by the day.'

His colleague didn't look as if she knew how to take this observation.

'Talking of sarge. . .' she said after a pause. 'You're not going to believe this, sir.'

'Try me.'

'Well, I made a call before, when we knew who the vic was, while you were sorting the cordon. I didn't want her family to hear it from a journo.' She had known the guvnor would hate the idea of Maria Hagan's next-of-kin being doorstepped by the *Gazette*'s trusty hacks and aimed to steal a march on them.

'Thanks, Kate. I'm ashamed I didn't think to check it out. That was well done.'

She blushed at the compliment but tried to conceal her pleasure with a show of insouciance. 'Well, get this, sir . . . Maria's mum lives at Rosemount.'

Now Markham's expression brightened for the first time that day. And even though Burton felt a brief twinge at the realisation that Noakes and not herself was responsible for the DI's look of happiness, she was unselfish enough simply to be glad that it was so.

'She's one of their publicly funded patients. Bromgrove NHS Trust's come on board in a big way, so Rosemount takes twenty percent of residents from there.'

'Any other relatives?' Markham asked.

'She divorced a while back. Her ex-husband was killed in a car crash and there aren't any children. There's a sister, but apparently they lost touch years ago. I've got family liaison working on it.' She paused. 'How do you want to play it, sir?'

'Let's sort the press conference first.' And Sidney. 'Then Doyle and Carruthers can crack on with taking witness statements. Depending on what Rosemount says, I'll pay a visit tomorrow morning.'

'I suppose you'll want to do that one on your own,' she said tentatively.

'Not at all, Kate. Three heads are better than one,' was the casual reply. 'I'm counting on you and Noakesy to come at this from your own, er, unique perspectives.'

His colleague's smile now was broad, unforced and full of confidence.

'Great, sir. I'll make sure sarge knows we'll be coming in.' She grinned mischievously. 'At least the DCI won't be able to say we fixed this to get him a ringside seat!'

Markham gave a grim chuckle. 'I doubt the coincidence of Maria's mother living there will go down well at HQ, but for once Noakesy's in the clear.'

* * *

134

The hastily convened press conference was every bit as excruciating as Markham had anticipated, 'Handy' Barry Lynch from the press office being, as Noakes might have said, about as useful as a chocolate teapot, seizing every chance to sidle up to Kate Burton instead of deflecting Gavin Conors and Co.

There was no doubting the *Gazette*'s number one 'reptile' smelled blood, pointedly asking if Bromgrove CID were 'out of their depth on this one' and suggesting they had been 'slow off the mark to accept there was a serial killer on their patch'.

Even worse was the fact that Mark Harvison and Shay Conteh appeared to be giving interviews left, right and centre on the station steps, slyly insinuating that Markham's team had been caught napping and were lazily targeting those 'in the public eye' rather than approaching the investigation with an objective mindset.

Burton fought a valiant rear-guard action, as Markham told her afterwards, throwing everything she could think of in the way of offender profiling jargon at a hostile audience. But blinding the hacks with science was clearly only going to buy the detectives so much time, as Sidney testily pointed out. 'I need results not cod psychology, Markham,' he hissed afterwards. 'Three deaths is a game-changer. . . serial killer territory. The Chief Constable' — aka God — 'is watching this one. You could say this is our Rubicon.'

'What does that mean?' Doyle demanded crossly in Markham's office after Sidney had disappeared.

Carruthers grinned. 'It's classical, mate. Julius Caesar and all that.'

His colleague was none the wiser.

'Point of no return,' Carruthers explained. 'Do or die.'

'Yeah,' Doyle protested. 'But it was a fricking wake. Nobody was clocking who pushed off early or who was holed up in the bogs . . .'

'Someone was clocking people's movements, sergeant,' Markham pointed out quietly. 'We have to pin those alibis down for the half hour when Maria Hagan met her end.'

The young DS flushed. 'Sorry, sir,' he mumbled. 'People just drifted off and did their own thing . . . all of 'em jittery after Rambert's murder, so most probably they didn't want to stick around.'

'No doubt, Sergeant,' Markham said, 'but we have to try to pinpoint someone who stood out.' Someone potentially on the knife-edge of rational conduct.'

'Sounds like Skelthorne and Chilton might fit the bill for that,' Carruthers said. 'After all, they don't have alibis for Hagan's murder.'

'True,' the DI said. 'And there was some kind of angry altercation between them in the banqueting rooms. I need to know more about that.'

'On it, boss,' Doyle assured him.

'Good.' Markham spoke with an assurance that he was far from feeling. 'I want you and Carruthers to probe the witnesses' accounts of their movements this afternoon, including catering staff, Mark Harvison and Shay Conteh. While you're doing that, Burton and I will liaise with Dimples with a view to pinpointing the time frame.'

'Between three and half past, right guv?' Carruthers asked.

'Yes. That's when her friends went to check on Maria,' Markham confirmed. 'Christina Skelthorne checked her watch and realised they'd hung around the buffet longer than they meant to.'

But by then, it was too late.

'Keep at it,' he continued. 'See who was still at the council offices. . . Was there anyone who peeled off and can't be accounted for in that half hour?'

Seeing that his subordinates looked less than enthralled at the prospect of drilling down into suspects' post-buffet movements, he exhorted, 'Even a few minutes absence might be significant. It looks like she died quickly.' He could hardly bear to think of those contorted features, glazed eyes and swollen tongue. 'So, if someone was out of sight on some pretext or other, then they're in the frame.'

Vigorous nods.

Markham's face as he turned to Kate Burton was an inscrutable mask.

'DI Burton and I will interview Maria Hagan's next-of-kin at Rosemount tomorrow.

Glances of intelligence passed between Doyle and Carruthers.

Noakesy's back in the game, was the stealthy telegraph.

* * *

George Noakes was indeed back in the game, and very much on his own inimitable terms, the DI reflected the following morning as he and Burton joined their old ally in the staff room at Rosemount Retirement Home where he was supervising the hanging of a painting that Markham recognised as *General Gordon's Last Stand*.

'Only a copy, obviously,' Noakes told them once matters were arranged to his satisfaction and the indefatigable administrator, a polite young woman as discreet as she was patient, had brought coffee and biscuits. 'But that other picture gave everyone the creeps, see, an' there's a budget for tarting the place up.' He surveyed the large canvas beadily with the air of a connoisseur. 'This one's way better cos it's like how they show him in that film with Charlton Heston and Laurence Olivier.'

Burton blinked uncertainly. 'I don't think *Khartoum* gets shown all that much nowadays, sarge,' she said. 'I mean, what with Olivier doing blackface and the rest of it.'

'More's the pity,' Noakes growled. 'S'pose these days, they'd want wokesters like Meghan Markle or Prince Harry in a face-off with the Taliban.'

'Don't know about that, sarge,' Burton grinned, 'seeing as it ends with getting beheaded and the body chucked down a well.'

'Sounds like you're really coming round to the general, Noakesy,' Markham observed pacifically.

'He were the business,' was the firm reply. 'The Chinese gave him a yellow jacket — s'like the Order of the Garter. . . it's a big deal when you get that.'

Burton cleared her throat, which never boded well.

'Gordon's a more controversial figure these days, sarge,' she said hesitantly. 'Cancel culture and all that.'

Noakes's pouchy features were obdurate. 'The bloke read his Bible for three hours a day an' couldn't tell a lie.'

Privately, Markham reflected that Gordon must have driven prime minister Gladstone and the rest of the Victorian politicos completely round the twist.

Burton preserved a respectful silence by way of an appropriate response to this revelation. Then she hemmed nervously. 'Wasn't there some kind of issue around his, er, interest in young boys, sarge?' she said. 'The ones he called his "Wangs".'

Markham's former wingman scowled at this reminder of aspersions cast on the Ultimate Imperial Hero. Having now come round to an appreciation of General Gordon's merits, he was having none of it.

'Folk have got mucky minds,' he growled. 'Jus' cos he organised ragged schools an' wanted to help lads make something of thesselves . . . like George VI and his boys' camps. . . Or the scouts.'

Burton didn't look as though she thought boys' camps or the scout movement offered a particularly helpful analogy, but Noakes's pugnacious expression convinced her that discretion was the better part of valour.

'Gordon said the body were corrupt an' only the soul mattered. He didn't give a stuff about money, women or fame.'

'Impressive, sarge,' Burton commented politely. 'He was definitely a one-off.'

'Too right,' the other replied, mollified. 'He were always for Christ and the Gospels.' Though neither proved much use against the Mahdi, Noakes had the air of a man sure of his ground. 'Gordon said, "All things are ruled by Him for His glory. It is rebellion to murmur against His will."'

Burton certainly had no stomach for any such murmuring.

'Amazing bloke,' she said, resolutely suppressing any PC concerns about predatory sexuality.

Noakes continued on his soapbox. 'It weren't all Pilgrim's Progress an' reciting the psalms. The general liked his cigs an' a drink. But he had standards, see . . . got dead upset when some Frenchie took him to see ballet dancers. Apparently, he couldn't stop necking brandy afterwards cos he didn't like women flashing their bits.'

Observing Burton's poleaxed expression, Markham was amused to wonder on what, from all the medley of General Gordon's sterling attributes, she would fix.

But his fellow DI had come a long way since the days when she hadn't known how to extricate herself from a set-to with the grizzled veteran.

'Wow, sarge. Hearing you say that takes me back to the Carton Hall case. . . burning ballerinas and all the theatre intrigue,' she said diplomatically. 'Gordon had a point about it being dodgy.'

Honour was satisfied, Noakes clearly appeased at such a good understanding between himself and Kate Burton. For his own part, Markham was touched at the genuine affection in his colleague's expression as she contemplated the old warhorse. 'I suppose General Gordon was a bit like Churchill,' she said by way of an olive branch. 'Er, fighting them on the beaches, that kind of thing.'

Noakes beamed. 'Zazkly like that,' he said. Wishing to meet her halfway, he said, 'He were quite PC an' all . . . wanted to end slavery in the Congo. Weren't no sissy neither.' *Perish the thought*, Markham thought suppressing a smile. 'Wanted to go sliding down Mount Ararat an' do Indiana Jones stuff.'

'I can see why you want to talk him up, sarge,' Burton said faintly. 'And that's a great picture . . .' Stifling any personal reservations, she added, 'I bet people will love it.'

Only those of a certain political persuasion, Markham thought in amusement before he deftly steered the conversation round to the current investigation.

Noakes listened intently as the DI went through the events of the previous day.

'That poor lass,' he said at the conclusion of Markham's recital. 'She must've had something on the scrote who did for her.'

'Or she could have found out something but not connected it to the killer,' Burton suggested.

Noakes considered this. 'Only they thought she was on to 'em and decided to take her out . . .'

'If she did know something, I don't see her keeping shtum and deciding to blackmail them,' Burton mused. 'It just doesn't fit with the kind of woman she was.'

Noakes nodded vigorously. 'Her mum's a nice woman,' he told them. 'Got Parkinson's, quite advanced. Memory-wise she's a bit all over the place . . . Karen the clinical manager's been in with her, kind of trying to lead up to the news about Maria . . . though really there's no easy way to tell someone their kid's been murdered.' Noakes glowered at *General Gordon's Last Stand* as if it would be a relief to his feelings to snatch up one of the Mahdists' spears and run the killer through with it.

'We'd better see her now,' Markham said gently.

The retirement home had lost none of its old-fashioned country house charm, Markham thought as they made their way up the stairs to the Bluebell Corridor. Despite its being the scene of a previous murder investigation, he found that Rosemount's aura of well-heeled tranquillity exerted the old familiar magic, jewel-coloured medieval knights and ladies in the stained-glass window as mesmerising as ever — and, he could tell, far more acceptable to Burton than any moustachioed Victorian buccaneers.

Mrs Hagan's room was cosy and intimate with its sprigged and striped wallpaper, chintz-covered chairs, painted, mirrored overmantel and framed copies of sentimental nineteenth-century Old Masters by the likes of Leighton and Rossetti.

The lady herself, slight and bird-like with vague blue eyes, was propped up in a winged armchair next to a two-tiered table whose surface was covered with miniature trinkets. Her room felt stiflingly warm, but the window was open and Markham could detect subtle scents of spring rising from the old-fashioned knot garden below.

Their interviewee was indeed disoriented and confused, to the point that Markham was by no means sure the news of her daughter's death had sunk in. She spoke of Maria 'loving Gino but not the other one' and 'hating the bitchiness'. Pressed gently by Burton with reference to the work environment, she appeared to zone out, rambling incoherently about people who would 'stab you in the back as soon as look at you' and colleagues who dismissed Maria as a 'mad old hag'.

'Don' sound like it were all sweetness an' light down at dress cutters central,' Noakes observed ruefully after they had left her, glad to be out of the stuffy cluttered room. 'But all them fashionistas are like that,' he pointed out. 'Same as in *The Devil Wears Prada* innit?' he added, comically proud of being (thanks to Natalie) au fait with modern(ish) trends.

'Well, it may have been some kind of generational clash,' Burton hazarded. 'Hagan, Skelthorne and Rambert against the young Turks. . . Osborne, O'Neill, Fenton and the rest of them. Kind of an ageist dynamic. . . and Maria sounded off about it when she visited her mum.'

'She said Maria loved Gino but not "the other one".' Noakes ruminated. 'Thass gotta be the Eyetie.' Belatedly he clocked Burton's wince. 'Sorry, luv,' though he didn't sound remotely contrite, 'but there's summat slippery about that one. . . reminds me of the bloke Princess Di was dating when she died — the one whose dad were always slipping her bodyguards briefcases of used fivers. . . y'know, like bungs to keep folk on side.'

'You mean Dodi Al-Fayed,' Burton said heavily.

'That's the fella,' Noakes beamed. 'Santini's the spitting image of him, 'cept for the specs.'

'We don't know why Maria Hagan might've been prejudiced against Mr Santini,' Markham said. With a sardonic curl of his lips he added, 'Perhaps it was just a backward resentment of foreigners.'

Sarcasm was invariably wasted on George Noakes.

'Yeah, well if you ask me, he needs watching.'

'All of them do,' Burton groaned, 'seeing as their alibis are all over the place.'

The trio wandered out to the forecourt, looking down towards the driveway with its gently waving pines and cypresses.

'Dimples says the lass died between three and half past, right?' Noakes demanded. 'So, what's the problem with their alibis?'

'It looks like people just drifted off from the wake . . . everyone doing their own thing,' Burton said ruefully. 'We haven't got cast-iron sightings of any of them covering the whole of that half hour and the council staff haven't been able to shed any light.'

'Too busy clock-watching,' Noakes grunted. Then, 'How about Harvison and Conteh?'

'Oh, Harvison was there all right, sarge,' Burton replied. 'But no one's swearing blind to being with him for the full thirty minutes.'

'Billy Nomates,' Noakes jeered.

'Something like that,' she sighed. 'And it's the same with Conteh. With the word "serial" being bandied around, suddenly everyone's clammed up. . . frightened of their own shadow.'

They began walking towards Markham's car.

'Come round to the Sweepstakes later after work, Noakesy,' the DI said. 'You can join me and Kate for a brainstorm.'

'I'll bring pizza,' Burton said with a sidelong smile at Noakes who looked delighted at the proposal.

'Great. We can watch some car crash TV and then plot our strategy,' Markham said warmly.

'Right,' Noakes sighed happily. 'See you later.' His shoulders in the garish check tweed jacket slumped. 'I've gotta do an emergency evacuation risk assessment with some twonks from the council. . . chuffing waste of time seeing as we did one last month.'

Markham grinned. 'Just channel your inner General Gordon,' he teased.

Rosemount's security manager looked as though a ravening horde of Mahdists was preferable to a posse of clipboard-toting council officials any day of the week. With another martyred sigh suggestive of infinite forbearance, he waved the others off and plodded back towards the house.

10. THE CHESSBOARD

Noakes had been worried lest Kate Burton's idea of a piz-za-fest might involve something vegan or wholesome, so he was vastly relieved to behold her triple pepperoni offerings with dough balls and garlic bread on the side. She laughed when Markham offered to rustle up some salad. 'It's all right, guv. The odd lapse from healthy living won't hurt me.'

'Too right,' Noakes affirmed, looking appalled at the idea of ruining prime takeaway with lettuce or 'rabbit food'.

Burton didn't demur when it came to accepting a glass of Markham's favourite Châteauneuf-du-Pape, downing her drink with a gusto that suggested she was glad of a chance to let her hair down. 'I got a cab,' she said defensively in response to Noakes's raised eyebrows, 'so I don't have to worry about driving.'

Or was there something else on her mind, Markham wondered as he gave her a refill. Her smile when Noakes mentioned 'Shippers' had struck him as somewhat strained, and now she seemed anxious to get off the subject of domestic arrangements, brushing aside enquiries about her future plans with an alacrity that suggested she was ill at ease.

Fortunately for her, Noakes wasn't inclined to waste much time on small talk, his mind running on their unsolved murders.

'Any joy finding out what Hagan an' Lucy were squabbling about at the wake?' he demanded.

'I've arranged to interview Lucille and Christina about that tomorrow morning, sarge,' she said patiently. 'No point pushing things while both of them were in shock. Plus, Santini's GP turned up and said they were in no fit state to blah blah.'

Noakes scowled. 'Pretty chuffing convenient if you ask me.'

'As far as those two are concerned, there's only what I overheard to go on,' she continued. 'That comment about how people should've shown Antonia Rambert some loyalty. And let's face it, Maria might just have been sounding off. She was pretty overwrought . . . didn't want to sit with them in church and seemed to be avoiding people.'

Noakes seized on the last comment.

'Yeah, that were odd, her giving 'em the cold shoulder,' he said. 'Like she were frightened of Santini. . . Even Carruthers thought he looked like a gangster with all that gunk on his hair.'

'Nothing like nailing your colours to the mast, Noakesy,' Markham said drily before adding with a glint in his eye, 'just because you feel cheated if you don't get change from a fiver when you go the barber's.'

The other self-consciously flattened his own hair down and made a futile attempt to brush dangling strings of melted mozzarella from his shirt front. 'Yeah well, there's summat dodgy about blokes who're into products.' He imbued the last word with a wealth of baleful innuendo.

'It's not so surprising when you consider Santini's line of business, sarge,' Burton said brightly. 'Talking of which,' she produced a DVD from the ubiquitous briefcase, 'a few years ago, the Confetti Club made this for Bromgrove TV — A kind of Valentine's Day special . . . The project never came to anything, but one of their researchers remembered it after your visit the other day.'

Markham was intrigued (and thankful to get off the subject of men's grooming). 'Excellent, Kate,' he said. 'Let's have a popcorn session and see if it throws up any clues.'

Forty minutes later, Noakes gave his verdict.

'Not bad.'

Markham and Burton exchanged conspiratorial looks. Hallelujah!

'You're right, sarge,' she said slowly. 'It was classier than I expected. It was interesting what that talking head from the university said about the Romans and Lupercalia.' Markham too had been intrigued to learn about the feast's origins in classical antiquity.

'They nicked the whole thing from the Christians,' Noakes was swift to interject, having frowned prodigiously through the section on pagan orgies. ''Cos there were three holy joes called Valentine including a bishop.'

'Right,' she agreed. 'I liked all the stuff about King Arthur and medieval romances.' Burton's voice was oddly wistful as she said this.

'An' then that weirdy idea about the first person you met that day becoming your valentine.' Noakes had evidently been much struck by the Restoration custom of 'valentine by lot'.

Markham smiled. 'Pretty high risk,' he concurred. 'What surprised me was hearing that the Victorians loved the idea of clandestine love-notes — cards made out of hair and all the rest of it . . . seeing as we usually think of them as being so prim and proper and anti-sex.'

Noakes pursed his lips. 'There's nowt anti-sex about a lass sending bits of her pubes through the post,' he observed disapprovingly.

'You're forgetting, this was the era of Lord Byron, Noakesy.'

'And a whole lot of other pervs . . . Mind you,' with a reminiscent smirk, 'them valentines with the insulting rhymes sounded good value.'

'Ah, the "vinegar valentines",' Markham chuckled. 'Definitely what I'd call top trolling.'

'You can see why decent folk didn't approve of all the shenanigans,' Noakes pronounced as though to ward off a hotbed of sin and vice, 'At least you know where you are with Christmas and Easter, but Valentine's Day's a whole different ballgame.'

'It's all to do with mysteries and secrecy,' Burton told them. 'Slipping anonymous messages into a pillar box. "The treasure-house of a thousand secrets, the fortress of a thousand souls",' she quoted softly.

Noakes, predictably, was less struck by G.K. Chesterton's sense of romantic possibility than by the potential for deviance and mischief-making. 'You don' want people sending creepy letters all over the shop,' he said stubbornly. Recalling his beloved true-crime documentaries, he added. 'Take serial killers. They start off with small-time stuff like pest mail an' nicking undies off clothes lines . . . then the next thing you know they're strangling an' chopping an' God knows what.'

Serial killers.

Those two words dropped into the easy banter like stones.

Uneasily, Burton asked with an attempt at lightness, 'Well, did you spot any apprentice serial killer on that DVD, sarge?'

Slowly, he answered. 'I reckon even back then, Everard had a problem with them youngsters who gate-crashed the funeral—'

'Jamie O'Neill and Joanna Osborne.' Burton nodded slowly. 'Yes . . . When Jamie cracked those jokes about Hallmark and Clintons, Gino didn't seem pleased that he was stealing the limelight.'

'It were awkward when the uni boffin got 'em talking about vinegar wotsits an' Ginelli said how about Miss Pushy, looking right at Osborne . . . You could tell him an' Santini had some private joke going on.'

'That felt uncomfortable,' Burton observed.

'Osborne gave Ginelli a right dirty look before she remembered she was on camera an' pulled a sickly face.'

'Hmm. There were digs at a few of the others too,' Markham pointed out.

'Yeah, the young lad who hasn't started shaving,' Noakes interrupted eagerly. 'Randy wossname.'

'Randall Fenton,' the other two said in unison.

'Randy didn't like Ginelli saying he could model for Cupid cos he looked about twelve years old,' came the retort. 'An' he looked like he wanted to sink through the floor when Santini told that story about him getting dumped by some girl cos he kept sending her crap poems.' He gave a wolfish grin. 'Shame we didn't get to hear a few limericks,' Noakes added, his own taste running to the kind of leery word-mongery that was unlikely to resemble anything penned by Fenton.

'That seemed more like banter than anything else,' Markham mused. 'It was quite affectionate really. . .'

'It was the same when Gino joked about Christina Skelthorne and the girls in repairs being addicted to Mills & Boon wedding stories,' Burton agreed. 'Preferably anything with a dashing billionaire bridegroom in the title,' she added with a chuckle. 'At any rate, all of that felt more relaxed than the spiky repartee with O'Neill and Osborne.'

'Everard did a hatchet job on old Claudia real goodo, though,' Noakes ruminated. 'Saying all her brides ended up being meringues, like the fat lass in the Hugh Grant film.'

'*Four Weddings and a Funeral*,' Burton piped up helpfully.

'He stayed just the right side of outright snide,' Markham pointed out. 'Careful to tie it in with the Victorian passion for lace and frills and fuss.'

'Yes, that was clever. . . talking about Princess Di and Victorian Revival in the nineteen eighties,' Burton said, 'so he kind of got it in about Claudia being old-fashioned and dated without sounding—'

'Like a complete bastard,' Noakes finished, nodding.

'This DVD was never shown, right?' Markham turned enquiringly to Burton who nodded confirmation.

'How come?' Noakes demanded.

'No idea,' she told them. 'Presumably Bromgrove TV were thinking about commissioning something but then got cold feet for some reason.'

'It's not a bad demo tape,' Markham said thoughtfully. 'Everard certainly comes across well.'

'Santini not so much,' Burton put in. 'Though he's got this mysterious aura about him — glamorous in a strange kind of way . . .'

Noakes snorted rudely.

'He's like that creepy hypnotist fella. . . the one who got into all that trouble cos he made some bloke think he were pregnant an' the papers made a big hoo-ha about it being shameful an' degrading. Mind you, nobody gives a monkey's now thanks to the LGBT lot, so these days he'd probably get a medal.'

'You mean Paul McKenna?' Burton enquired faintly.

'Thass the one . . . became a sleep guru or summat daft once he'd stopped convincing folk they were freaks.' Noakes thought for a moment. 'An' then there's Rasputin. . . Yeah,' with conviction, 'Santini's got the same shifty glittering eyes.'

Burton shivered involuntarily at this reference to the notorious Russian holy man who had cast a long shadow over their previous investigation at a local psychiatric hospital. Markham also flinched at the recollection.

Noakes was gratified by their reactions and burrowed into his armchair with the air of a born storyteller.

'Yeah, I can tell you remember the mad monk,' he said. 'D'you know, he were a horse thief to start with an' then some of the villagers in Siberia or wherever he lived punished him by doing summat horrible to his privates, so he went round all the time with a permanent stiffy. It were a different colour from the rest of him. An' he went round flashing in nightclubs shouting, "Through this I rule Russia." Then after he got murdered, they pickled it an' put it in a museum.'

Burton looked decidedly wan at these revelations, as though she was regretting the pepperoni, but rallied bravely.

'Oh, come off it, sarge, that's just one of those myths. . . When he'd eaten the cyanide cakes and drunk the poisoned madeira, they shot him and chucked him in the river—'

'And then they burned the corpse,' Markham concluded. 'So that tale about the museum exhibit has got to be hokum.'

Noakes looked as though he wanted to say, if it's not true, then it ought to be.

'It was fantastic, though, the way they just didn't seem able to finish the man off,' Burton conceded. 'Those stories about his eyes opening and him leaping up when they thought he was dead . . . like something out of *Fatal Attraction* or *Nosferatu*.'

'As I recall, Rasputin was a magnet for emotionally fraught women,' Markham said thoughtfully.

'Jus' like Santini,' Noakes shot back with conviction.

'I'd say they both fall some way short of the Harvey Weinstein benchmark,' Markham pointed out caustically. 'And in Rasputin's case, he was smeared by some appallingly racist bigotry that bordered on pornography.'

'Not surprising with them eyes an' that beard,' his friend insisted stubbornly. 'Plus he went round groping an' raping women like Mister Tickle on steroids. Remember that Boney M song about him being like the world's greatest lover . . .'

'Not exactly a classic of the genre,' was Markham's sardonic response.

Burton giggled suddenly.

'What?' Noakes demanded.

'Just remembering those ridiculous outfits,' she said. Another giggle. 'I read somewhere that Rasputin was totally uncouth with the most terrible table manners, and that's why all the aristos couldn't stand him.'

For a moment, Noakes looked affronted as though he suspected a personal allusion but, belatedly realising what she had said, Burton was alert to the danger.

'The thing is,' she went on hastily, 'like the guvnor says, it's easy to be prejudiced against people just because they're a bit different. . . Though I can see why you think Santini is sinister, sarge. The man's definitely got some kind of strange charisma. Perhaps now he's out of Gino's shadow, he'll be the next big thing.'

Noakes's thoughts turned to the boutique's senior personnel. 'Mebbe the TV people never went ahead with the programme cos they got spooked by Rambert an' Hagan,' he suggested. 'Them two looked dead uptight and snotty . . . like they'd wandered in from *Songs of Praise* or summat.'

Markham smiled. 'I think they just weren't as comfortable with the format as some of the others,' he said. 'Not part of the media generation, which is why they came across as stiff.'

'Mind you, they were left out of things a bit, so p'raps that's why they got the hump,' Noakes persisted. 'Kind of hanging around like spare parts. Everard an' that smarmy presenter didn't really bother with them.'

Burton was struck by this. 'Yes, considering that Antonia was into textiles and the history of fashion, she would probably have had something to say about Valentine's Day trends.'

'I think it may have been down to ageism,' Markham pointed out ruefully. 'The assumption that only media savvy, photogenic millennials or generation Z could possibly be worth a producer's attention.'

Noakes was sympathetic. 'Guess that's why they looked so down-in-the-mouth then,' he said. 'Though Hagan got her two pennyworth in once Osborne stopped yakking.'

'Yes, but Everard and Santini gave her a look like they kind of wanted her to shut up,' Burton said.

'Maria was somewhat trite,' Markham commented. 'And they would have had the commercial demographics in mind. . . even the historical section was soundbite-friendly — nothing too heavy or demanding.'

Noakes returned to his initial query. 'So what scuppered the programme?' he demanded. 'Cos something must've gone amiss.'

Burton sighed. 'Not necessarily,' she said. 'There could have been an issue with scheduling, or someone new came in and then the project just gathered dust . . . any number of reasons.'

'Or Claudia Everard kicked up a fuss and got it shelved,' Noakes hazarded.

Burton shrugged. 'We've got no evidence that happened, sarge. I'd say it's more likely the moment passed — February came and went, so a feature on Valentine's Day wasn't buzzy any more. And then everyone forgot about it.'

The other grunted, clearly preferring more sinister scenarios.

'Still, it made interesting viewing,' Burton said, 'seeing the Confetti Club people all together like that. And the lingering shots of antique frocks looked good. That footage they spliced in from the V&A was pretty impressive.'

Noakes perked up, sharing Burton's keen interest in history.

'Strange how folk never really bothered with wedding dresses till Queen Victoria came along,' he said. 'That's when the craze for big white numbers started, though not everyone could splash out on a new outfit. My mum got married in her best dress, which made sense cos it were navy so didn't matter about stains. She looked champion,' he added as though daring them to challenge him. 'Much better than Vicky any road. . . they called her the Royal Dwarf. . . If she came on *Say Yes to the Dress*, they'd be asking,' adopting an exaggerated falsetto, '"Are You Wearing the Dress or Is the Dress Wearing You?"'

Burton chuckled, the red wine inducing an unwonted mellowness. 'Well, according to legend, she was buried with her wedding veil over her face, so at least the couturier must have got something right.'

'Oh aye, cos she fancied getting married again in heaven.' Noakes grinned evilly. 'Imagine the shock for old Albert when he lifted it an' got an eyeful.'

Mischievously, Markham reminded him, 'Doesn't the Good Book say there will be no marrying nor giving in marriage in heaven?'

Noakes, as ever, was determined to have the last word. 'Yeah, but Vicky thought that didn't apply to royalty,' he sniffed. Then, wary of further ontological debate, he changed the subject. 'You got anything else on Harvison an' Conteh?' he asked hopefully.

'There's a rumour that Harvison and Martin Carthew were friendly at one time,' Burton said.

Noakes's head come up. 'You mean Claudia's toyboy?'

'For want of a better word, yes . . . But I can't pin it down to anything more than membership of Medway Golf Club and mixing in the same circles.'

'The funny handshake brigade,' the other said dourly.

'Quite possibly, sarge, but there's no law against it. And as for Shay Conteh, he's got a slick solicitor onside courtesy of the Students' Union. . . dropping lots of not-so-subtle hints about oppressive police tactics.'

'Harvison an' Conteh were there in the same building as Hagan when she snuffed it,' Noakes persisted.

'Along with everybody else,' Burton reminded him. She ruffled her fringe restlessly. 'Joanna Osborne and Jamie O'Neill went their separate ways after the wake . . . straight home to, in their words, "crash". Claudia Everard and Martin Carthew left in his car sometime after three. As for Lucille and Christina, well you know about that. . . theoretically, there was opportunity, but we don't have a motive.'

'How about Count Dracula?'

'If you mean Mr Santini, sarge, he went down from the banqueting suite to the mezzanine for a bit to clear his head then headed back to the boutique . . . the shopping centre CCTV shows him clocking in at quarter to four.'

'What about this mezzanine thingy then . . . anyone see him there?' Noakes pressed.

'It's really just a landing between the second and third floors. . . there's doors that open onto a little roof terrace with a few chairs and tables. He went out there for ten minutes or so . . . had the place to himself.'

Noakes's sour expression said, *More's the pity.*

'Harvison and Conteh were in the building too,' Burton continued. 'Legitimately in both cases. Their meetings were over by three. Harvison says he went to the vending machines in the basement and got himself a coffee. According to Conteh, he hung on in the seminar room for a bit to check his phone messages.'

'Mister Bleeding Popular,' the other commented tetchily.

'Well, it sounds plausible enough. It's that kind of place, sarge. Lots of events and things going on. . . all these conference rooms and break-out spaces . . . nobody logging visitors' movements once they're in the building — no reason to . . .'

Until now.

'I've checked with the people who were at those meetings. A few are reasonably positive Harvison and Conteh were where they say they were but no one had eyes on them for the whole of that half hour between Maria's friends leaving her in the Ladies and finding her dead.'

Noakes's frown deepened.

'There's witnesses to say that Harvison and Conteh were both off the premises by ten to four,' she said. 'Harvison visited Bargain Booze in Lance Lane and Conteh called into the Students Union. So we can place them after they left the Town Hall Extension.'

'Jus' not before then.'

'They would have known the details of Gino Everard's funeral and the wake,' Burton said. 'After all, there was a notice about it in the *Gazette*. If either of them is our killer, they could've decided to stake out the banqueting suite using the cover of their meetings . . . hoping for a chance to get near to Maria in a busy venue where there was a pretty good chance of them blending into the crowd.'

Noakes visualised the scenario. 'It would have felt like all their Christmases had come at once when they saw Lucy an' Chrissy dump her in the bogs.'

'The corridor on that floor was dim and her friends were distracted,' Burton said. 'They might not have noticed someone lurking in a doorway watching them. With Maria being drunk and incapable, they just wanted to park her and take a load off.'

'Their guard was down, and they wouldn't have registered the danger,' Markham said gravely.

'For whatever reason, the killer needed to take Maria out in a hurry,' Burton said. 'They saw a chance and they seized it.'

Noakes wasn't finished. 'How about Mister Too-Young-To-Shave, the one who writes dodgy poetry?' he demanded.

'Randall Fenton hung around to check on Mr Santini,' Burton replied. 'Wasn't sure where he'd got to, so he just,' she air quoted, '"drifted around for a bit then decided to call it a day".'

'Anyone see him drifting?' was Noakes's sarcastic rejoinder.

'One of the caterers mentioned he was wandering round like he was in a bit of a daze,' Burton said.

'What time was this, Kate?' Markham wanted to know.

'She thinks it was just after three. And then not long after, Lucille saw him drifting around the foyer when she came back up from having her cigarette . . . thought he looked a bit rough. She was going to have a word with him, but then he looked at his mobile like he was checking a text from someone . . . so she figured he was all right.' She gripped her brow between her fingers, thinking hard. 'Technically he could've done it, but from the timings it doesn't seem likely. Also, if we're linking this to the break-in at the shop, then he's not our man because the person on CCTV was average height and—'

'Fenton's a beanpole,' Noakes concluded glumly. 'So, we've got sweet FA,' he burst out. Then, 'What about the *Gazette* hack?'

'The people on reception think Danielle Rigsby left shortly after three,' Burton said, 'but that's only an approximate timing.'

'What a bleeding shambles,' the other groaned. 'It feels like they're all pieces on some pigging chessboard . . . I need another beer, guv,' he added sheepishly as though to rinse away the taste of failure.

'Help yourself, Noakesy,' Markham said affably. The other duly padded out to the kitchen.

He wandered over to the bay window and rested his forehead on the pane for a second before turning back to Burton.

'We're missing something here, Kate,' he said. 'Some piece of the puzzle that we haven't identified.'

'Maybe things will be clearer when we interview Lucille and Christina tomorrow, guv?' was all the consolation she could offer.

'D'you reckon they're holding out on us?' he asked.

'It could be they were just embarrassed about workplace bitchiness,' she answered. 'If the youngsters were in the habit of whingeing about older colleagues, then they might feel bad about it now.'

Noakes came back from the kitchen. He looked disappointed, as though he had been hoping to detect signs of Olivia's presence among the guvnor's groceries.

'Watcha going to tell Sidney?' he asked baldly. 'Cos you can bet his missus an' her posho friends don' like the thought of someone in their fave shop being a serial.'

'I'm flat out of ideas right now, Noaksey,' Markham said heavily. 'I guess it's a case of going back through the witness statements and hoping we can break someone's alibi.'

'There's a memorial service for Antonia Rambert on Thursday, boss,' Burton said apologetically.

The day after tomorrow, he thought grimly. And there was still nothing to show for their enquiries.

'Where?' he asked resignedly.

'She was a Quaker, so it's at Friends House in Medway.'

Noakes looked interested on hearing this, as though he rather fancied putting out ecumenical feelers.

'Midday, guv,' Burton elaborated. 'With coffee and biscuits afterwards.'

'Not a funeral then?' Noakes liked to be clear on these points.

'No, sarge. Her body won't be released for a while yet, but in the meantime, they wanted to have some kind of respectful celebration of her life.'

'I've never been to a Quaker do.'

'They don't have hymns or anything like that,' she said.

Markham suspected that in Burton's eyes this was a definite bonus, given the buttock-clenching embarrassment attendant on Noakes's uniquely operatic approach to Hymns Old and New.

'I'll be there then,' he said firmly.

'Great, sarge,' came the meek reply.

'Better be getting off now,' Noakes said. 'Ta for the pizza an' beer.' In the hallway, he turned to Markham. 'You all right, guv?'

'Hanging in there, Noakesy.'

'There's no need to worry about Sullivan, you know,' the other said shuffling his feet. Having bonded with the teacher over five-a-side, he had consulted their teammates. 'Degsy says he's jus' doing his knight in shining armour thing.'

Thank you, Degsy! Markham didn't know whether to laugh or cry.

'Good to know,' he said gravely. The idea of Noakes and Degsy embarking on some sort of pastoral intervention really didn't bear thinking about . . .

Burton didn't know what to make of Markham's odd expression when he rejoined her in the living room, but he adroitly turned the conversation away from himself.

'So, how are you, Kate?'

'Oh, you know, guv.'

It was the same evasive brush-off he had employed with Noakes.

For a long, emotionally charged interval they contemplated each other.

If ever something had been going to happen between them, he thought afterwards, then that was the moment.

Outside, the wind was getting up. The living room curtains were drawn back disclosing storm-tossed trees, the pale underside of their leaves showing like the shimmer of ghostly souls. Burton's lips were half-parted, and she seemed to Markham in that instant curiously like a penitent steeling herself to confess some guilty secret.

Then the landline rang, shrilly and insistently, and the mood was broken.

He made no move to answer the telephone and eventually it stopped.

'I need to be going anyway, sir,' she said in tones that could have sounded something like a sob, as though acknowledging that things had somehow shifted between them.

He wanted to cry, 'Don't go!' and heard his unspoken words filling the silence.

But then, as if some screw was tightening in his back like the wind-up key in a mechanical toy, he heard himself offer to call her a taxi.

In an equally colourless voice, she accepted.

The danger had passed, and the status quo was restored.

11. QUICKENING FOOTSTEPS

The interview with Lucille Chilton and Christina Skelthorne the following day failed to yield any useful leads, though it gave an insight into the depressingly feline world of bridal couture.

Although the two women had presented a united front in the immediate aftermath of Maria Hagan's murder, relations between them appeared to have cooled significantly since then, their body language suggestive of mutual suspicion and mistrust.

'What did Maria mean by saying people should have shown more loyalty towards Antonia when she was alive?' Burton pressed them.

Obviously discomfited that this exchange had been overheard, Lucille sought to retrieve the situation, smoothing her russet mane with nervous fingers and studiously avoiding her colleague's eyes.

'Chris nicknamed her Minnie the Moocher — you know, from that song in The Blues Brothers. . . only she changed the lyrics to her being a red hot hoochie coocher.'

The other shot her a resentful glance.

'It was just a bit of fun,' Christina told the detectives, clearly embarrassed. 'Antonia could be a bit of a snoop sometimes. She was always running to Gino and dropping people in it.' Colouring, she added, 'Plus, she didn't always back us up in front of difficult clients.'

Doyle leaned forward. 'How do you mean?'

'Well, some of the women who come in are whiny, entitled, spoiled brats . . . pretty much the same as what you see in *Say Yes to the Dress* and those reality shows . . . rude like you wouldn't believe.'

Carruthers was sympathetic. 'I could believe it,' he said kindly. 'When my girlfriend went shopping for a bridesmaid's dress, she couldn't get over what went on in some of the stores she visited . . . tantrums and meltdowns and divas having strops all over the place.'

Christina smiled at him gratefully, her colour subsiding somewhat.

'Too right,' she said with feeling. 'The thing with Antonia was, if a client or wedding planner was making things difficult or just being a twenty-four- carat bitch, she always sided with them. It wasn't just a case of her deciding that "the customer is always right" . . . you felt she got some sort of kick out of making us look small, like we didn't know what we were doing.'

'Perhaps she felt threatened and insecure,' Carruthers suggested. 'She might've thrown her weight around to shore up her credentials in case Gino and Franco decided she was past her sell-by date.'

'She was only a few years older than me.'

'Yeah, but retail and fashion are cut-throat, right? You seem pretty chilled, but maybe Antonia didn't have your confidence.'

Hearing this astute observation, Markham decided that perhaps Carruthers wasn't as lacking in empathy as he had previously imagined. Certainly, he was successful in putting Christina Skelthorne at ease, the pretty saleswoman's manner was less defensive than at the start of the interview. 'Antonia had bags of experience,' she told them. 'And what she didn't know about design and textiles wasn't worth knowing. I

160

think she planned to do a foundation course at the university, leading to a fashion history degree or something like that.'

Lucille rolled her eyes. 'Yeah, she could bore for England about lace appliqué and satin bodices. Always banging on about tulle and gazar and all that. Kept pestering Gino to design something "medieval" like Queen Guinevere might wear.'

'So, Ms Rambert was by no means on the scrapheap,' Markham said lightly.

'Oh no,' Christina said hastily. 'But she could be tricky . . . kind of spiky . . . and almost sneaky at times.'

Doyle latched on to this. 'Sneaky?'

'She earwigged and seemed to know everyone's business,' Lucille said bluntly. 'There was the time when she snitched to Gino about Jo Osborne thinking about a move to Happy Ever After in Medway. Jo was livid about that.'

'And she made sly little comments about Jamie modelling himself on Gino,' Christina added. 'I mean, him and Randall both kind of hero-worshipped Gino, but she enjoyed making Jamie squirm about it.'

'She went easy on Randall because he wasn't as cocky as Jamie,' Lucille informed them.

'Look, we all had issues with Antonia at one time or another,' Christina admitted. 'And maybe Maria was right about saying we should've reined it in. She was a kind soul, which was probably why she didn't like us taking the mick.' A sidelong glance at Lucille. 'But we all did it. D'you remember Jamie's name for Antonia . . . HMV.'

Doyle was intrigued. 'HMV?'

'His Master's Voice, because of the way she trailed round after Gino making cow's eyes at him,' Christina said acidly.

'That was banter,' Lucille insisted. 'Just Jamie having a bit of a laugh.' Defiantly, she added, 'Franco didn't mind us making jokes. He knew we needed to let off steam sometimes and turned a blind eye. Jo called Maria the Mad Cow behind her back cos she was so mumsy and always dishing out advice.' Uncertainly, she added, 'Mad Cow. . . like in BSE, mad cow disease.'

'Hilarious,' said Doyle with his best deadpan expression.

'Maria eventually twigged to it,' Christina said flatly. 'I got the feeling she didn't like the way Franco let people badmouth senior staff. Felt he should have been more like the boss . . . Gino didn't play favourites or let anyone overstep the mark.'

'What about Maria's private life?' Carruthers asked with the air of one clutching at straws. 'Any blokes on the scene?'

It was almost comical to see their incredulous expressions.

'God no!' Lucille exclaimed with the condescending pity of one to whom Maria Hagan doubtless appeared ancient. 'She was well past all that.'

Christina seemed to intuit that Kate Burton was less than impressed by the casual disparagement, hastening to explain, 'With being divorced and then what happened to her husband — the car crash and everything — she didn't socialise all that much.'

'How about Antonia?' Doyle enquired.

This time, Lucille knew to be more tactful.

'Well, she had to look after her mum. And there was her reading and history, stuff like that.' It was clear that the young PA regarded such pursuits in the light of a prophylactic guaranteed to extinguish any prospect of romance.

'I think she might have met someone at the university,' Christina said unexpectedly. 'She had this kind of cat-got-the-cream expression when she talked about doing a degree.'

'Nah,' Lucille snorted in derision. 'Books were her thing, not blokes.'

Afterwards, Doyle said ironically, 'Who'd work in bridal sales? They're worse than a bunch of primary school kids.'

'We learned that Antonia was a busybody, though,' Carruthers pointed out. 'So she could've been on the killer's trail.'

'D'you reckon she found something out and then shared it with Maria, so then Maria had to die too?' Doyle mused.

'That's one possibility,' Markham said. 'Or they could have made discoveries independently of each other.'

'And tried blackmail?' Burton asked.

'I can't see that happening with either Antonia or Maria,' Markham replied. 'They were way too straight for anything of the kind.' In customary fashion, he walked across to his office window before wheeling round on his colleagues. 'I think the killer must have managed to raise a doubt in their minds.'

'You mean so they weren't sure they'd got it right, boss?' Burton asked. 'Worried that they might be jumping to conclusions?'

Markham nodded slowly as he returned to his desk. 'We've seen it time and again,' he said. 'That fatal hesitation . . . people's reluctance to see what's staring them right in the face.'

'And when they finally cotton on, it's too late,' Doyle supplied the epitaph.

'I think these were two middle-aged women who inadvertently stumbled upon clues to murder,' the DI said. 'Only, in each case for some reason they couldn't follow the thread to its logical conclusion.'

Outside his office window, overcast skies threatened rain and the tinnitus-buzz of lunchtime traffic floated in from the high street mixed with shrieks and yelps from a neighbouring school playground: 'Done You, one, two, three!' It sounded like a hard-fought game of Relievo was in progress, and for a moment Markham was transported back to a time of innocence and invincibility when all that mattered was running till your lungs burst. His murder victims too had known those milestones of childhood before their encounter with a killer brought them a headstone saying 'RIP'.

Doyle's discreet cough recalled him to the present.

'Could Antonia have got it on with Shay Conteh?' the young detective asked. 'If Christina's right about her meeting someone at the university, that could be a link.'

'Conteh says not,' Burton replied wearily, 'and nothing's turned up to show they knew each other. If there was

163

some mystery man on the scene, she took good care to be discreet about it.' The DI paused, revolving something in her mind. 'I think you're right about blackmail, guv,' she told Markham. 'Not their style. But the killer must've been really plausible . . . so Maria and Antonia decided it couldn't possibly be them.'

'Maybe they dropped a hint about something incriminating? Some juicy secret or other,' Doyle surmised. 'Antonia and Maria would've been mega-flattered at thinking they were in on it.'

'If they had bugger-all else in their lives, it isn't surprising,' Carruthers observed brutally. 'He played them like a violin.'

'You're forgetting, Dimples says it could be a woman,' Doyle pointed out.

His colleague looked sceptical. 'Just doesn't feel like it to me,' he said finally. 'Plus, all the women in that shop come across as too dippy.'

'Which leaves Randall or the Prince of Darkness,' Doyle shot back. 'Only we haven't got anything on either of them.'

'There's Harvison and Conteh too,' Burton observed.

Carruthers nodded. 'They're bully-boys all right. I can just see Conteh coming up on someone from behind and choking the life out of them.'

Having sent Doyle and Carruthers back to the drawing board, Markham braced himself. 'Time to brief the DCI,' he told Burton who gave him a pallid smile.

At least Sidney was relieved that 'blackmail in the shires' formed no part of their hypothesis but looked decidedly jaundiced at the lack of progress.

'What now, Inspector?' he demanded irascibly. 'As things stand, it would appear there's no viable suspect in the case.'

No need to spell out that the media, most notably the *Gazette*, was growing increasingly restive.

'Next steps?' Sidney honked as the silence stretched.

Some sort of *Crimewatch*-style diversion usually did the trick in these circumstances.

Kate Burton was primed and ready. 'Real-time motion reconstruction for local news bulletins, sir,' she said brightly. 'The council's onside and we're confident it will jog people's memories. 'Three-dimensional mapping should produce results.' Unless they bollix it up, she thought grimly.

Afterwards, Markham asked, 'Was all of that for real, Kate? I mean the time and motion stuff with the council.'

'Absolutely, sir.' Forehead puckered, she added, 'Their facilities team are right on it. It's a case of nailing down witness statements. And then I'll sort something for the Bromgrove Newsround slot on Friday.'

Markham had feared that the DCI was going to threaten them with Superintendent 'Blithering' Bretherton (Carruthers' uncle no less) who these days resembled Sidney's evil twin or some character-actor version of a tax accountant, with a little fringe of short hair surrounding his shiny pate and a beaky nose which he had a habit of jabbing in people's faces. Ponderous and fatuous all at once, he was never a congenial prospect to the detectives. However, by some fluke of station Kremlinology, the spectre of Bretherton never materialised, and the two detectives were able to escape from the DCI's office with promises of a fresh media initiative.

Preparation for this was an activity which took the rest of the day and felt utterly futile in the final analysis.

'We've got zilch,' Doyle exclaimed when the team reconvened at the end of a long dispiriting overhaul. 'Everard's wake was just this crummy little affair at the town hall, and nobody really gave a stuff.'

'But the killer slipped in there somehow,' Burton said, 'and silenced Maria Hagan. . . the same way they got to Antonia Rambert, like a thief in the night.'

'It's the memorial service for Antonia tomorrow,' Markham said wearily. 'Twelve noon at Friends House in Medway.'

'Are we all going to that then, guv?' Doyle enquired, with the air of one who would prefer virtually anything — even root canal work — over this trip to a Quaker outpost.

'Yes, Sergeant, we are,' Markham replied firmly. 'We need a reset. Maybe having the suspects together once again will produce a breakthrough.'

Doyle and Carruthers looked mutinous but refrained from outright rebellion.

'Noakesy's joining us,' the DI added.

Signs of reanimation on Doyle's part, though Carruthers looked less than enthralled.

'Is it full on prayers and hymns, boss?' Doyle asked with more than a hint of trepidation.

'No hymns, just a mixture of silent prayer and intercessions,' the DI told him, not without a certain sly amusement at the horrified looks of his subordinates. 'I understand a local elder will be taking the service.'

'Well, you know what they say about respecting your elders,' Carruthers quipped.

Despite the feebleness of the pun, Markham was pleased to see Doyle and Burton exchange indulgent smiles. Clearly the new member of the team was growing on them.

After his colleagues had gone, Markham dug out the email he had received from the 'lead attender' at Friends House, his gaze resting on a simple biblical citation at the bottom:

'For now, I shall sleep in the dust; and thou shalt seek me in the morning but I shall not be.' Job 7:21.

Three innocent victims were gone to dust, but the team could still make them count in the present, so that they stood for something more than a footnote in the annals of time.

* * *

The Quaker Meeting House in Medway was located at the end of an unpretentious Victorian terrace in an agreeably leafy cul-de-sac.

Markham filled Noakes and the others in as they sat outside in his car on Thursday 14 April watching mourners arrive.

'It's quite informal and unstructured,' he advised. 'Quiet reflection and thanksgiving unless the spirit moves someone to speak.'

'Like in tongues?' Noakes asked warily.

Having duly noted the memo about casual dress being acceptable, he was smartly attired in fawn sports jacket, dun checked shirt and flannels. Rather a preponderance of beige but infinitely preferable to the politburo suits he sported at Rosemount, Markham thought wryly.

'Don't worry,' the DI told him. 'Quaker worship is very undemonstrative and low-key. Nothing charismatic or "happy-clappy",' which he knew was total anathema to his friend. 'Apparently it's a case of listening in the stillness—'

Noakes remained apprehensive. 'Listening for what?'

'Your inner voice,' Markham said unperturbed. 'Or whatever puts you in touch with the sacred, I suppose.'

'Thass too wishy washy,' the other said firmly. 'There should be rules, see. You know where you are with rules.'

'Judi Dench is a Quaker,' Carruthers said much to Markham's amusement, as though the DS thought Noakes's good opinion might be secured by learning that 'M' was onside.

'Oh aye.'

'They're big on nonviolence and the peace movement,' Doyle put in.

From the way Noakes's mouth turned down at the corners, Markham could see it wasn't an angle which held much appeal for this particular ex-soldier and stalwart of the local British Legion.

'David Maxwell, who's taking the service, plans to keep it simple,' the DI reassured them. 'There'll be a period of silence followed by a couple of readings as it's by way of being a memorial for Antonia. Then coffee and biscuits afterwards, with everyone invited to sign the visitors' book.'

'Happen it won't be so bad,' Noakes conceded. 'Weird to think of Rambert wanting to sit around an' tune into nature or whatever they do. She didn't *look* hippy-dippy . . .

more the type who'd want bells an' smells an' everything done proper.'

Markham felt a pang at these words, realising how little they knew of the woman's character or interior world.

'Right, let's get in there,' he said briskly. 'Obviously silent prayer rules out our gawping at attendees, but I'd like you to be on the alert for anything that strikes you as unusual.'

Just over an hour later, the service was over and the detectives safely back in Markham's car comparing notes.

'Sad that she didn't have any family there,' Carruthers commented.

'Her brother couldn't make the trip,' Markham said quietly, having made a condolence Zoom call to her chilly sibling who, though perfectly correct in his demeanour, had exhibited few outward signs of grief. It had been the same with Maria Hagan's sister, another semi-detached relative with 'mobility issues'. Mind you, the DI reflected, one shouldn't make assumptions about what occurred in families. He was only too grateful that nobody other than Noakes and Olivia knew the half of what had gone on in his own . . .

'A bit creepy with all them chairs in a semi-circle like a séance or summat,' Noakes said. 'I was worried folk would hear my stomach rumbling.' As it was, his beloved George boots had performed a symphony of squeaks by way of counterpoint to the readings and prayers.

'At least there was a half-decent turnout,' Doyle said. 'Including the chippy journalist.'

Danielle Rigsby had struck Markham as decidedly ill at ease, but in fairness most of the non-Quakers had appeared equally awkward and at a loss as they sat in the nondescript meeting room with its heavy damask curtains, pleated lampshades, bland furnishings, sad electric fireplace and flock wallpaper the colour of Noakes's suit. The only bright point was a little ivy-clad courtyard visible through French windows where a variety of stone pots and ceramic planters held cheery clusters of narcissi, daisies and gerberas.

Unsurprisingly, there was no sign of Jamie O'Neill or Joanna Osborne, but the rest of the boutique's personnel were all present and correct, somewhat subdued by virtue of the occasion but none exhibiting any unusual signs of disquiet. Claudia Everard and Mark Harvison didn't attend but Shay Conteh was a late arrival, slipping in after everybody else.

Now Noakes asked, 'How come the boxer were there?'

'Yeah,' Doyle turned to Burton. 'I thought Conteh said he didn't know Antonia, ma'am.'

'He could have been lying about that,' she said slowly.

Three pairs of eyes were fixed on her.

'Go on, Kate,' Markham said, seeing that she appeared troubled.

'Well, when they wheeled in the coffee and biscuits, I went up to him and said something like it was nice of him to come seeing as he didn't know her.'

'And?' Noakes demanded impatiently.

'He didn't turn a hair . . . Said some mate of his from the Christian Union who met her at an Open Day told him about it, so he decided to come along too, show a bit of solidarity.' She frowned. 'Plus, his involvement with Women Together and the anti-violence movement made it seem like the right thing to do.'

Markham gave her a searching look. 'Sounds fair enough on the face of it,' he said.

'Yes, and he introduced me to his friend, so that part was true,' Burton agreed.

Noakes looked more like a bulldog than ever. 'So, what's the problem then?'

'When we were signing the visitors' book, I noticed the way he signed his name with these extra twiddles for the letter A.' She whipped out her notebook and pen. 'Look,' scribbling quickly, 'something like this. . .'

And she showed them what she meant, drawing the initial with its distinctive curlicues and the wavy line at the bottom.

As they looked at her blankly, she said, 'It's Gaelic lettering. Quite distinctive calligraphy.' Of course, calligraphy was one of Burton's interests, so she was bound to have been struck by the signature.

'Is he Irish then?' Noakes sounded bewildered. 'Don' sound like an Irish surname,' he added doubtfully.

'Shay's a variant of Seamus or Shea,' Burton told them. 'I heard him telling someone his mother was Irish and his stepfather Nigerian.'

'Okay, so he's got poncey handwriting,' Noakes went on. 'What of it?'

'I remembered I'd seen that handwriting before,' she explained patiently. 'In a penguin book on Antonia's bedside table at the house on Bromgrove Rise where we found her body. There was some graffiti inside the back cover, a Latin inscription: *Ad Astra Per Aspera*. It translates as "Reach for the stars no matter how hard the journey" . . . kind of an inspirational quote. Each letter A had the same flourishes as Conteh's signature in the visitors' book. Very distinctive.'

'Okay, so maybe they did know each other,' Doyle said slowly. 'He could've panicked when she was killed and lied about it, like an automatic reflex in case we got hung up on the whole sex angle, and then he had to stick to his story.'

Markham recalled his initial impression of Conteh's hard-to-define charisma and that striking classically Celtic colouring of a boy on a school trip to some provincial museum, he had once seen a painting of the Greek god Pan, half-man, half-goat — a dark reddish-gold figure with horns and hooves whose slanting cobalt-blue eyes looked sideways out of the canvas with a sly challenge. 'Pan was a cunning trickster,' the guide had told them with the weary apathy of one accustomed to inflicting culture on cohorts of juvenile delinquents. 'He was lustful and sometimes cruel. On one occasion he arranged for his followers to tear a nymph apart after she rejected his advances.' Of course, the hapless instructor had lost his sniggering audience at 'lustful', but the painting made an impression on Markham who had a disagreeable sensation of something sinister and vaguely malevolent.

Certainly, Conteh was nothing if not outwardly personable. Noakes had thought he looked like D. H. Lawrence. But, looking back, was there not something Pan-like about his slim oval face with those slightly protruding ears and the cold blue eyes with their unreadable expression . . . perhaps even a hint of cruelty in the well-formed mouth?

It had seemed incredible to Lucille Chilton and Christina Skelthorne that Antonia Rambert should have been romantically involved with anyone, but Markham remembered the woman's Anna Wintour grooming, sharp tailoring and excellent legs. It wasn't inconceivable that the 'cat-got-the-cream' expression Christina had described was the product of sexual intrigue and that Shay Conteh was Antonia Rambert's secret lover.

Or they could simply have been friends and then she discovered another side to his personality — a homicidal rage that led to the murder of Gino Everard. So, then she had to die too . . .

Doyle was watching him expectantly.

'You're quite right, Sergeant,' he said. 'It might be perfectly natural for Conteh to lie, on the basis that a connection to Rambert would put him in the frame.'

'But we've got to confront him with it, right?' Noakes said eagerly.

'Undoubtedly,' the DI said. Then, almost reluctantly, 'I didn't particularly take to him. But those first two deaths — particularly Antonia's — and the vandalism at the boutique exhibited an element of unhinged theatricality which somehow doesn't seem to fit with Conteh's temperament, at least not with what we've seen of it so far. Decking Antonia's body out in that bridal gear and strewing the shop with mysterious symbols is the knife-edge of rational conduct. . .'

'Conteh's an academic type,' Noakes countered. 'If he were swapping boffin books with Rambert an' spouting geeky Latin quotes at her, he'd likely get off on dress-up an' costumes an' things.' Markham's former wingman then looked somewhat queasy at the thought of this intellectual hinterland.

'Or maybe he staged all the artistic stuff to get us thinking it couldn't possibly be him, Mister Sports Science. . . the boxing champ,' Doyle suggested.

'I know what you mean about the first two murders, boss,' Burton said suddenly. 'The Miss Havisham stuff and that business in the shop felt neurotic and crazy. Like the work of a woman . . . a woman scorned.'

The other three frankly boggled before Noakes said scratching his chin, 'Ain't that sexist or discrimination or summat — saying it's so screwy it has to be a woman.'

Burton could see he wasn't trying to be offensive or pick a fight but was genuinely bewildered.

'It's just a hunch, sarge,' she replied mildly. 'Just something about those crime scenes. . .'

'What about Hagan?' demanded Carruthers. 'The way she died had "bloke" written all over it.'

'Dimples couldn't rule out a woman,' Burton reminded him.

Suddenly Noakes said, 'What if *two* of 'em are working this?'

For a moment Markham felt as though ice-water had lodged in his spine and Doyle's face jerked with alarm, both men recalling all too well a previous investigation which had involved just such a scenario.

'Who do you have in mind, Noakesy?' the DI enquired steadily.

'What about Claudia Everard an' her toyboy?'

Burton was startled. 'Martin Carthew? The lawyer?'

'Why not?' Noakes went on stubbornly. 'I can see him sneaking up on folk from behind.'

'Or maybe Santini's pulling the strings somehow,' Doyle mused. 'Like Svengali. . . manipulating one of the women. You could say Chilton and Osborne are "women scorned"—'

'Seeing as he gave one of them the brush-off and got rid of the other,' Carruthers finished.

'And don't forget Skelthorne,' he continued. 'She came across as downright shifty about the whole setup, like she had something to hide.'

Doyle was hitting his stride now. 'Or it could be Jamie O'Neill. Him and Joanna Osborne are pretty chummy, so maybe they're the double act.'

'O'Neill's too wussy to have done Hagan,' Noakes objected. 'An' the lass don' look like a fruit loop.'

There's no art to find the mind's construction in the face, Markham thought grimly as he recalled some of the Lady Macbeth types he had encountered over the years.

'One step at a time,' he told the team. 'Kate, I want you to get Mr Conteh in and see what he has to say about a relationship with Antonia Rambert.'

'Even if he admits to knowing her, it doesn't make him the murderer,' Carruthers pointed out.

'Quite,' Markham agreed. 'It's a case of shaking the tree to see where it takes us. If you're right about an accomplice, Noakesy, then maybe this will rattle them into giving something away.'

Suddenly, two police cars shot past with sirens blaring. Markham stiffened in his seat as though it portended ill for the current investigation.

Relax, he told himself, it's just another local call, nothing to do with the boutique murders.

He willed his heartbeat to return to normal and smiled at his colleagues.

'Right,' he said, 'back to the station via Rosemount before they start wondering why you're playing hooky, Noakesy.'

His friend's lower lip shot out.

'What about the interview with Conteh?' he demanded.

'Kate'll brief you later. Conteh's not going anywhere and we'll mount discreet surveillance on him.' Whether Sidney liked it or not.

Something told Markham that the next twenty-four hours would be crucial.

But as to where the breakthrough would come from, he had no idea.

He only knew instinctively that the hour of reckoning was close at hand.

12. TURNING POINT

'Conteh was smooth as a pair of roller skates, guv,' Kate Burton told Markham later as they enjoyed a drink together back at his apartment in The Sweepstakes.

Markham was surprised by the speed at which his colleague downed her goldfish bowl sized gin and tonic before readily accepting a refill. Such gay abandon being contrary to her customary abstemiousness, he had a feeling that something was wrong.

Amused by her description of Shay Conteh, he played along, however.

'I take it you got nowhere with him?'

'He was super cool. Couldn't say for sure if his and Antonia's paths had crossed — occupational hazard of student politics blah blah blah.'

'Lawyered up?'

'And how! Same as before. . . whizzy brief courtesy of the Students Union. Mister hotshot legal eagle — dead courteous while hinting he'd throw the whole Human Rights Act at me if I dared to suggest his client was of anything less than unimpeachable character.'

Markham grimaced sympathetically, taking a gulp of his Châteauneuf-du-Pape.

'A dead end then.'

'That entry in the visitors' book at Friends House didn't seem to bother him at all, boss. He just looked at me like I was some kind of thicko and said obviously second-hand books had all kinds of marginalia in them.' She sighed deeply. 'I feel a total prat for getting so excited about the handwriting in the first place.'

'Nothing to be ashamed of, Kate. I'll confess, I was hoping this might be the breakthrough we needed.'

His fellow DI's glass was empty again. He was reluctant to seem to be plying her with alcohol but sensed she needed to confide something. Accordingly, he poured her another modest measure of Gordon's with a waterfall of Schweppes.

'Let's forget the case for now,' he told her. 'How are you?'

'To be honest, guv, Nathan's a bit fed up with me,' she said.

'How so?'

'Well, he reckons I should be getting over dad by now . . .'

Markham remembered their investigation at Sherwin College in Oxford when his colleague had opened up about her childhood and the father, now deceased, who meant the world to her.

'You're still struggling?' he said very gently.

'It's just that everything seems somehow flat and monochrome these days, guv. No colour, no definition, no clear edges, nothing . . . Like I'm watching things in analogue while everyone else has switched to digital.' She screwed up her face as though trying not to cry. 'Dad kind of held everything together. . . made everything fine. The world was okay cos he was in it. . . I remember nights at home in winter when it hailed, just knowing he was along the landing made me feel so safe, so protected.' She blushed furiously. 'Sorry, guv, you'll think I'm nuts.'

'Try me.' And now his voice was tender. Also, he was angry at himself for failing to have noticed that she was in difficulty. 'Go on.'

'It's like I'm hollowed out,' she said slowly, 'kind of numb and weightless . . . going with the flow, only nothing feels real anymore. As if I'm looking at everyone else through a sheet of plexiglass or something.'

'Dissociation, Kate,' he said softly. 'A coping mechanism. It's nothing to be ashamed of.'

'Towards the end, Dad's big thing was cosmology and destiny,' she said dreamily, as if he hadn't spoken. 'I can still see him sitting in his shed with the hens — Mum never came there — going on about how everything in the universe was connected and I was on the side of goodness and beauty. He never wanted me to join the police but later on, he came round to it . . . said that danger and violence are the price we pay for being curious and self-aware and I should help turn bad into good.'

It struck Markham that this was how he himself coped with the destructiveness he witnessed as a detective — by telling himself that in mitigating the awfulness of the human condition, he was part of an unfolding process which ultimately embraced everyone and everything.'

'Dad said crime's the flipside of our being addicted to beauty and risk-taking,' she continued. 'Like it's the price of humans being alive, our destiny, so we have to enter into it.'

'An interesting philosophy.'

'He started going to church again,' she confided. 'Talking about how we came from the stars and everything was part of a pattern. Mum thought it was his meds, but I reckon it was a religious conversion or something. . . Any road, I made sure Father Casey from St Anne's kept an eye on him.' And now, finally, her voice broke. 'So, everything was all right and Dad made sense of it all in the end.'

Markham found himself momentarily unable to speak, his throat closing over as he heard his lost brother's eager tones: 'The planet's aeons old, Gil. Just think of it! We all came from this incredible supernova, carrying the Big Bang wherever we go, with fourteen billion years' worth of elementary particles inside us!'

He found his voice. 'Sounds like your dad cracked it, Kate.' Whatever 'It' was.

'I reckon so, boss. He said the whole point of being human was that we're the only species able to appreciate the planet and wonder at it, and it would be pretty sad if no one was there to realise how special it all is . . . It doesn't even matter that we know we're going to die, because otherwise we wouldn't understand the preciousness of life, the universe and everything.' She took a deep breath. 'That's why he said I shouldn't hold back or hide my light under a bushel . . . because life's an adventure and this is the only time I have to show myself and make a difference.'

'Excellent advice, Kate. As Walt Whitman said, despite all the sordidness and mire, what counts is that the powerful play goes on and we can contribute a verse.'

'I remember that poem. Robin Williams quotes from it in *Dead Poets Society*.' Her voice was stronger as she went on, 'I think Dad found God . . . He didn't start reciting stuff from the Bible or anything embarrassing like that. He just seemed settled about things in his own mind — and he told me and Mum he wasn't going to be snuffed out and there were surprises in store for him . . . said he understood how everything fitted together and I wasn't to worry.'

'There you go, Kate. He obviously had every confidence in you.'

'Yes, but I can't stop wishing I knew more about how it was for him at the end . . . that I'd taken more trouble to understand where he was coming from.' There was a treacherous wobble in her voice. 'Maybe he felt lonely, working it all out by himself like that.'

'Perhaps that was what he wanted. Perhaps there was no need for words, because he knew you were on your own journey, and he saw everything panning out just the way it ought.'

A shaky laugh. 'There were these lines on a cheesy card someone sent my mum after Dad died: "Listen for my foot-fall in your heart, I am not gone but merely walk within you".

A bit death-is-nothing-at-allish, but it's kind of right? He's there all the time now . . . even if I just re-read one of the books I did for English A level, it feels like a gift from Dad.' She chewed her lower lip. 'Nate thinks I'm being self-indulgent. And he doesn't have much time for what he calls "superstitious mumbo jumbo". We got into a silly argument about it the other night.' She hesitated before plunging on. 'Do you remember when we investigated that religious order, the one with all the relics, mementoes of that saint?'

'How could I forget. Noakesy went into it all so thoroughly, that at one point I thought he might defect to Rome!'

She gave a smile. 'Well, Father Casey brought Dad one back from some pilgrimage he went on . . . don't remember which saint it was from . . . Anyway, Dad really liked it. He said people in the Middle Ages had the right idea when it came to cherishing relics — splinters of the cross, saints' clothes or whatever — because that's what you should do with stuff that's been so close to extraordinary people. He didn't think it was morbid or creepy at all.' Her lips curved in a reminiscent smile. 'He said maybe if folk understood that the Earth and everything on it — including humans — are relics of billions of years of cosmic development, they might be more respectful towards the planet and stop screwing it up.'

'Extinction Rebellion and the likes of Greta Thunberg would agree with him.' Markham hesitated. 'I'd have thought Nathan was fairly eco-minded if it came to that.'

'Oh, he doesn't mind saving the planet. He just got impatient with me for being "mystical" and dragging religion and my dad into it like he's some kind of spook. Thinks that's neurotic and unhealthy.'

Markham wondered if there was more to this, since it was unlike Nathan Finlayson to be intolerant. Could it be that Finlayson, like Olivia, sensed unfinished business between himself and Kate Burton, sensed that they were more to each other than colleagues?

Or was it presumptuous to make such an assumption, seeing that Kate was now engaged to the psychologist? To all intents and purposes, their relationship was a great success, so was he reading too much into what sounded like a mere blip?

And yet, as they talked, he experienced a sense of well-being and kinship that he had never felt with anyone else, not excepting Olivia and Noakes. He and Kate Burton were somehow on the same wavelength, and he found her infinitely simpatico in a way that he would not have known how to explain. It was the conviction that they somehow completed each other. Like now, when by lifting the veil on her personal life she touched a chord deep inside him. Something similar had occurred during that investigation in Oxford, when her diffidence had fallen away in their stake-out of the Latimer College folly.

'If your dad's haunting you, Kate,' he said lightly, 'then it sounds like he's an exceptionally benevolent ghost.'

'I remember Mum saying when someone asked the Queen Mother if loss gets better, she said, "It never gets better, but you get better at it."'

'A wise observation.'

The doorbell went.

'I might have known Noakesy couldn't stay away,' he said easily, moving to answer it.

But it was Olivia who stood there. His ex looked thin and pale but, in his eyes, beautiful as ever. The timing, however, could not have been more unfortunate.

'Hi there, Gil,' she said. 'Just wondered how you were doing.'

He felt a flare of triumph at these words.

So Mathew Sullivan wasn't the be all and end all to her, and she still felt something for him.

As they contemplated each other wordlessly, there was the sound of a mobile in the background followed by low, murmured conversation.

Kate Burton appeared in the hallway. 'Sorry to interrupt, boss,' she said with a shy duck of the head towards Olivia who ignored her with queenly disdain. 'There's been an incident at the Mitre Hotel in town. Doyle's down there now. . . he thinks you should take a look.'

'Why?' For the life of him, Markham couldn't help sounding sharp. Hating himself, he saw Burton recoil slightly, as though he had struck her. Meanwhile, Olivia looked from one to the other with a cynical expression curling her lips. It was obvious she believed he and his visitor had been doing something more than talking shop and it didn't help that, under her ironic gaze, Burton looked guiltily self-conscious, turning an unbecoming red like a lobster suddenly flung into boiling water.

'Kate and I were supposed to be analysing the boutique murders but somehow strayed into metaphysics,' he said in an attempt to retrieve the situation.

'Metaphysics. Really?' she said quizzically, raising an eyebrow. 'Quite the kindred spirits.' With a thin smile, she added, 'I've come at an inconvenient time, so I'll push off and let you . . . get on.' There was a sardonic emphasis on the last two words.

Nothing to do but to acquiesce. 'My apologies, Liv,' he said lamely. 'Duty calls.'

'Doesn't it always.'

And with that, she was gone.

Burton was flustered. 'I didn't mean to, er, mess your plans up, boss,' she said.

There was a flush on the high cheekbones, but Markham had himself well in hand now.

'Not at all, Kate. Nothing that couldn't wait.' Only a crucial chance of clearing the air with Olivia.

Get a grip, Markham, he told himself. *Get a grip*.

'What's happened at the Mitre, then?' he asked.

Burton clicked into professional mode.

'A woman name of Veronica Urshell's been strangled. At first, from the way she was found, it looked like some kind of sexual assignation gone wrong. But it turns out there's a connection with the Confetti Club.'

'Ah.' Markham began to see why they had received the call-out.

'Veronica lived in Marbella, but her daughter Michelle's getting married later this year and wanted Mum over here for the final dress fitting. So Veronica booked into the Mitre where she turned up dead this afternoon.'

'Presumably those were the sirens we heard earlier.'

'That's right, sir,' came the crisp response. 'Michelle's best friends with Natalie Noakes and got on to her after they found her mum. When Noakes heard, he alerted Vice there was a potential link to our case.'

'Okay, Kate. Let's head to the Mitre,' he said. 'Get Noakesy and Natalie to meet us there.' With a supreme effort, he forced Olivia's image from his mind, though he was in turmoil after her unexpected appearance at his door. Did this mean there might be some way back for them? Or was she now more convinced than ever that he and Kate Burton were inextricably entangled or "an item"? Had she come to tell him that she and Mat Sullivan were now a couple, or had she wanted to return to The Sweepstakes?

It was futile to torment himself like this. Extraneous emotions *had* to be suppressed if he was to stay focused and nail the boutique killer. It was his professional duty, and personal considerations would have to take second place. *Don't they always*! Olivia's scornful tones echoed in his head even as he prepared to lead the team into battle.

* * *

'Okay, Natalie, deep breaths,' Markham urged, 'deep breaths.'

'C'mon, luv,' her father added. 'There's nowt to worry about. We jus' need to know what happened with your mate Michelle.'

Michelle Urshell being hysterical and under the care of a doctor meant Natalie Noakes was currently their best hope for a lead.

The apple of Noakes's eye looked as though she had been pulled out of a pub or nightclub (eminently possible), with panda eyes and streaky make-up. Notwithstanding which, she had sobered up sufficiently to be a cogent witness. Markham was amused to note that Doyle, who had been on the receiving end of Natalie's amorous advances in her salad days, practically flattened himself against the wall as his colleagues gently coaxed the relevant facts from her.

'Shell said her mum kind of freaked out after the dress fitting this morning.'

'Why was that?' Burton asked.

'She thought she'd seen someone she knew and it upset her cos of something that happened years ago.'

'What kind of something?' Burton pressed.

'She never said. . . Afterwards, it seemed like she'd got over it. . . told Shell it was all a silly mistake and she'd got the wrong end of the stick. Shell figured maybe hearing about the murders creeped her out, so her imagination was working overtime or something. She was a bit nervous like that. Anyway, it didn't seem like there was anything to worry about. Veronica was going to have a bit of a lie down. . . watch some telly, have a bath. . . They planned to go out for dinner later. Then when Shell couldn't get hold of her, she knew something was wrong.'

Leaving Natalie to the care of hotel staff, Markham, with Burton, Doyle and Noakes made their way to Veronica Urshell's room on the thickly carpeted well-lit third-floor corridor with its tasteful black and white pictures showing Bromgrove in the 1950s.

Dimples Davidson was waiting for them, looking down at the middle-aged woman's nude body sprawled face down across the double bed, her shoulder-length chestnut hair (newly highlighted, Markham observed with compassion) spread over her shoulders.

Gently moving the hair away, Dimples exposed the neck with its tell-tale livid weal. It appeared to be disjointed, indicating a neck fracture.

'They've tried to make this look like a sex attack,' he said grimly, 'but there's no evidence of that actually being the case.'

'No signs of a struggle,' Burton said, 'so looks like she let whoever it was into her room.'

'It must've been the person she recognised at the Confetti Club,' Noakes said slowly. 'They clocked her reaction. . . thought she might connect them to the murders an' go to the police.'

'But why would she think they were implicated?' Doyle asked.

'Cos she knew summat about their past . . . an' if she told what she knew, it would be all up with them.'

'I imagine they knew Veronica was staying here from her conversation with Michelle while they were in the shop,' Markham said. 'So it was just a question of coming to the hotel after work.'

He turned to the pathologist. 'Time of death, Doug?'

The pathologist, unusually for him, didn't tut-tut or demur, his bluff features grim as he contemplated Veronica Urshell's supine form.

'Around seven o'clock, seeing as she's still relatively warm to the touch and that fits with the rectal temperature.'

'Okay, somebody from Reception must've noticed them downstairs,' Doyle observed eagerly. 'I mean, people can't just wander in off the streets. They'd need to ask which room Veronica was in.'

'Not if she'd mentioned her room number while she was in the boutique,' Markham said. 'I think she probably let it slip on purpose so the murderer would know where to come.'

Doyle said, 'You mean like an *invitation?*'

'Yes, a signal that she wanted to talk,' Markham replied. 'According to the head receptionist, it was really busy down in the lobby this evening, so if someone just came in purposefully with a crowd of people and went upstairs — like they knew what they doing — then none of the staff would think to challenge them.'

'Why the chuff would Veronica let a killer into her room like that?' Noakes demanded, mopping his forehead vigorously with a grubby handkerchief as he scowled round the overheated, stuffy room. 'I mean, if she'd recognised someone who had a dodgy secret, then she must've known it were dangerous.'

'Don't forget, Michelle said Veronica laughed the whole thing off after they visited the boutique,' Burton pointed out. 'Talked about it being a silly mistake and said she'd got the wrong end of the stick. So presumably she'd convinced herself she was overreacting and letting her imagination run away with her? She might even have felt a bit foolish about it all. . . wanted to be reassured—'

'By a bleeding killer,' Noakes finished bleakly. 'But yeah, it could have happened like that.'

'It's a comfortable hotel in the centre of town,' Dimples said unexpectedly. 'She could've felt lulled into a false sense of security. Looks like she'd had a couple of drinks from the minibar,' he said, gesturing to the tray with its glass and empty bottles on top of the fridge. 'So, she threw caution to the winds and let curiosity take over. Maybe she felt titillated by the idea of pawing through someone else's secrets . . . it made her feel powerful and superior.'

It was a perceptive analysis, Markham thought.

'What was the point in taking the poor cow's clothes off?' Noakes burst out. 'I mean, they must've known we'd make a connection with the other murders.'

'They didn't know what, if anything, Veronica had shared with her daughter,' Markham said. 'According to Michelle, it was after the dress fitting that Veronica "freaked out", so the killer figured it was worth a shot to try and make it look like this was a middle-aged woman who had arranged some kind of sexual encounter. The mere fact of her visiting the Confetti Club would just be coincidence, nothing more. At the very least, a sexual angle would muddy the waters . . . have us chasing our tails.' The DI paced the thick-pile carpet restlessly. He turned to Burton. 'We need to speak to Michelle urgently,' he said. 'I want you to clear it with her GP, do whatever you have to, Kate, but please sort it. . . Time's running out and she might hold the missing piece of the jigsaw. Doyle, get back to base and update Carruthers. The two of you can draft a briefing note for the DCI so he knows the score.'

Now that the case was finally gathering momentum, he wanted Sidney in the picture.

* * *

Michelle Urshell was a wispy looking girl with a thin, narrow face and a curtain of long brown hair which Markham guessed she liked to hide behind. Her parents were divorced, but her dad — a beefy building contractor — admitted them to his daughter's flat and then commendably made himself scarce on the pretext of sorting tea. Noakes's presence — thanks to the connection with Natalie — seemed to reassure her and, though her eyes were puffy and red-rimmed from crying, she was composed and collected.

The missing piece of the jigsaw emerged in answer to a question from Burton.

'I understand your mum had rather a nervous temperament, Michelle. Is that right?'

'Yeah . . . Apparently she'd always been like that ever since her best friend went missing in their last year at secondary school — Medway High.'

A misper, thought Markham. *An unsolved crime. Here it was. At last.*

'Do you feel able to tell us about it?' Burton asked gently.

Seeing Michelle's bewilderment, Noakes said, 'Probl'y seems daft, us making a big song an' dance about something from way back. But we reckon that thanks to your mum, we can maybe put a murdering lowlife behind bars. We can't bring her back, luv, but we can make sure she didn't die for nothing.'

It was blunt and awkward, but this appeal by the big, shuffling father of her best friend — squeezed into his armchair like a bullock in ballet shoes — did the trick.

'Her friend's name was Clare Kenworthy. Well, actually mum said there were three of them. They were into clothes and makeup and boys, all the usual stuff.'

They held their breath.

'Clare was really pretty — dainty with soft curly dark hair, big brown eyes, and a heart-shaped face. She got engaged to Denis — all the girls were mad about him, but he only had eyes for Clare. Then she entered this local *Beautiful Brides* contest just before Christmas. Everyone said she was a dead cert to win, but one day she suddenly disappeared . . . just didn't come home from school. It was three years before they found what was left of her inside an abandoned steel locker behind the old Medway reservoir.' She shuddered. 'Right at the back of a chalk pit covered with undergrowth. . . It was only the size of a wardrobe . . . or a coffin. But there was a key and a padlock. . .' A quick indrawn breath. 'Some workman decided to take a look inside before it went to the dump . . .'

'I remember,' Noakes said gruffly. 'CID bollixed up the search an' went on a wild goose chase to Old Carton.' Heads had rolled, he reflected, but it had been small comfort to the Kenworthys. He laid a meaty hand on Michelle Urshell's arm with a delicacy that no one in CID (bar Markham) would have realised possible. 'It wouldn't happen today, luv. No wonder your poor mum were freaked out.'

'It really got to her, Mr Noakes,' the girl said earnestly, as though they were the only two people in the room. 'I know she had these nightmares about yellow-brown bones and horrible spawny brain tissue. . . the head coming loose from the spine with tufts of black hair attached and empty black eye sockets grinning back at her . . . Clare really looked after her teeth — her dad was a dentist — and mum couldn't stop thinking about how all that flossing ended up.' The very definition of PTSD. 'The locker was on its side . . . so it must have tipped over when Clare was trying to get out . . .'

Noakes held her glance steadily, though Markham knew he was cursing the hideous ineptitude of bygone policing.

'You need to forget about all of that,' he said as tenderly as if this was his own daughter. 'Jus' remember, we're going to make everything right. Your mum fretted about Clare never getting justice, didn't she, but now they're together an' they can count on us to get it sorted. We're gonna stop the pain an' sadness an' make it all square in the end.'

Michelle Urshell smiled tremulously at the big, uncouth retired policeman — the Red Tomato of CID legend.

'I know you will, Mr Noakes,' she said.

Once again, Markham felt his throat constrict and his eyes prickle.

In the end, it was as simple as that.

* * *

Afterwards, things moved fast.

'I've got hold of Miss Sexton, the woman who was Clare Kenworthy's headteacher at Medway High, boss,' Burton said looking fired up as the team convened in Markham's office. 'She's got a name for us — the third girl who hung out with Veronica and Clare.'

Doyle and Carruthers leaned in while Noakes, very much the elder statesman, watched proceedings with arms folded across his chest.

'*Cerys Skelton*,' Burton announced. 'When I showed her a picture of the boutique staff, she picked Cerys out right away on account of a birthmark next to her collarbone . . . a *wen*, she called it.' Burton pulled a face. 'I had to listen to her banging on about why the parents didn't get it sorted. Apparently, there was some "good-natured teasing".'

Doyle struggled to get his head round this. '*Hold on a moment, ma'am*,' he interjected. 'Are you saying Cerys Skelton is *Christina Skelthorne* . . . as in she changed her name?'

'Yes,' Burton confirmed. 'Back in the day, Cerys Skelton was best friends with Veronica Urshell and Clare Kenworthy. Apparently, staff called them the Three Musketeers. But the classmates dispersed and lost touch after Clare was murdered.'

Noakes was catching up fast.

'Okay, so the chief witch recognised Cerys as being one of the Three Musketeers,' he grunted.

'The *headmistress* told me Cerys Skelton was part of a gang with Veronica Urshell and Clare Kenworthy,' Burton said austerely. 'Then they drifted apart and went their separate ways towards the end of the upper sixth . . . that's how it goes with teenage girls.'

''Specially when one of 'em's a psycho who murdered her bestie,' Noakes said dourly.

Doyle's face was a picture of honest puzzlement. 'But why would Skelton kill Clare Kenworthy?' he asked.

'Jealousy,' Carruthers told him earnestly. 'They were all mad about this Denis bloke, remember, but he made his choice . . . and it *wasn't* Cerys.'

'Well, it wasn't Veronica either,' Doyle objected. 'But *she* didn't go tonto.'

Carruthers twitched the horn-rimmed specs in a manner normally calculated to annoy the hell out of his colleagues. On this occasion, however, they remained an attentive audience as he propounded his theory.

'That's because Veronica didn't have a screw loose like the other one,' he said. 'Sounds to me like Clare getting engaged and the *Beautiful Brides* competition may have triggered something with Cerys—'

'A psychosis which made her want to harm her friend?' Burton enquired eagerly.

'Well, something that skewed her perception at any rate, ma'am,' he replied. 'Which meant she wasn't rational on the subject of weddings and all the rest of it . . . had some kind of obsession or kink or whatever you want to call it. And then later on something else happened which made things even worse. . .'

Carruthers paused, his face troubled.

Burton was watching him closely. 'Go on, Sergeant,' she encouraged him. 'If you've got an opinion, we want to hear it.'

Doyle nodded vigorously. Meanwhile, Noakes eyed the DS beadily as though reserving judgement.

'Maybe Cerys went through something like my Kim,' he said. 'Snotty bitches making her feel like shit.' He flushed. 'Excuse my language, but it made my blood boil when Kim told me how some of the salespeople spoke to her. She couldn't imagine getting ready for your wedding and taking that kind of abuse. . . stuff about having a melon sized body and the wrong shaped head—'

'*Hey, what if that's it!*' Doyle exclaimed.

'Eh?' Noakes stared at him.

'Let's say Cerys had this kink or what have you — some hang-up from when she was a teenager. . . something that led her to murder her friend when they were schoolkids—'

'Emotional retardation,' Burton interjected, anxious as ever to find the right psychological label. 'A form of arrested development that meant for some reason she couldn't cope with watching one of her peers attain personal fulfilment.'

'Yeah, that's it,' Doyle replied, happy for once to accept his colleague's intellectualising. 'So, what if she was this emotionally twisted adolescent who never really grew up and couldn't handle normal social interactions — didn't understand sex or what made other people tick — and then she ended up being humiliated in a boutique like the Confetti Club—'

'*Woah*, hold on,' Noakes cut in. 'You mean she rocked up somewhere to buy a wedding dress an' some smart alecs made her an' her parents feel like rubbish an' it flipped a switch, so then she felt like going out an' killing folk?'

'Weddings can be an ordeal for some families,' Burton said thoughtfully, 'because they're a kind of going public . . . *exposure*. When our next-door neighbours' daughter got married, the parents got so wound up I really thought her mum was going to have a breakdown. You never know what goes on behind closed doors. If the family dynamic was peculiar in some way, then what comes naturally to most people might have been traumatic for them. And if Cerys internalised everything and had psychological issues to start with, well, you can see there might be a problem.'

'*Too right, ma'am*. With some women, an episode like that'd be enough to tip them over the edge,' Doyle said with a fervour which indicated he was not without personal experience in the field. Markham knew there had been turbulent times with his previous girlfriend Paula — the one who had forced him to choose between her and CID — but the young detective was now in calmer waters.

'You could well be right,' she murmured. Then to Markham, 'The fat wars can get vicious, boss . . . remember the *Beautiful Bodies* case.'

'It doesn't even have to be about size,' Doyle went on, 'though God knows the body positive people and plus-size bloggers are right when they call retailers out for fat shaming. It could just be that Cerys had the same kind of crappy experience as Carruthers' girlfriend. . . But like you said, ma'am, there was stuff in her past — family stuff, too — that meant *she* wasn't equipped to deal with it and ended up with a complex about bridal designers.'

'Like Gino Everard,' Burton said flatly.

'*Exactly*, ma'am.' Doyle was delighted his superiors were cottoning on so quickly. 'If Cerys Skelton *is* Christina Skelthorne, there's got to be mental issues galore.'

'We don' know she killed Clare wossname,' Noakes said belligerently. 'All we've got is this headteacher woman chunnering on about the Three Musketeers an' airy-fairy bollocks.'

'You've got to admit there's something seriously *weird* about Skelton ending up in a bridal shop, sarge,' Doyle insisted.

'Not just any old shop,' Carruthers pointed out, 'but one connected with three more murders.'

'Remember Ted Bundy,' Burton said suddenly.

She and Noakes were true-crime aficionados who had bonded over intense discussions about serial killers and their pathologies, so mere mention of the prolific American murderer immediately riveted his attention.

'What about him?'

'The criminologists and psychologists think it was being turned down by a wealthy Californian socialite when he was just twenty which triggered something in him.'

'That an' the porn,' came the dour response.

'Obviously it wasn't the only factor,' Burton said patiently, 'but later on, when his life was on more of an even keel and he'd acquired a veneer of sophistication, he sought the woman out again and made her fall in love with him, just so that he could drop her — *reject* her — the same way she had rejected him.'

'Kind of like a kid getting his own back,' Noakes agreed. 'Yeah, he said being rejected by his first girlfriend was the pits and his lowest time ever . . . so then he started hunting women who looked like her . . . slim prom queen types, with long hair parted in the middle, the same way she wore hers.'

'That's right. Your average young guy would *never* have reacted like that. But for someone like Ted Bundy, who as a child most likely had undiagnosed Socio-Emotional Learning Disorder — SLED,' Burton could never resist an acronym, 'it was catastrophic. The difficulty dealing with adult relationships and the loss of self-esteem when he struggled at university led to a fractured personality: the public Ted who seemed in control of his life and the private Ted who resented women and found the world a frightening place.'

'Bundy killed hundreds of women, didn't he?' Carruthers said ruminatively.

'Figures vary,' Noakes told him. 'Anything from thirty-six to three hundred.'

'*Jesus*.' Carruthers registered Markham's flinty expression. 'Sorry, boss.' Hastily, he turned to Burton. 'You're not saying Skelthorne's some kind of female Bundy are you, ma'am?'

'No,' Noakes answered for her. 'She's saying that getting dumped by Denis could've messed with Skelthorne's head an' then maybe later there were some kind of mega-embarrassing incident around wedding dresses an' all of it set her off, which is how she ended up topping Gino Everard.'

'That's *it*,' Burton said with satisfaction.

It wouldn't be the first such private bedlam the team had encountered, Markham thought with a shiver.

'Presumably Cerys Skelton changed her name to Christina Skelthorne to distance herself from the past and construct some sort of credible public persona . . . a mask of sanity,' he said. And despite the horror of these murders, he felt profound pity as he reflected on the mock acculturation their newly minted prime suspect must have endured; almost like an alien life form acquiring appropriate behaviour through mimicry and artifice, fighting to suppress deviant impulses that raged beneath the surface.

'Skelthorne don' zckly cast weirdy vibes or owt like that,' Noakes said finally, dishevelling his hair in time-honoured style.

'She's done a good job of reinventing herself all right,' Doyle concurred. 'Only—'

'Only what?' Noakes demanded.

The DS was thinking of Christina Skelthorne's demure prettiness and delicate hands with their slender, tapering fingers and well-kept nails. 'She's so well-groomed — like she's come straight from the manicurist — it's hard to imagine her garrotting folk and lugging bodies around.'

'She's a gym bunny,' Carruthers reminded him. 'I remember someone mentioning it when we were taking statements after Antonia Rambert's murder. One of the backroom kids said something about her signing up for these hardcore workouts — scary bootcamp affairs with dumbbells and bench presses . . . the whole nine yards.'

'Also, if she had a psychotic break, there could have been a surge in energy,' Burton observed. 'And according to Dimples, the element of surprise was a major factor with these murders.'

'The timing for Hagan was pretty tight,' Doyle demurred.

'But she had the opportunity,' Markham pointed out. 'None better once she and Lucille had deposited Maria in the Ladies and Lucille sheered off for her cigarette break.'

'She must've figured she was home and dry,' Burton mused, 'and then got the mother of all frights when Veronica Urshell turned up at the boutique.'

'D'you reckon Veronica ever suspected her old schoolmate of having killed Clare Kenworthy?' Carruthers asked.

'Well, Michelle never mentioned anything to that effect,' Markham said.

'And the headteacher Miss Sexton didn't say anything about Cerys having raised red flags,' Burton pointed out.

'Maybe Veronica's PTSD or repressed trauma or whatever it was had something to do with anxiety about Cerys's role,' Doyle hazarded.

'So Cerys went and became Christina to draw a line under all the bad stuff,' Carruthers recapitulated. 'Tried to start over. . . only for some reason she couldn't keep a lid on it.'

'I think that's right,' Markham agreed. 'She may also have wanted to make it difficult for Veronica Urshell to track her down . . . though there was little to be feared from that direction with Veronica settling in Spain.'

'It was a million to one chance Veronica turning up at the Confetti Club,' Doyle said. 'The shock could've been enough to send Cerys/Christina round the twist again, what with worrying Veronica might be going to expose her and thinking about Clare Kenworthy after so many years.'

'How about this for a scenario,' Markham said. 'Veronica wasn't able to hide her feelings of shock when she suddenly encountered Cerys at the Confetti Club in her new guise as saleswoman Christina Skelthorne. Maybe seeing Cerys in the context of a *bridalwear* shop brought a host of latent fears and suspicions surging up—'

'Cos of the way Clare Kenworthy died. . . her engagement and the *Beautiful Brides* contest?' Noakes interrupted.

'Yes, and also possibly because hearing about the murders of Gino Everard and the others made her suddenly fearful of Cerys . . . what she might be capable of,' Markham continued. 'According to her daughter, Veronica subsequently made light of it and said it was all a mistake. This could have been partly because she didn't want to spoil Michelle's excitement about her wedding by discussing ghoulish topics, but also because she wasn't ready to admit even to herself that her old friend could be a four-times killer.'

'You mean she wanted Cerys to convince her there was nothing in it,' Burton concluded.

'Exactly.'

'What went wrong then?' Doyle asked. 'Couldn't Cerys have talked Veronica round, persuaded her that she'd got it all wrong . . . *nothing to see here move along. . .?*'

'She'd be the kind to talk a good game,' Carruthers agreed. 'Which means she must have lost control of the situation somehow.'

'Perhaps Veronica blurted out something that made her panic,' Burton surmised. 'Or she could've pressed Cerys's buttons and said the wrong thing . . . triggered a violent response.'

'Or Cerys may just have felt it was too great a risk to let Veronica live,' Markham told them. 'Especially if she tapped into Veronica's underlying fears about her. She may also have hoped to throw sand in our eyes by posing the body in such a way as to suggest a sexual encounter gone wrong or, in the event that the police *did* decide to connect the murder with the Confetti Club deaths, a sex-fuelled killing spree.'

Carruthers whistled. 'If you're right about all of this, she's some piece of work, boss.'

As always, Noakes got down to brass tacks. 'How do we nab her then?'

'I was just coming to that.'

* * *

Two hours later, seated with Noakes and Burton in the DCI's office, Markham watched Sidney pick his jaw off the floor.

Finally, 'Are you *serious*, Inspector?' the DCI demanded. 'Assuming this woman *is* in fact your killer, how can you possibly be sure she will go after Natalie?'

'Cos my Nat an' Shell Urshell are *like that*.' Noakes crossed the pudgy index and second fingers of his right hand and waved them aloft with a view to confirming the closeness of their relationship. 'If Nat gets in touch with Carrie—'

'*Cerys*,' Markham and Burton said with one voice.

'Yeah, thass right, Cerys,' Noakes ploughed on unabashed. 'Well, if Nat tells Cerys she knows all about the Clare Kenworthy story an' she figures whoever killed Clare killed Shell's mum along with Everard an' the rest of 'em, then Cerys'll most likely try to shut her up—'

Sidney said testily. 'But that doesn't make Natalie a threat . . . Cerys can always respond that *yes*, she and Veronica Urshell and Clare Kenworthy were friends at school — as confirmed by their headmistress — and *yes* it no doubt gave Mrs Urshell a jolt to recognise a face from her past, but that's got nothing to do with Mrs Urshell's murder which was most likely sexually motivated.'

'I ain't finished,' Noakes said huffily, ignoring Sidney's basilisk glare. Slimy Sid wasn't the boss of him anymore, so he could *chuffing well button it*. 'My Nat could say she kept asking Shell's mum about it over the years — emailing her 'an all that — cos she were mad keen on true crime.' Like father like daughter, Markham thought, exchanging a knowing glance with Burton. 'So eventually Mrs U let her in on something private.'

'*Private?*'

'Thass what I said,' Noakes admonished the DCI with some hauteur. 'Summat Mrs U never told the police back then, a clue from Clare. . . from beyond the grave.'

The DCI unbent a fraction. 'What sort of clue?'

Noakes tapped the side of his bulbous nose. 'Nat can say she never put it together till now, but she's convinced she knows who the killer is . . . wink wink nudge nudge.'

'That sounds somewhat nebulous, Serg— er, Noakes.' Sidney's frown was something to behold. 'In the first place, why should Cerys assume that Natalie is in possession of information which directly implicates her? And secondly, why wouldn't Natalie go to the police if she believed she knew who was responsible for so many heinous murders. . . the more so, given your own background in CID?'

'Cerys'll be well paranoid by now,' Noakes pointed out. 'Not thinking straight. She'll reckon my lass has rumbled her. An' she'll peg Nat for a glory-hunter. . . wanting the credit for bringing in a serial killer an' solving the wedding shop murders all by herself. Nat can spin her a yarn about wanting to show everyone she's more than jus' a pretty face, that she's got plenty between her ears . . . looking to impress her mum an' dad.' Markham heard the poignant subtext even if Sidney was oblivious.

'Nat was always soft-hearted,' her father continued. 'Piece of cake for her to give Cerys the idea she's worked out it's her, but she wants her to do the right thing an' turn herself in — social conscience thingy an' all that.' Touchingly, he burst out, 'Nat can do this, boss.' Somehow Noakes had found it in him to address Sidney in the old way.

And Sidney was not immune to this appeal. 'I don't have a daughter, Noakes,' he said. And Markham sensed a world of loss behind the words. 'But I know how close you are to yours. It makes me the more reluctant to expose her to the risks of an entrapment scenario.'

Noakes flapped a hand in the direction of Markham and Burton. 'Them two'll see her right, boss.' The Yorkshire accent was very pronounced, as always with Noakes in times of high emotion.

Sidney looked at the former DS. A long, penetrating look that Noakes returned without flinching.

'Inspector Markham,' the DCI said finally, 'Noakes has surpassing trust in you and DI Burton. I trust you will prove worthy of his faith.'

'You can depend on it, sir,' was Markham's quiet response.

'All right, Inspector, do as you see fit. But keep me posted please.'

DI and DCI locked eyes. 'You won't regret it, sir.'

Sidney sought to break the intense atmosphere. 'Three against one,' he honked ruefully. 'The odds are against me.' His gaze rested on Noakes, his old nemesis, with something curiously like affection. 'If you make a mess of this, you know what you can do with those consultant timesheets,' he said with clumsy jocularity.

'You don' get rid of me that easily, I'll be back, guv.'

Guv.

Tribute proffered and accepted, they left Sidney's office, ready for the final act.

13. CHECKMATE

'The DCI's right about the difficulty of making this convincing,' Markham said to the team during their council of war a short time later. 'Natalie has to give Cerys the impression that Veronica Urshell shared something personal which made her wonder about Cerys . . .'

'Otherwise she'll smell a rat,' Carruthers finished for him.

'Correct, Sergeant.'

Burton was thinking intently. 'I checked in with Cerys's headteacher Miss Sexton to find out some more about the "good-natured teasing" she said went on. She told me Clare's nickname for Cerys was "Anne Boleyn", so maybe that could be Natalie's way in.'

Noakes looked at the DI as if she was nuts.

'Hold on a minute. *Anne Boleyn!* One of Henry the Eighth's wives. . . who got her head chopped off! What's *she* got to do with anything?' he demanded.

'Hear me out, sarge. . . Cerys has a wen on her neck — like a mole — the same as Anne Boleyn.'

'Hey, I remember that from when we did the Tudors at school,' Doyle said eagerly. 'Didn't Anne Boleyn have six fingers on her right hand too, so they thought she was into witchcraft and all sorts?'

'Maybe that's how she managed to snaffle Henry,' Carruthers mused. 'In the films they always make her look gorgeous. Angelina Jolie in a headdress . . . but with the birthmark and gammy hand, she must've been quite ugly in real life.'

'It was probably just a minor blemish, but then her enemies blew it up into something to support the witchcraft story,' Burton said. 'And she wore chokers and high necks to cover the mole or goitre or whatever it was.'

'Calling someone "Anne Boleyn" ain't the worst, though,' Noakes said dubiously. 'I mean, there's ruder nicknames than *that*.' His expression suggested that he had been called a few juicy ones in his time.

'Assuming this was a teenaged girl insecure about her body image and plagued by jealousy, then it might have been enough to make her secretly *hate* Clare Kenworthy,' Burton replied. 'Just being reminded of it should press Cerys's buttons,' she explained patiently, 'and hopefully bring back all the bad feelings — trigger a reaction.'

'Okay, I'm with you now,' Noakes said slowly. 'But how's Nat going to make a connection between this Anne Boleyn stuff an' thinking that Cerys is some mad killer?'

'She can pretend she's doing a Psychology foundation course — hoping to go to university to do a full-time degree — and one of the modules is all about PTSD and repressed memories. So *that's* when she got interested in the Clare Kenworthy story — which she already knew about from her best friend Michelle — and asked Veronica if she minded talking about it. They wrote to each other, swapped emails, that kind of thing. And that's when Veronica opened up and told her about the nickname. Natalie could tell something was niggling her . . . that she was having all these doubts and flashbacks about Cerys . . . to do with the Anne Boleyn name-calling, as if it was somehow *connected* to Clare's murder.'

'But isn't that all a bit, well, tenuous?' Carruthers objected. 'I mean, wouldn't the school or the police have picked up on anything suspect going on with the girls?' he added. 'As in bullying or fallings-out . . . stuff like that?'

'I remember taking a shufti at the case files cos of the Medway connection. The SIO back then didn't know his arse from his elbow,' Noakes growled.

Before he could embark on specifics, Burton hastily resumed, 'As far as anyone knew, all the kids got on just fine . . . Plus, Cerys's parents swore blind she came straight home the evening Clare went missing and the police never challenged them about it.'

Doyle was appalled. '*Christ*, you don't reckon they *knew?*' Aware of Markham's cool gaze, he hurried on. 'We're talking *murder* here!'

'I doubt we'll ever find out what the parents knew or suspected,' Burton said sombrely. 'The point is, Natalie can say Veronica hinted to her that Cerys knew more about what had happened to Clare than she ever let on . . . that maybe Cerys had just wanted to scare Clare or pay her back and then it all went wrong . . . And now to top it all, Natalie's found out from her dad, who's *ex-job*, that the woman she knows from the Confetti Club as Christina Skelthorne and Veronica's old schoolmate Cerys Skelton are one and the same, so it all *fits*.'

'*Hmm*. Is Natalie going to come right out and accuse Cerys of killing Veronica and doing the boutique murders?' Doyle asked. 'It'd be pretty kamikaze to try and talk a serial round on her own and—'

The young DS broke off suddenly. Markham was sure he had meant to say that not even Natalie Noakes was that stupid, before remembering her father was sat right next to him.

'Initially, Natalie can let Cerys think she believes Veronica's murder was a sex crime,' Burton said. 'Nothing to do with Cerys. It's only as things progress that the penny drops.'

'What about Everard, Rambert an' Hagan?' Noakes countered. 'If she thought Cerys did them three, she'd never agree to meet up on their own.'

'Natalie has to start by giving Cerys the idea all she can think about is Clare Kenworthy. . . that she's starry-eyed about solving the mystery and becoming the next female Cracker — everyone at the university thinking she's brilliant, a feature in the *Gazette*, "local girl makes good" . . . one in the eye for everyone who thought she wasn't bright enough for higher education. *I know, I know, sarge,*' forestalling Noakes's objection to this last, 'it's just about her needing to come across as obsessed with the Kenworthy case, so to start with she hasn't a notion of Cerys being involved in the boutique stuff.'

'But someone who'd killed once could kill again,' Carruthers pointed out. 'Surely she'd have that at the back of her mind.'

'Not if she's got a one-track mind and can only think about Kenworthy,' Burton assured him. 'And not if she drops a hint that she has it from her ex-policeman dad we're looking elsewhere for the boutique killers. . . at competitors of Gino Everard or the ex-wife and her partner, for example.' Burton's tone rang with confidence now. 'At first, she comes across as totally oblivious to the danger. Then as they talk and she realises how disturbed Cerys is, *that's* when it dawns on her what she's got herself into but by then, Cerys has decided she can't afford to let Natalie leave the shop alive.'

'It just might work,' Carruthers said, highly impressed that his colleague appeared to have thought of everything.

'*It'd better,*' Noakes rumbled, 'seeing as it's my lass we're using as bait.' The missus would *crucify* him when she found out, but hopefully they'd be home and dry by then. And, to tell the truth, he was proud that Markham believed his Natalie could pull this off.

'Tomorrow's Good Friday,' Markham said. 'As I recall, the unit next door to the boutique in the shopping centre is currently empty, which makes it an ideal observation post.'

'And the boutique's closed tomorrow because Franco Santini won't trade over Easter, so that works in our favour,' Burton advised.

'Excellent. Right, I want both shops wired for sight and sound by five o'clock tomorrow afternoon, which is when Natalie will arrange to meet with Cerys.'

'On it, sir. And I'll get the profilers to prepare a water-tight script.'

He noticed she didn't mention Nathan Finlayson but made no comment, though a narrow-eyed glance from Noakes showed that he had clocked the omission.

'Make it good, Kate. We need Cerys to decide that having Natalie at large shooting her mouth off, blabbing about flashbacks and recovered memory, is too great a risk.'

* * *

The plan worked even better than Markham had dared to hope, with Natalie giving her pitch-perfect impression of a ditsy true-crime addict (well, he supposed heredity had to count for something), hinting strongly — with a mixture of maudlin sympathy and prurient interest — that she knew Cerys was somehow connected to the mystery of Clare Kenworthy's disappearance.

But the killer would not be rushed.

'Look, I made a new life,' she said evasively. 'Only moved back here when I was pretty sure the past was buried. New name and everything.'

As advised, Natalie backed off, careful not to press too insistently lest the other's suspicions were aroused.

'What made you go into this?' she asked, gesturing round the showroom.

A sudden change came over Cerys at that point, so that the slanting green eyes seemed to turn black. From their vantage point, the detectives heard a distant, stony inflection in her voice that made it sound almost as though she was drugged or sleepwalking.

'My mum and dad were elderly parents. Well, when I say elderly, I mean they had me in their forties, so they were ancient compared to everyone else's. It made me feel

203

embarrassed sometimes when I was growing up, how fussy and old-fashioned they were.' Her face was working uncontrollably now. 'But they wanted the best for me. They were thrilled when I became engaged to an accountant who worked in dad's department . . . I didn't love him, but we got on okay and it seemed to be expected somehow. It felt good to be the same as other girls and I even started to get excited about the wedding which was going to be,' she affected an *ee bah gum* accent, 'a "Bit of a Do".' Suddenly her voice hardened in a way that gave Markham a chill. 'We decided to make a day of it when we went into town to choose the dress. Back then, the poshest shop around was Healy's Heavenly Brides . . . They were hucksters really, but in those days, it was *the* place to get kitted out.' A muscle was leaping at the corner of her jaw. 'So off we trooped — me, Mum and Dad — all dressed up to the nines . . . ready to show that we were as good as anyone.'

There was silence, as though the speaker had gone deep into herself where no one could reach her.

'What happened?' Natalie asked in a small voice.

The other sounded oddly flat and toneless. 'Oh, what you might expect. The sales staff were snotty and stuck-up, cut us right down to size. I wouldn't have minded so much for myself, but they took the mickey out of Mum and Dad — like they were special needs or some kind of simpletons. The head saleswoman kept looking us up and down and implying everything was way out of our league . . . Then when I was in the changing room, I heard a couple of them laughing at us and imitating my mum. When she was nervous, she overdid the gracious lady bit. . . The manager — this jumped-up oily git who thought he was God's gift — was really rude about my size, because in those days I was a big girl. He made snide remarks about stuff like back cleavage and needing a fireman's lift to get me down the aisle.'

She paused, and took a deep breath.

'It was really *humiliating*, and I remember just feeling smaller and smaller and smaller, like something was draining out of me. I literally felt it slip away from me like in those old movies where you see a ghost lift out of the body lying on the ground. Mum and Dad seemed to shrink too, almost as if they were trying to fade into the wallpaper. When we got out of there, Dad kept saying his money was as good as anyone else's and they could keep their overpriced tat . . . but I could see how ashamed he was.'

Hearing this, Markham was reminded of Burton's theory that this was an unusual family and somehow set apart. It sounded as if they could have been cheerfully confident within the security of their home but were easily intimidated and deflated off their own patch. He supposed it was unlikely they would ever find out what exactly had transpired in Cerys Skelton's home life, but he would have given much to find out.

Natalie appeared genuinely interested in finding out how the story concluded. 'Where did you go in the end?'

'I found this other place where there weren't too many skinny girls around. Getting Hitched, it was called. Of course, the marriage itself never lasted cos neither of us had a clue. . . felt like it was jinxed from the outset.'

'Bad luck having an experience like that,' Natalie said hesitantly.

'It wasn't the only rotten experience by a mile. But I've never forgotten it. . . never forgotten the smarmy manager with his hard insincere face. . . That's one reason I went into bridal retail, because I was determined not to let other brides feel the way I did.'

Suddenly her voice became a hiss. 'Nobody would ever have treated *Clare* like that. *Clare* the fashion plate . . . *Clare* the golden girl. . . the one Denis chose. . . She laughed at me when I said I fancied entering a beauty contest like the *Beautiful Brides* gig. She tittered and said didn't I think I was a bit *chunky* to be putting myself forward for the likes of that . . . apparently, when Denis called me statuesque, one of the sixth-form lads said you'd have to be *desperate*. . .'

'Girls can be right bitches,' Natalie said, with the self-consciousness of a former queen bee.

'*Too right*. Well, you know about the *hilarious* Anne Boleyn gag, of course, but the other stuff brought everything to a head,' Cerys said. '*Everything.*'

Markham sensed a wealth of meaning in that one word.

As if a switch had been flipped, with clinical detachment, she added, 'So that was it. I killed her. . . got her out to Medway reservoir on the pretext that I wanted to show her something no one else knew about . . . she was such a *romancer*, it worked a treat. I bashed her over the head with a log, so it was a piece of cake after that. She was kind of gurgling and moaning after I got her into the locker, but I didn't wait around to see things pan out.' The casual reference to Clare Kenworthy's lonely death in her metal coffin was chilling and Markham marvelled at the dissociation. Presumably part of Skelton's pathology was an ability to compartmentalise; like other killers he had encountered, she erected a necessary wall of dispassion in order to cope. It was notable too the euphemistic way she spoke of 'things panning out', such phraseology indicative of the abnormal remove she felt from her twisted acts.

'No one saw us together — I took good care of that — and Veronica told the police she thought Clare might've gone out to Old Carton after school, so that's where they looked. Nobody but me knew about the chalk pits. It was my special place, so I knew they wouldn't find her till it was too late.' She recited a gleeful mantra that made Markham's gorge rise. 'Nobody saw anything. Nobody heard anything. There wasn't a body. The earth just opened up and swallowed her down.'

Natalie gulped. 'So, *you* killed her.' And then, as though with dawning horror, her voice a whisper, 'Oh my God, what about all those others . . . was that you as well?'

'Team effort, darlin',' came a silkily caressing voice from behind her. 'You see, *I'm* the muscle.'

Randall Fenton appeared from the backroom area, sauntering in with a charming smile which didn't reach his eyes.

There was no sign of the former spindly gaucherie, the supervisor's stoop-shouldered bearing and stuttering diffidence replaced by an easy assurance and lazily proprietorial attitude as he beckoned to Cerys who readily joined him, slipping into his embrace with the air of one who felt she belonged there.

Markham felt Noakes stiffen beside him.

His former wingman had been right about an accomplice, only never in a month of Sundays could they have imagined it would be Fenton. Now, however, Markham could see the sinuousness that had gone unnoticed beneath a convincing impression of shambling gawkiness. He could see too that Fenton was handsome with his piercing blue eyes and sensitive, well-moulded features; by keeping his head down and gaze averted, he had successfully averted the detectives' attention from his striking looks.

'Everard,' and there was a biting contempt in Fenton's tone, 'kept my girl down. Kept me down too, the ponce.'

So, his puppy-dog devotion to the designer was all an act. Or was it? Could Fenton have made a play for Everard even as he pursued Cerys?

Cerys broke into Markham's thoughts. 'It was the same with that witch Rambert. She got off on making people feel small.'

Natalie found her voice.

'Was that why you killed her?'

Fenton's face darkened.

'That and the fact that she poked her nose in where it wasn't wanted,' he snarled.

'After we did Gino, Randy sent me a picture of Leonardo da Vinci's Vitruvian Man,' Cerys said. Seeing Natalie's incomprehension, she added condescendingly, 'That's the famous drawing of a wavy-haired nude man inside a circle and a square with his arms and legs in two positions.' She sniggered. 'Only Randy superimposed Gino's face on him—'

'Well, the hair was a dead ringer for his stupid bouffant,' Fenton interjected sardonically.

'Randy did a hangman doodle — y'know, a little gallows with a noose — and stuck the picture underneath so it looked like Gino was swinging there . . . and signed it.'

'Our own private code to celebrate killing the bastard. Only Rambert saw it — that was *careless* of you, babe — and got the wind up. Tackled Cerys about why we kept it secret that we were a couple . . . what were we doing making a sick joke like that blah blah.'

Cerys took over the narrative. 'The picture made her suspicious,' she said. 'But Randy turned on the charm and convinced her we knew something that could lead to the killer. . . that we were frightened and wanted her advice.'

Fenton scowled, his expression ugly. 'The old bat loved the intrigue. I think she was secretly hoping we had something on Franco . . . We couldn't risk letting her talk about the drawing and our being a couple.' A high-pitched snicker which was shocking in its shrill malice. 'Giving her that *Princess Bride* makeover was a bonus.'

Natalie licked dry lips. 'And Maria Hagan?' she asked faintly.

Fenton's lip curled. 'Another one who didn't know when to leave well alone.'

Cerys pouted. 'Would you believe, Antonia couldn't keep shtum . . . told Maria that she thought Randy had some kind of sick obsession with Gino and knew something about the murder—'

'So we had to go through the whole fricking charade again with *her*,' Fenton exploded. 'As in spin this yarn about knowing stuff but being scared. Problem being, we couldn't be sure she bought the story . . . so that meant another one for the chop, karate chop in her case and then. . .' He mimed strangulation.

As Natalie looked at them aghast, Cerys said, 'Maria getting blotto at Gino's wake was a stroke of luck. Once Luce was on her fag break, it was just a question of texting Randy *Thunderbirds Are Go!*'

'Yeah, and didn't I have to move like the clappers, babe,' he murmured into her hair.

Slowly, he disengaged himself from Cerys and contemplated Natalie.

'That just leaves the problem of dealing with you,' he said pleasantly. 'Let's see. I think *you're* going to slash your wrists and bleed to death right here in the shop leaving a letter saying you've decided to check out cos life ain't worth living any more. Yep, that should do nicely. . . With you being one of Gino's groupies, the fuzz'll probably throw unrequited love into the mix and start looking at *you* for the murders.' He intoned with mock-solemnity, '*Killed herself while the balance of her mind was disturbed.*'

Markham saw that Noakes was clenching his fists.

'*Steady,*' he whispered. '*Steady.* I want a confession for Veronica Urshell.'

Natalie, ever the policeman's daughter, knew what was required.

'Was it also *you* who killed Veronica then?' she asked tremulously, looking as though she might vomit.

'He did it for *me,*' Cerys said abruptly. 'I knew Ronnie had recognised me the second she walked into the shop with that mousy daughter.'

'And then when that stupid cow from repairs started babbling on about the murders, the blood drained from her face and she stared like you were the devil incarnate,' Fenton said bitterly.

'Yeah, it was obvious Ronnie was having a lightbulb moment,' Cerys went on. 'Suddenly I just *knew* she was remembering everything that happened with Clare.' Her expression was withdrawn, remote, as though she was travelling back into the past.

Fenton snapped his fingers in front of her face like a hypnotist, and she came round with a start.

'Ronnie made a point of saying the hotel name and what room number it was,' she resumed, 'so it was obvious she wanted to talk . . .'

'She was half sloshed when we rocked up,' Fenton gloated. 'Been busy raiding the minibar. Didn't check the spyhole but let Cerys in when she heard her voice in the corridor.'

'She knew the game was up as soon as she saw us together and Randy forced his way in.' Cerys's voice was unsteady as she said this. 'There was no point even talking to her.'

'Not that we tried,' her lover said. 'All over in seconds. Just a case of making it look like she was some pathetic middle-aged woman on the pull.'

'How did you know she wouldn't have told Shell she'd recognised you . . . talked about you and Clare Kenworthy?' Natalie asked Cerys.

It was Fenton who answered. 'We didn't,' he said bluntly. 'But either way, a bit of window-dressing wasn't going to hurt. If her mum came across as a sex-starved lush, then there was less chance of CID taking anything the daughter said seriously.' He grinned, making Markham think of a basking shark. 'You didn't really enjoy that part, though, did you doll?' he taunted Cerys. 'Not as tasteful as messing around with dinky party bags and painting red hearts on the dresses here.' He shook his head like a kindly uncle. 'You and your weird little games.'

It was obvious from his lover's taut expression that she was acutely uncomfortable with this teasing, a strange, mottled stripe suddenly appearing on her skin as though invisible nails were digging into it. Clearly whatever kink lurked within Cerys's tortured psyche, Randall Fenton indulged the fetish while at the same time twisting the rack.

Fenton picked up a pair of tailor's shears from the table at Cerys's elbow and casually passed them from one hand to the other as though testing their weight.

'Perhaps when we've done the messy bit, we can do a bit of dress-up,' he murmured eyeing Natalie speculatively. 'You've really got quite a look of Elsa in *Frozen*.'

Markham's upraised hand gave the sign.

Now!

As the team burst into the shop from next door, with Noakes in the lead, Fenton pulled Cerys into his body and without a word drew the shears fiercely across her throat before a uniformed officer pinioned him.

It was the work of seconds, but afterwards Natalie described it over and over to anyone who would listen as being like a film in slow motion. *Romeo and Juliet* gone wrong.

Before they dragged him away, Fenton locked eyes with Markham as if he were the only person there. 'I had to do it,' he said, blue eyes awash unfocused with tears. 'She was sick . . . so many demons. Prison would have killed her.'

* * *

A fortnight after the horrifying conclusion to the Confetti Club investigation, the team, together with Noakes, sat with drinks outside their favourite pub The Grapes on a Saturday afternoon, enjoying what Noakes called 'proper Easter weather'. He had very definite ideas about the demarcation of the seasons and heartily disliked how 'you don' get proper summers an' winters anymore,' reminiscing fondly about the heatwave of '76 and the cold snap of '81. It was the one area where he and Greta Thunberg saw eye to eye.

It was unusual for them to adopt the 'continental' habit of al fresco drinks, but the day was so mild that the temptation had proved irresistible.

The Grapes was an old-fashioned hostelry awash with nineteen-seventies retro décor, mixed with nautical curios and patriotic memorabilia collected by the fearsomely bee-hived landlady Denise whose *tendresse* for Markham ensured they were always received as honoured patrons. The pub's multiple nooks and crannies, along with all its quirky fittings and uneven floorboards in the back parlour that were as creaky and sloping as those of any quarterdeck, gave the place a delightfully eccentric character. The fact that Bromgrove's upwardly mobile young executives had yet to be seduced by its unique ambience was a definite plus as it meant that the police were rarely bothered by importunate eavesdroppers or would-be alpha males looking to pick a fight and impress their girlfriends. Though if it came to that, Denise was rarely at a loss when dealing with 'upstarts who needed taking down a peg or two'. *Have a Go If You Think You're Hard Enough* was a refrain rarely heard in her premises.

The landlady was currently undertaking a programme of cautious renovation entailing a certain amount of anxious consultation with her favourite inspector, to the ill-concealed amusement of his male colleagues. But Markham retained an impenetrable composure throughout all the discussion of carpet swatches (Prince of Wales feathers in the front room now due to make way for tobacco twisted pile), while Burton, following his lead, gamely reviewed design ideas with a zeal likely to earn Denise's eternal regard. The other three showed belated interest in mooted plans for a new 224-inch giant television behind the bar, regarding the current model as something of a let-down when it came to enjoying the footie. Denise informed them she would have to see what her accountant Mr Blake (widely rumoured to be her lover) had to say about that and she wasn't making any promises, a Spenlow and Jorkins-style diversionary tactic that struck Markham as being worthy of Slimy Sid at his slipperiest.

So, the Gang of Four and Noakes were content to linger in the little screened seating area with just two tables (the pub being sans beer garden), Denise having assured them she would keep other customers at bay for the duration.

'What d'you think Fenton meant by "so many demons"?' Doyle asked as they savoured their drinks and grazed happily on a platter of bar snacks ('brain food', their bosomy hostess had told Markham with a wink).

'Gotta be Skelton's kinky hang-ups about brides an' wedding dresses an' all that,' Noakes grunted, rapturously making short work of a scotch egg. 'He said she liked playing "weird little games", remember . . . so most probl'y all sorts.'

'Rituals no one else knew about,' Carruthers said sombrely, 'except for Fenton.'

'I still can't get my head round it, though,' Doyle said, spearing some breaded halloumi fries. 'Skelton an' Fenton come from bog standard ordinary backgrounds. There weren't any . . . what does Shippers call 'em . . . *psychological markers* to make people notice they had problems.'

Burton was now so resigned to her fiancé's less than flattering nickname, that she no longer bothered to protest at the allusion to serial killer Harold Shipman.

'Yes, but they thought of themselves as being social zeroes,' she said thoughtfully, stirring her gin and tonic with one of Denise's garish Queen Elizabeth swizzle sticks. 'And according to Fenton's secondary school form teacher, there was some gossip about him hurting family pets. So there must've been a sadistic streak there from early on.'

Doyle gulped down his Grolsch. 'Yeah, I get the jealousy — Skelton having this *Ugly Betty* resentment against Clare Kenworthy and then she flipped . . . somehow rationalised it by telling herself Kenworthy was a bully who had it coming. . . managed to get her life back on track—'

'Till the disastrous shopping trip with her mum and dad set her off or triggered something,' Carruthers interjected. 'So mentally she ended up in a bad place and started fixating on weddings and bridal stuff again.'

'I think that's right,' Burton agreed. 'And somehow Gino Everard became a blame figure — a scapegoat — for everything that she felt had gone wrong in her life . . . Everard with his *mwah mwah* air kisses and hand waving and flamboyance.'

'But Everard wasn't like the slimeball who cut her parents down to size,' Carruthers pointed out. 'That's what Kim remembered — how *nice* he was . . . And he didn't want the TV people making the wedding show pilot into some kind of blood sport, pitting mums and daughters against each other. Santini had no problem with that if it boosted the ratings, but *Everard* wasn't having any.'

'Yes, but you've got to remember, Cerys only had a fragile grip on reality,' Burton said. 'Never really evolved beyond the pre-adolescent phase. . . constantly feeding on negative energy. It made her vulnerable to Fenton who enjoyed dominating her and found that he got a real kick out of killing people.'

Noakes broke off from the scampi bites to observe, '*He'll* be able to handle prison, but she'd never have coped. He got that much right, the sick twist.'

'Wouldn't she have got a hospital order?' Doyle asked.

'Not necessarily,' Burton replied. 'With borderline personality disorder — which is probably what she had — there's a lot of disagreement about how far sufferers can be considered responsible for their own actions, especially where they're high-functioning—'

'Some folk said Princess Di had BPD,' Noakes cut in. 'Not my missus, though,' he added hastily.

'Nathan says probably most of us have borderline traits to one degree or another,' Burton commented.

Noakes's expression suggesting he didn't particularly like that diagnosis, she continued pacifically, 'Princess Diana's an interesting example, sarge. I remember reading a description of her as having "emotional haemophilia" because the usual clotting defence mechanisms didn't seem to work.' Aware that Doyle and Carruthers were exchanging glances of the *What-The-Hell-Is-She-On* variety, she concluded, 'Whatever the psychiatrists came up with, the strength of public feeling would have meant a prison sentence for Cerys.'

'Thank chuff her poor parents aren't around,' Noakes said through a mouthful of scampi. 'They sounded like salt of the earth . . . didn't deserve to have her turn out a fricking serial killer.' He swallowed, took a swig of Ruddles and looked round at his friends. 'All we know is, these days *Nobody is safe.*'

Now Markham spoke. 'Don't be such a prophet of doom,' he admonished. 'All things work together for good in the end.' As he said this, he shot Burton a complicitous glance that made Noakes eye them both suspiciously. But, 'Oh aye,' was all he said in a tone of profound scepticism before turning his attention to the pork scratchings.

'The DCI was most impressed by Natalie's coolness under pressure,' Markham went on, causing Noakes's countenance to brighten. 'Even joked about putting her on the payroll.'

'Yeah, well, my lass has got her head well screwed on.' Thankfully, Muriel had been so delighted with Natalie's sudden celebrity that she was prepared to overlook having been kept out of the loop. 'An' now she's fallen out with the Eyetie, we don' have to worry about self-marriage ceremonies or any of that malarkey,' Noakes announced happily.

'How did Mr Santini and Natalie come to fall out?' Burton enquired curiously.

Noakes tapped the side of his nose enigmatically. 'Saw through him in the end, didn't she,' he replied. 'Plus, that Rick Jordan's come to his senses an' told his mum to butt out, so looks like everything's kushdi again.' Doyle looked profoundly relieved to hear there was no prospect of Natalie turning her attention to CID. There was only so much excitement a bloke could take, and he doubted Kelly would necessarily appreciate the nuances of his history with the pneumatic Miss Noakes.

Eventually Burton, Carruthers and Doyle melted discreetly away, leaving Markham and Noakes together. 'I heard Claudia Everard an' Santini are going into business together,' Noakes said idly. 'An' Shay Conteh and Mark Harvison have complained to the PCC.'

'Correct on all counts, Noakesy.' Markham replied, smiling as he watched pupils from the local secondary school hurtling towards the bus stop a little further down the road, ties being loosened and skirts rolled up in the time-honoured proclamation of youthful defiance. Seeing the students was a sudden reminder of his estrangement from Olivia, on whom he had not set eyes since the awkward encounter when she had interrupted his colloquy with Burton. At the thought, his smile faded.

'Them complaints are dead in the water,' Noakes said consolingly, mistaking the guvnor's downcast expression. 'Sidney's so chuffed about that *Copper of the Year* feature the *Gazette* did on him, that you could strip naked an' jig down the high street for all he cares.'

It was quite true, the DCI being mightily delighted at a satisfactory conclusion to the boutique murders, with no fingers being pointed at any luminaries in high places.

''Course he took all the credit as per usual,' Noakes sniffed. 'An' it makes me wanna puke the way he spouts all that psychology guff like he invented it hisself.'

'A small price to pay for professional amity, Noakesy.'

As indeed it was.

'Thanks to Kate's unbounded talent for quoting great chunks of the *Harvard Review of Psychiatry* by heart, we can now count on unlimited credit with Sidney for being at the cutting edge of developments in criminal profiling.'

Noakes grinned but the piggy eyes were shrewd.

'A little bird told me her an' ole Shippers are having problems,' he said.

'That may well be but,' Markham's voice held a warning, 'I try to stay clear of my subordinates' personal lives.'

Noakes heard the faint chill in the guvnor's voice as a warning to back off in short order. Being ex-army, he knew when to beat a tactical retreat. But he knew there was mischief going on. Mischief that involved Burton, the guvnor and Olivia. He was determined to get to the bottom of it.

But for now, they could bask in the knowledge of another investigation completed and a job well done.

'D'you reckon there's any chance of Fenton lifting the lid on what really went on, guv? Seemed to me like mebbe there was a whole other story with him an' Ginelli.'

'You could well be right, Noakesy, but I think Mr Fenton will want to keep his secrets close.'

'Yeah, jus' like Ian Brady,' said the indefatigable true-crime specialist. 'Thass why they reckon he wouldn't tell that poor Winnie Johnson where him an' Myra Hindley buried her lad . . . cos it meant he still had the upper hand. An' all the time, he kept photos to remind hisself where the poor little sod was buried.'

'Yes, but at least we've put Fenton where he'll never be able to hurt another living soul.'

'I'll drink to that, boss.'

Noakes took a long draught. Then, 'Weird that in the end Anne Boleyn were the key to it all,' he said.

With her head tucked underneath her arm
She walks the bloody tower
With her head tucked underneath her arm
At the midnight hour.

The boutique killers had paid their account in full. Justice was done and the victims could finally rest in peace.

THE END

ALSO BY CATHERINE MOLONEY

The Joffe Books Story

We began in 2014 when Jasper agreed to publish
his mum's much-rejected romance novel and it
became a bestseller.

Since then we've grown into the largest independent
publisher in the UK. We're extremely proud to publish
some of the very best writers in the world, including Joy
Ellis, Faith Martin, Caro Ramsay, Helen Forrester, Simon
Brett and Robert Goddard. Everyone at Joffe Books loves
reading and we never forget that it all begins with the
magic of an author telling a story.

We are proud to publish talented first-time authors,
as well as established writers whose books we love
introducing to a new generation of readers.

We have been shortlisted for Independent Publisher
of the Year at the British Book Awards three times, in
2020, 2021 and 2022, and for the Diversity and Inclusivity
Award at the Independent Publishing Awards in 2022.

We built this company with your help, and we love
to hear from you, so please email us about absolutely
anything bookish at:

feedback@joffebooks.com

If you want to receive free books every Friday
and hear about all our new releases, join our mailing list:
www.joffebooks.com/contact.

And when you tell your friends about us, just remember:
it's pronounced Joffe as in coffee or toffee!

Milton Keynes UK
Ingram Content Group UK Ltd.
UKHW041446090724
445399UK00023B/198